Praise for Margo Lukas' *Half Moon Rising*

"Margo Lukas has done an excellent job of creating fantastic characters and a memorable plot that readers won't soon forget."

~ *Angel, Romance Junkies.*

"…Margo Lukas has one really big trump card up her sleeve – Half Moon Rising is a fantastic story. It's most enjoyable – I cannot stop reading once I begin."

~ *Mrs. Giggles, Romance Novel Central.*

"This fast paced and creative story will keep the readers guessing until the very end."

~ *Anita, The Romance Studio.*

"Half Moon Rising is a novel of suspense and excitement that grabs you from page one."

~ *Dana, Fallen Angel Reviews.*

"One of the best werewolf stories I've read…"

~ *Gail, Rites of Romance Reviews.*

Half Moon Rising

Margo Lukas

A Samhain Publishing, Ltd. publication.

Samhain Publishing, Ltd.
512 Forest Lake Drive
Warner Robins, GA 31093
www.samhainpublishing.com

Half Moon Rising
Copyright © 2007 by Margo Lukas
Print ISBN: 1-59998-634-5
Digital ISBN: 1-59998-491-1

Editing by Anne Scott
Cover by Anne Cain

First Samhain Publishing, Ltd. electronic publication: March 2007
First Samhain Publishing, Ltd. print publication: October 2007

Dedication

For Michael, Sophie, and Audrey

Chapter One

Runaways.

She spied the three street kids standing at the end of the bar sneaking pretzels into their pockets. Kids trying to be normal teenagers, at least for a few hours. As hard as it was not to reach out to them and lead them home, tonight she couldn't. Tonight she had her own problem to solve.

Outfitted in her usual jeans and gray, five-dollar T-shirt, CJ Duncan perched on the last barstool with her back resting against the black cinderblock wall. Her long blonde hair was pulled back into a sloppy knot at the base of her neck with a few strands loosened to frame her face.

Just enough dangly gold jewelry adorned her ears and slender neck to fit in, but not enough to stand out. It was a cover she had perfected.

The real target of her surveillance shoved his hands in his pockets and attempted to talk to a mini-skirt-wearing girl who writhed on the dance floor next to him. The two teens were a contrasting couple. She was pale white with a pixie blonde cut, while he had shaggy black hair and a deep tan.

In CJ's opinion, he was better looking than the average teen boy, with a well-built frame he would grow into in about five or six years. She noticed too much stoop in his shoulders, too much shuffling of his feet. He didn't seem to have the self-confidence to go with his looks.

He hadn't been hard to track down after she picked up his trail outside East Seattle High. For someone else, his side trips to the mall and coffee house might have made tailing him difficult.

Not for CJ. She could track anyone.

He had been at this packed teen dance club for over forty-five minutes. The place reeked of sweat and someone nearby had overdosed on cologne. With practiced effort, she put the odors out of her mind.

CJ had been shocked the first time she caught sight of the person who had left the scent trail so like her own. She had expected to find an older man outside the high school complex. There had been no mistaking the modern, glass building as the same one she had seen in her recent visions.

She had flown to Seattle to find her father. Her unexpected visions hadn't come with instructions. That is, if they had any meaning at all...

Truthfully, her priority was getting rid of these creepy hallucinations wrecking her life. A private detective could only endure so much disruption. CJ refused to accept she could do nothing to stop them.

A large shadow momentarily blocked out the neon light from the low club ceiling. She kept her eyes ahead and the kid in her field of sight.

"They've got better drinks in the tavern upstairs," a deep voice said. "Interested?"

CJ didn't look at the man planted on the barstool next to her. She didn't respond to his invitation. It was a big city. People could be ignored.

"You came here for the music." He leaned over to her, as if revealing a secret. "Me, too. Who needs a melody?" His voice was clear. Commanding. A shiver of sensual awareness snaked across her skin. CJ crossed her arms in front of her chest, wishing she had worn a padded bra.

"Not. Interested." She laced her tone with annoyance.

The man didn't take the hint and leave, but instead swiveled to face the bar. He ordered lemon water. Encounter over.

His voice...and her reaction...made her curious. A side-glance revealed a man wearing a dark, pinstripe suit stretched across broad shoulders as he leaned on the bar. His dark hair was cut short. Its natural wave curved over his collar. From the edge in his voice, she wouldn't have been surprised to see him in biker's leather.

She didn't mind a ride on a Harley now and then.

But he was just another suit. Some banker or overpaid manager killing time as he waited for his kid, like the other adults who converged by the club's entrance. At least he hit on her and not some teenage girl.

Curiosity satisfied, she turned her full attention back to the boy and caught him glancing at his watch. He likely had to leave soon. With a quick survey of the perimeter, she verified the exit locations. Only four.

She hoped he was heading home after the club. Two days investigating dead ends around the city didn't sit well. Not one damn bit. She now had less than two weeks to get some answers, before she had to be back in Minneapolis.

This kid was beginning to look like her last hope.

A rumble of an aluminum barstool was her first signal the man next to her was spinning back in her direction. Shit. He was turning too fast. Before she could move out of the way, his

9

lemon-spiked water drenched her T-shirt. The cold water made the stretchy fabric cling to her body and her lack of a sturdy bra even more apparent.

Idiot.

In a flash he tried to blot at her stomach with his handkerchief. Instinctively CJ curved her body away before he made contact. She jerked her head upward. Now she'd get a good look at the oaf and tell him to buzz off.

His thirty-something face was definitely not the middle-aged wannabe Romeo she expected. Damn. Not at all. The guy was fine. *Dangerously* fine.

CJ's body responded with *that* pleasurable tingle of anticipation, just as it had from his voice. It had been a while since one look made her feel like this. But this club was not the place, and not the time. She pushed her rising lust for him back down. Again.

She couldn't afford to look at him long. The kid would be leaving soon. Only a quick once-over…

She indulged herself.

The blue recessed lights over the bar made an indigo glow around his handsome face. The subtle waves of his hair caught the lights, revealing glossy dark hair with highlights. A few strands drifted down over one eyebrow, refusing to stay contained in the conservative haircut. Shadowed hollows under his high cheekbones gave way to a classic square jaw with one shallow cleft in the center of his chin.

His lips were locked tight, the bottom one sensuously full. The kind of lips that made a woman think about deep, long kisses.

CJ did not want to think about deep, long kisses.

She mentally shook herself and turned her gaze to the gold eyes staring down, directly into hers.

Something in his gaze wasn't right. It wasn't, "Hey, babe. Look at me." She expected a sleazy leer from a man who had just propositioned her for a drink upstairs.

Her old survival instinct from years on the street bristled to attention.

His expression held nothing flirtatious. His yellow eyes were almost piercing, watching her face intently, studying her as she studied him. Man, she needed to get a fix on this guy, but she had to keep her attention on the kid.

This club was sensory overload.

And it certainly wasn't like her to get distracted by a man. Ever.

"Here, take my handkerchief." He quickly stood and moved in front of her, blocking her view of the floor with his large frame. Very large frame.

He positioned himself too close to her own stool to allow her to stand without touching him. His head almost brushed the low ceiling of the bar.

CJ was an easy five-feet-eleven. Her annoying stranger had to be at least six-four.

He offered the white square of useless fabric. As she looked down at the handkerchief it hit her—what he had done. He had her cornered with the bar to her side. The wall pressed to her back.

This wasn't good.

CJ rose from her stool, prepared to push him out of the way and sidestep him. She had to regain her visual on the kid. Before she made her move, he grabbed her arm. Tight. His face rigid as he attempted to pull her closer to his body. He didn't want her to look around him.

CJ didn't budge. She moved a leg back, getting ready to use the leverage of his own arm to throw him to the floor. Her next move would be to duck her shoulder, shift weight and throw him…

Instead the edges of her sight blurred. Closing in on her narrowing lens of focus, the haze cut off her ability to see. Her sight. It was always the first sense to go.

Damn, not now. Please, not now.

She was lost in a blurry mass of shapes and light before she finished her plea.

When she refocused her eyes, the man and the club were gone. Only a soft halo of neon lights surrounding a bare piece of meadow remained. As she stared into the serene meadow, a blindingly white wolf with bared teeth emerged from the fog. Its growl shook the ground. Her body flooded with fear but, caught in the vision, she stayed rooted to the spot.

The white wolf. The wolf always growled. At her? At something else? She never knew.

She listened to the menacing snarl for what seemed forever…yet slowly, the guttural warning became a beat. A steady pulse…like music. She grabbed onto the sound and concentrated. The growl faded.

The wolf. *Not real.*

She forced herself to look away from the animal. She peered at the shapeless fog trying to see buildings, landmarks…sometimes they were there. But tonight only impenetrable fog swirled around the wolf.

She listened to the pounding beat, hearing it growing louder. *Music,* that was something different.

The club had music. The club was reality. More real than anything her eyes were showing her. She couldn't panic. Not this close to finding who she needed. The insane scene unfolding in front of her had to end.

She began her countdown. "Ten, nine, eight..." Just as she had practiced, she slowly pictured herself in the scene she was witnessing. She imagined taking a step backward from the wolf with each count.

"...seven, six, five, four..." Now she could hear the words of the song, too. "...three, two..." A wave of pungent cologne engulfed her.

"One." She shouted the number above the din of the club. The wolf and the haze were gone. She leaned back and steadied herself on the barstool.

"Lady?" A voice called her. She turned to the speaker. The bartender stood behind the counter, eyebrows drawn together in a frown.

She ran to the edge of the bar and scanned the dance floor. *Nothing.* She checked each exit. *Nothing.*

The man with the golden eyes wasn't anywhere in sight. Neither was the kid.

છ૭ૹૅૠ

"Geez!" The kid looked nervously in the sideview mirror, watching the empty street behind them. He slammed the dash with an impatient fist. "Drive faster. What if she's following us?"

In response to the kid's irritating command, Trey Nolan flicked on his signal, pulled into the next side street and brought his black Jeep to a dead stop.

There was only the hum of the vehicle's motor for a good minute before Trey spoke. Let the kid sweat.

Once he decided Mario had realized his error, Trey lowered his voice to a threatening growl. "First, don't tell me how to drive. Second, she is not following us, and third, the next thing out of your mouth had better be a damn good explanation why you weren't at your computer science club meeting." Trey glared at the teenage boy hunched over beside him. *What had Mario been thinking?*

The kid sunk farther into the Jeep's bucket seats and picked at a non-existent thread on his green cargos. "You aren't going to rat me out to my brother are you?"

Mario's desperation weakened Trey's anger, but he could not be too easy on him. The two of them didn't live in that kind of world. Mario had to understand that cruel fact and stop breaking the rules.

Trey rubbed his jaw and thought about the kid's question. He was on dangerous ground coming between the two brothers. "Mario, I don't know what I'm telling your brother. Once you give me the truth, I'll let you know."

"So, I was supposed to be at the meeting. No big deal."

"No big deal?" The loud words filled the car. *Why couldn't the kid get it?* "Disobeying your brother is always a big deal."

Trey gripped the wheel tighter, trying not to picture his hands around Mario's neck. "Computers are the reason you are at that high school. I stuck my neck out. Convinced your brother, and the rest of the Elders, you had to be in the best college prep program for computer science in the city, instead of training at the compound." Trey consciously lowered his voice. He didn't need to upset Mario anymore than he already was.

It wasn't easy. Trey had enough on his mind. Mario's frantic text message had been the last thing he needed. "If you don't develop your computer aptitude, who knows where Lazlo will place you? You don't have the...well, to put it bluntly, the control to join me at the firm as a security operative. But if you learn computer programming you could get away from your brother. I could assign you anywhere in the world."

"Yeah, yeah. I know all those things. I think about getting away from Lazlo all the time." Mario traced an aimless design on the Jeep's window with his finger. "It was a girl, okay? I know they're not important to you, but this one is worth the risk."

Trey felt like a hard-ass, but Mario had to toe the line. Their kind did not like rebels. "So what you're telling me is you skipped the meeting to be with your girl at the club."

Mario clenched his teeth and smothered a swear word. "See, that's the problem. She's not my girl. She thinks I'm a dweeb because I never go out."

Trey took in the young man next to him. Mario had every reason to be angry. Trey understood hopelessness.

The boy was handsome with his dark, Mediterranean looks. No one could argue he wasn't. Plus, he had no acne, he was tall, smart. If Mario were allowed, he could be the captain of the football team and the king of the school. But his brother would never tolerate such average teenage dreams.

It would've done Mario a world of good to succeed in this school. Mario's angry words stirred deeply buried memories. Trey, too, remembered the torture of not being normal like all your friends.

Trey looked down the quiet street softly illuminated by decorative lampposts. Every twenty feet a neat mailbox stood at the end of a driveway. A normal American neighborhood full of normal American people.

Mario was only kidding himself if he thought his life could be like these people's.

Trey could tell Mario the truth. Give the kid some hope he'd get through these crazy years where life seemed to pass you by.

The Jeep's dashboard clock showed nine o'clock creeping up. He needed to get Mario home soon, if they wanted to keep this quiet from Lazlo.

The pep talk would have to wait. Trey had some questions for Mario about the lady at the club.

The stunning blonde woman had clearly spooked Mario. His text message had been short and urgent. *Help. Woman chasing me.* Trey had gotten the alarming note on his cell as he returned to his office for some late night work.

Mario had been right. The lady had reacted with aggression when Trey blocked her in the corner, so Mario could escape. Trey hadn't picked up enough clues about her before she spaced out into some kind of trance. He had decided to get Mario out while he could and ask questions later. Something important had happened tonight, Trey just wasn't sure what it was.

"Let's talk about the blonde woman. When did you notice her?" Trey asked.

Mario shrugged. "Not too long after school. When I couldn't lose her at the mall, I freaked. No way it was a coincidence she was always fifty feet away from me. That's why I texted you. I hid my phone in my pocket the whole time. She didn't have a clue what I was doing."

Trey caught the defensive tone in Mario's voice. He needed to hear some praise. He sure didn't get it from anyone else at home. Softening his tone, Trey said, "Yeah. Smart. I'm sure she had no idea you were on to her. But do you have any clue why she'd follow you?"

Mario scoffed and glared at Trey as if he had just asked if two plus two was four. "Duh. Because she thought I was dog food. Didn't you sense it?"

Trey stiffened at Mario's accusation. "Dog food" was their unique slang for a target during operative training. He had missed something. Something important. "Back up—"

"She's a freak'n werewolf, Trey. A werewolf." The weight of the problem now on Trey's shoulders, Mario collapsed back into his seat.

Trey did the same, his mind suddenly full of the implications of what Mario had told him. *It couldn't be.* Mario had to be wrong.

But what if Mario wasn't wrong?

What if she was a werewolf? Her very existence could set back Lazlo's plans for months. Trey's pulse quickened. She could be just what he needed to buy some time for his other project to come through.

Trey put his hand to his chest. The stone hidden beneath his broadcloth shirt reminded him of his greater mission. Yes, not much longer and he could reclaim all that was rightfully his. She would be the perfect distraction.

His mood lifted as a plan of action formulated. He had to find this woman.

"My brother's gonna flip when he finds out—"

"We're not going to say a word to Lazlo." Trey lowered his voice so Mario knew exactly how important this was. "Because then we won't have to tell him about your little mini-skirted side interest at school, will we?"

Mario let Trey's words sink in as he glanced in the sideview mirror. The inky blackness spread like a cape behind them. "You think she isn't going to find us?"

"I think we'll find her first. It will give us the advantage." Trey clasped his hand over Mario's shoulder to give some comfort to the shocked boy. "Don't look so worried. How much trouble could it be to track down a lone, female werewolf?" Trey shifted the Jeep into gear and pulled back onto the street. "Especially for a smart couple of werewolves like us?"

Chapter Two

CJ looked skyward at the dark wall of the fifteen-story building. A cocky smile escaped. It had been a long time since a man outmaneuvered her. Considering that very thing occurred two nights ago, she was determined not to let it happen again any time soon. Her imminent midnight trip to Trey Nolan's top floor office would make sure of it.

The white handkerchief had been quite useful in tracking down the identity of her golden-eyed man. Turned out he was the president of Guardian International, which according to the web, was a premiere provider of bodyguards for the elite of the business world.

No doubt the building was wired with the latest in high-tech security hardware. She may not have even attempted this fact-finding mission, but for the unusually warm April day with temperatures soaring into the eighties. On her stakeout that afternoon several office workers had yanked open their windows to let in fresh air. If a window could be opened from the inside, well, CJ knew ways to make it open from the outside.

CJ took a deep breath. The odors of the dank alley penetrated her mind. She absorbed the scent of cats, rats, stale water and burned fuel. Putrid urine and decaying garbage, but no trace of Trey Nolan. Good.

She would not be caught off-guard.

CJ took his handkerchief from her small duffle bag, folded it, and stuck it in a zippered pocket of her black, form-fitting climbing pants. She'd never forget his scent, but she wasn't taking any chances. Chalk bag, flashlight and other necessary equipment hooked in place on her belt, she hid the duffle holding her street clothes under some loose cardboard on the side of the alley.

She had been in plenty of trash-strewn alleyways in her years as a missing persons investigator, but never with such a distracting handicap. She would be glad when this night was over and she could stop tracking Trey Nolan.

CJ didn't waste time daydreaming. She wasn't *trying* to imagine his long arms wrapped around her. Or his face thrown back in orgasm.

The cursed handkerchief was the problem, or rather the aroma it carried. His fragrance made her body respond in a way few in-the-flesh men ever had. Her nipples tightened, her belly warmed and her panties grew damp each time she sniffed the small cloth to verify she was tracking the correct scent.

With her body aroused by his smell, her mind leapt forward with images of Trey naked and ready.

CJ put her hand over the pocket. Leaving it in the alley was a possibility. With the handkerchief so close, his heavy masculine musk called to her. It was richly complex with spicy undertones and something else, an essence visceral and dangerous to her self-control.

His odor lacked the mask of cologne or shampoo she found lingering on the typical male. Instead, Trey's own woodsy essence dominated. It marked his territory in an eerily animalistic way. This, unluckily for him, made him quite easy to pick up among the downtown crowds and track to his penthouse office.

She remembered the embarrassment of letting him corner her in the club—a rookie's mistake. More humiliating? He had witnessed her enthralled by one of her visions.

She patted the pocket and decided to keep the handkerchief there. If she found what she wanted in his office, she might just leave it as a calling card. A not-so-subtle reminder she was not to be underestimated.

CJ monitored the windows dotting the concrete wall.

The last light on the second floor went out. The guard had made his rounds. It was time for her to turn the tables on Mr. Nolan.

She wrapped a chalked hand around the nylon rope attached to an anchor on the five-story building across the alley and gave a tug. It was firm. The rope would be her safety net in case something happened on her upward climb.

Like having a vision one-hundred feet above ground.

She grabbed a hold of the rim on the garbage dumpster and in one fluid motion landed on top. Her hand reached out for the closest concrete ledge.

A sharp vibration rapped against her thigh.

Damn. She hadn't switched her cell phone off. Who was calling her now?

She had it out of her pocket and to her ear in a second.

"Are you okay?" asked Roz, her roommate and closest friend in the world. Her voice came through the small phone tight with a fretful tone.

"I'm fine. I told you I'd call you when I knew something for sure." CJ repositioned her feet on the dumpster so she could lean against the building. She didn't want to cut off Roz's call. Experience had taught her Roz could drive herself crazy with worry. "I'm in the middle of—"

"Something dangerous. I know. I did a reading."

Now that irked her. What Roz did for a living was her business, but CJ did not like it when she brought her psychic mumbo jumbo home. She had seen enough real evil in the world; she didn't need any made-up monsters.

"Oh, CJ. I didn't mean to. Really, I didn't," Roz pleaded.

"So it was an accident?" Yeah, right it was.

"Your mom called, then I finally cleaned out the dishwasher and found your coffee mug, and my Tarot deck was still on the table."

At the mention of those damn cards, CJ's irritation grew.

"I'm sorry, you hadn't called for three days. Three really long days." Roz paused. "But, I saw something evil. Like big, bad and scary evil."

CJ took a breath. This wasn't the time to argue about their differing opinions on the existence of the supernatural. She loved her roommate, but sometimes her imagination was too much. "Let's skip the scary evil for now. You said my mom called?" Karen Duncan didn't hover in her daughter's life, but she checked on CJ by phone every few days.

"Oh, yeah. The cruise is going fine. Time of her life. Don't worry, I covered for you. Told her you were in Chicago on a job."

"She didn't ask any questions about how I was doing? About the visions?" CJ's mom had been in a stew about them, especially after the meds didn't stop them. CJ had kept their increased frequency a secret the last few weeks. Giving her mom a cruise for her and two of her friends had been Roz's idea. Maybe her roomie flaked out over picture cards, but she always came through with a clever idea in a pinch. Roz got Karen out of town so CJ could go on this trip without interference.

"She's your mom. Of course, she asked. I told her what I knew. That nothing had changed." Roz's voice went a pitch higher, a sure sign she was annoyed. "Which by the way is the truth. Are they still happening?"

"I had a bad one the other night. Lost a few minutes."

Roz hesitated a second before she asked, "Have you found out anything about your dad yet?"

CJ debated how much to tell Roz. She shifted on the dumpster and did a quick visual check of the building. The lights were off; she probably had an hour before the guard did another round.

Her experience told her to end the conversation now and get on with her climb. But Roz would just keep calling. Persistence was her roomie's middle name.

"No, but I picked up on some kid, maybe a relative, the other night. He was at a building I've seen a couple of times in my visions. A high school. I tailed him to a teen club." She hoped Roz didn't make her explain how a building in her vision actually existed in a city she had never visited. She wasn't ready to answer that question.

Roz's squeal sent a cat hidden under the dumpster skidding down the alley. "How did—wait, you smelled him, didn't you? He smelled like you."

"Yes, he was...similar to me. But I lost him when I had the vision. I haven't found a fresh trail for two days. It's like he's disappeared."

The kid had disappeared, as if he knew she could smell him. That inconvenience had left Trey Nolan's handkerchief as her only lead.

Roz interrupted her thoughts, "Do you think this relative smelled you? Maybe he inherited your...ah gift, too."

She hated discussing her odd, but useful genetic quirk out loud. Her mom and Roz were the only ones she had ever told about it. "I don't know. He was young, got an older guy to help him get away."

Roz's heels clicking on their hardwood kitchen floors echoed through the phone. "An old guy? CJ, listen to me, you should come home. Now." Roz's tone held a tinge of panic.

"This change of tune doesn't have anything to do with the...what did you call it? Big, bad and evil thing?" She touched the slick pocket that held Trey's handkerchief. His scent flowed through her mind. It was strong, attractive, but different, too. She sensed something different in Trey. But evil? She had encountered every imaginable vice on the streets—pimps, pedophiles. True minions of hell who reeked of their perversions.

No, Roz was just overly worried. Spooked by those crazy Tarot cards. CJ should have called her earlier.

CJ waited for Roz to keep arguing her point. The little redhead could hold on to an argument like a pit bull.

A few seconds passed before Roz responded. "Well, there *is* a chance I projected my worry on your reading."

"Yeah." CJ rolled her eyes. Miracles never ceased. She moved the cell phone to her other ear. "That's exactly what you're doing. Now stop worrying. I find people for a living. I know what I'm doing." She reached and checked the distance to the first window ledge. Only a few inches beyond her fingertips. No problem. She had a great vertical jump.

"Okay, you're a big girl, but stay alert." Roz's tone became firmer. "Call me if you need help. You'd be surprised what I can do."

CJ inwardly ignored Roz's offer. Roz was as intimidating as a puppy dog. "Well, I'm not going to find out anything if I don't get going. I'd like to get done before the sun rises. And don't ask me anymore about it. I won't tell you. Call you in the next few days, okay?"

After making absolutely sure it was turned off, CJ flicked the phone shut, certain she had put Roz's fears to rest.

She didn't want to think about her own fears.

CJ rested her head against the cold, rough concrete of the building. The scratch of the surface against her skin focused her thoughts. A dark city. A mission. A kid to track down. These were familiar. This was her normal life. Breathing deeply, she pushed her questions from her mind.

She eyed the ledge she had checked out before. Almost without effort, she bent her knees and launched from the dumpster to grasp its sharp edge in a chalked hand. Her other hand followed immediately, her feet now braced against the building. Slowly she lifted her torso higher using her arms, until she could pull one leg up onto the ledge.

Calmly she closed her fingers around a vertical ridge on the window's side. Gaining a toehold with her other foot, she eased herself to a standing position.

Her breathing was quiet. Steady. She studied the thirteen floors looming above. It was a classic early twentieth-century structure with art deco elements across its facade. Plenty for her to make her way to the top floor and pry open the windows to his offices.

Fifteen minutes later, she reached the top floor without a misstep. She shimmied across the row of windows. Bingo. She found one left unlocked. She loved it when people made her job easier.

CJ wiped a hand across her pants to shake off the chalk and slipped on a thin, cloth glove. Her feet and other hand holding her firmly in place, she inserted her jimmy tool between

25

the sashes of the window. It didn't take much effort before the bottom window rose enough for her to fit her hand beneath it. It glided upward with a firm shove.

As she gained access to the Guardian's penthouse offices, she scanned the shadows of the room she entered. Her rubber-soled feet gripped against smooth tile and the unmistakable stench of bleach stung her nostrils. A restroom. Staying flat against the outside wall she scanned the ceiling for cameras or the telltale red blinking light in any of the air vents.

The room appeared to be clean of any surveillance equipment, so she stepped away from the wall. On closer examination, she discovered the reason for the lack of cameras. The ornate marble and brass fittings revealed it was most likely the private bathroom of Trey Nolan, which meant his office probably was right out the next door. She wished she had time to do a proper casing of the building, but she didn't want his trail to grow cold.

She flashed her light around the room. A small armoire stood next to a corner shower stall. Taking a plush hand towel hanging from a brass ring, she held it close and drew in its aroma.

It was there. His scent. Beneath the chemical-created floral fragrance and the smell of strong masculine soap, he left his mark. Warm heat pooled low in her belly. She tightened her muscles, trying to stop her body's sexual response. She inhaled slowly and exhaled through her lips, making her body return to her command.

His scent.

She had smelled it a dozen times in the past twenty-four hours and yet, her reaction only grew more intense. It was maddening. Crazy. An attractive man could be dangerous to a woman. How many women had found themselves helplessly trapped because they let their desire for a man short-circuit their brains? Too many. And it was only the smell of him pushing her buttons.

Heaven help her when she faced the man again.

She quietly opened the drawers beneath the marble-topped vanity looking for any personal items. Anything with traces of her half-brother.

No luck. Every item was Trey's.

She looked down at the last drawer she had pulled out. A razor, one comb, a toothbrush and a capped tube of Crest. All Trey's. No lipstick, no long hairs lingering on his comb. She surmised women were not common visitors to his personal bathroom. Maybe he wasn't the lady's man his dark good looks had led her to believe. Interesting.

Having examined the contents of the room, she crept closer to the door and sniffed, but the bleach from the cleaning staff still hung too heavy in the air. She resorted to placing an ear to the door to listen. It felt unnatural to trust her hearing, but the next room appeared to be as empty as the bathroom. She pushed the light on her watch. Ten till one. She prayed she hadn't put herself at risk talking to Roz.

She cracked the door ajar and listened again. Nothing. The room she entered was dark except for a sliver of light shining in through a draped window. A thick carpet cushioned her steps as she closed the door behind her.

She did another quick fan of the office with her flashlight. She saw his desk across the room with several shelved cabinets behind it. A good place to commence her search. Only one object sat on the desktop.

She found the massive piece of furniture to be dark wood with a black stone top. Her light found the item placed off to the side, and she stifled a laugh with her hand.

A teddy bear sat smiling at her. She observed the otherwise bare surface and wondered at a man with only a stuffed animal on his desk. She snatched the bear to read the tag hanging from its shiny ribbon collar. In childish print, it read, *Dear Mr. Nolan. Thanks for saving Mommy. Love, Alexandria.* So he had seen some action as a bodyguard before becoming the CEO. That would explain how he got her brother out of the club so quick.

She slid a gloved hand to the desk's top drawer and found it securely locked. A test of every other drawer on the desk and the cabinet behind revealed the same.

She wasn't surprised. Trey Nolan didn't seem like a man to let his secrets be discovered easily.

Putting the pencil-thin flashlight between her teeth, she pulled a needle-shaped tool and a small wire from a pocket. With practiced skill, she worked on the first large drawer in the cabinet behind Trey's desk. She toiled in silence for a few minutes, trying to figure out the mechanics of his lock. With a click and an almost undetectable release of pressure, the heavy drawer pulled free.

It didn't hold anything useful, just meticulously filed technology manuals and procedural binders. The next few drawers held much of the same. But on the fifth she found the company promotional materials. She pulled out the first file dated the previous year. The flashlight illuminating the pages, she flipped through the glossy-paged booklet. There were several photos of tall men and women, wearing dark sunglasses and black suits.

A shiver ran down her spine. She recognized the hard set of their faces. Their alert postures. A look she had practiced for use on the street. A look that came easily to her. She had learned early most smalltime pimps were cowards and with that same bodyguard posture she could maneuver a runaway girl out of a dangerous situation.

She put the brochure back in the file. She doubted her brother worked for Trey. No, more likely Trey was protecting the kid. Did her father have enemies after his family? Is that why her mother left Seattle before CJ was born? She needed a customer list for Guardian and it didn't seem to be in this cabinet.

She contemplated Trey's bare desk. Surely he needed a computer to run a company this size? She slid her fingers across the surface, pleased when she detected a narrow indention at the back. His leather chair swung easily to the side, allowing her to crawl beneath. A search of the bottom panel revealed a button. With one touch, a slim screen emerged.

If she could just find the mouse and the keyboard she might get somewhere. CJ plopped in Trey's leather chair and began working with her tools on the drawers of his desk.

A sharp odor broke her concentration. She stilled the needle and wire.

Smoke.

CJ stood from the chair while she slipped the tools back into her pocket. Her sensitive nostrils quivered. Whatever burned, it was close. The odor settled in her mind. Sweet, slightly waxy. Candles.

She turned to face the draped windows of Trey's office. The air in front of them remained calm and empty of smoke. She closed her eyes shutting out any other stimuli and focused on the smoke smell. She moved from behind the desk to walk the perimeter of his office. Bumping her knees and skirting large objects she reached out with her nose. The heavy, sweet aroma hit her like an invisible wall.

Her eyes flew open. She stood in front of framed photographs hung in a decorative grouping. She plucked the nearest from its hanger. Nothing. She grabbed the next and found what she expected.

Neatly hidden in the pattern of the faux-painted wall was a small hole with a glass lens. A glance at the framed photo revealed a corresponding hole. A very well-camouflaged peephole.

She leaned forward to see if any light was reflecting from the room on the other side of the peephole, but the smoke was now coming into the office, surrounding her in its thick fog. Its smell swelled inside her head, but incredibly her lungs didn't burn with the effort of breathing the strange smoke.

She cupped her hands around the peephole to see if she could make out any reflected light through the lens.

Instead of a distorted reflection of a regular room, the sight before her was as clear as day. Standing motionless, with black smoke swirling around its body, the familiar white wolf glared at her with its icy blue eyes. But this time there was only silence from the creature, when before it had filled her mind with growling. No bared teeth. No ears flattened back in agitation.

It simply gazed at her. Trapped in the animal's stare, a creeping dread came over CJ as, slowly and gracefully, the wolf lay down on the floor. With a final gesture it curled a lip, flashing a series of sharp teeth, before placing its large head on crossed paws.

CJ's eyelids grew heavy. Darkness enveloped her.

୧୬ଡ଼ଔ

"Comus mir sawl. Comus mir lupus potére. Comus mir sawl. Comus mir lupus potére."

Trey Nolan sat cross-legged on the hardwood floor in his hidden room, safe from discovery by his pack. He paid no attention to the wrinkles creased in his finely tailored blue pants. For comfort he had shed his suit jacket and shirt, the garments placed across the single bed he had tucked away to the side of the room. His Italian loafers lay next to the door to his small sanctuary.

Except for his lips, the flicker of twelve candle flames was the only movement in the room.

Bought during a business trip to Mexico City, the new candles gave off intense heat...much stronger than he had ever felt from normal candles. The owner of the occult shop, a small, elderly, indigenous woman, had pressed upon him specific instructions to place them in a circle around the spell maker. She promised these candles would amplify the power of his ancient amulet. Considering the amount of pesos he had parted with, he did not want to be disappointed.

He wasn't.

The flames grew in size as he repeated the memorized chant. Over and over he spoke the magic words. Willing the supernatural realm to give back the power he had been destined to possess.

As a werewolf, he did not go easily into the trance of chanting, not like he imagined real wielders of magic to do. Instinctively he held onto an awareness of his physical surroundings. The heat from the candles drove his inner temperature higher, but no sweat eased his body. Though he had not shape-shifted, the spell made his inner wolf dominate his human systems. Unable to sweat through his human pores, he opened his lips and panted to cool his heated body.

31

The power he sought was worth any discomfort.

"*Comus mir sawl. Comus mir lupus potére. Comus mir sawl. Comus mir lu—*"

A muffled crash in his outer office snapped Trey's focus from his incantations. The candles still flickered with light but without his mind as its portal, the magic he had conjured was gone. The only trace of the spell was the unnatural heat emitting from the object that hung in the center of his bare chest.

He placed a hand around the golden amulet. "Damn."

This time he had been close to reclaiming his rightful powers. With the intensifying candles he had almost breached the metaphysical wall separating him from his true werewolf potential. His body had coursed with supernatural energy as he chanted.

And the scent.

That beautiful, overpowering scent.

The candles melted beneath their fiery wicks and released their sweet aroma...and he had smelled it. The fleeting odor burned into his brain.

If anyone asked him, he wouldn't know how to describe it, but he knew it was there.

A precious memory. A recollection of a fragrance to reinforce what he always believed in his heart to be true.

Magic was the answer. *His answer.*

Before he could continue with his spell, he needed to make sure he was alone. Being ninety-nine percent sure the room was airtight wasn't good enough. If anyone in the pack discovered his magical experiments, he'd have to answer to Lazlo, the Alpha Leader. After being bested by Lazlo during the Succession Challenges, he doubted he'd survive the encounter.

Trey quickly blew out his circle of candles and rose from the floor.

He had worn the gold and red stone piece continuously for the past several weeks, hidden safely beneath his suits. In stolen moments, when no one from the pack was near, he practiced his chant. Whispering his spell and wearing the amulet, he could feel his werewolf gifts just out of his reach.

Tonight had been unique.

Energy coursed through him tonight. It had given him a chance to smell.

He dare not risk the amulet now.

Taking it off, he placed it in a velvet-lined box. The small box he locked in a drawer of an antique apothecary cabinet shoved against the wall. He tucked all but one of the candles into a basket and slid it beneath his bed. The last candle he kept in his hand.

The evidence of his disobedience safely put away, he stepped to the peephole to survey his outer office.

A crumpled form lay sprawled on the carpet directly in front of his peephole. Broken glass from a photo frame caught the shiny beam of a slim flashlight on the floor next to the body. The small bit of illumination showed the end of a light-colored ponytail peeking out from beneath a dark knit cap.

It was her.

He marveled she appeared unconscious. He had never heard of a narcoleptic werewolf, but then her very existence was a mystery. Why not one more?

He found his shirt, jammed his arms through the sleeves and quietly entered his outer office using his secret entrance inside the office's small coat closet. In a firm voice he commanded, "On." The inset fixtures above soaked the room in clear, white light.

On a silver tray on a side table next to the door, he placed one of the candles, just in case he had to explain any odors clinging to his clothes.

He walked silently to where the woman lay. She was rousing herself as he crouched at her side.

Bending down, he grabbed her wrist. He pulled the intruder to her knees, an arm twisted with a gentle pressure behind her back. She was tall for a female, so it would be to his advantage to keep her on her knees.

Blue eyes flashed up at him in anger. The scruffy knit cap pulled tight, covered all of her hair except for the stray ends of her ponytail. Even with the ugly cap and angry eyes, the woman was a beauty. A compulsion to see her hair made him yank the cap off. A long, platinum blonde ponytail uncurled down her shoulder.

The sensual cascade of hair made him shift his stance to accommodate his growing appreciation of her beauty. He had never seen a werewolf with such icy pale eyes, or fair hair. The New World Pack didn't have any wolves with this coloring.

"Who are you?" Trey spoke firmly, but he didn't shout. The room was silent except for their breathing.

She pulled away but didn't try to yank out of his grip. "Get your hands off me before you regret it."

The slim smirk that appeared on her face might have intimidated a lesser man. He increased the pressure on her arm. "I highly doubt that. You had better answer my question or I'll call in the guards." He had to be careful provoking her if she was truly a werewolf, but showing weakness on his part could be just as dangerous.

"You let underlings do your dirty work?" she asked.

"Believe me, if I wanted to harm you we wouldn't be talking. But seeing as you appear to have a problem with faint—"

"A temporary problem. I'm far from helpless."

"I'd never assume you were helpless. Too bad you had such a *temporary problem*. I might not have heard if you hadn't fallen."

She shrugged.

She was lying. Werewolves didn't just faint for no reason. If their bodies suffered any trauma they shifted forms. The shift always healed them, as long as it wasn't a head wound. Severe injury to the brain could make a werewolf lose consciousness. Her head showed no signs of trauma.

Trey crouched closer. "You're lucky I didn't see the need to take you out immediately." He paused, watching her face for any sign of fear. He saw none. She was a tough cookie all right. "But I have a right to know who you are and why you are in my office in the middle of the night."

She blew a loose strand of hair away from her eyes and twisted to face him as best she could in her awkward position. "Fine. Let me go and I'll answer your question."

He had established his ability to subdue her. Most female werewolves wouldn't directly challenge a larger male, but he had to keep in mind her pack could be different. Only he didn't want her to fight back. His martial arts moves were limited in their effectiveness against the supernatural strength of his kind. He had learned that lesson at the hands of Lazlo.

"Yes. But first I need to do some checking." Still holding her arm and with efficiency from years spent as a Guardian operative, he patted down her slim body. Her curves were subtle, but there. He slid behind her and, as he patted down her backside, he enjoyed how the gentle roundness of her pert behind fit nicely in his hands.

35

"Enjoying yourself?" She twisted her head to look over her shoulder. Her eyes cold and sharp.

"Yes, I am." He saw no reason to lie.

He found no weapon, but one pocket revealed his carefully folded handkerchief from the night before. It had been foolish to leave it with her at the club, whether she was werewolf or not.

His own search for her hadn't gone well, so he supposed fate was on his side with that little slip up. He tucked it into his front pocket. Her eyes watched his gesture with an expression he couldn't identify. Her lips parted as if she wanted to say something, but instead she closed them and directed her gaze back to the floor.

Satisfied she carried no weapons, Trey released her arm and stepped back. Not too far back. He didn't want her out of his reach. "Now you will answer my questions."

The woman sprang from her knees to her feet in a movement reminiscent of their kind. He had mastered the move himself through practice. She turned to face him square and planted her feet wide. She brought the arm he had twisted in front of her and made a point of kneading out any soreness he had left.

He didn't drop his cautious stance. It was common strategy, appear weaker then strike. Perhaps the fainting was part of her ploy as well. But her disorientation at the club hadn't seemed planned.

Whatever problem had caused her to pass out, she was fully alert now. Her gaze didn't waver from his face.

He couldn't say the same for his stare.

She was as tall as he recalled, even with the ridiculous rubber-soled shoes she wore. The endless stretch of black, from her fitted pants to the body-clinging spandex top, reminded him more of a nubile feline, than the hearty canine women of his pack.

"The name is CJ Duncan. I'm from out of town."

"Out of town? Anywhere more specific?"

She waited to respond, her face guarded. "I think you coastal people refer to it as flyover country."

This CJ wasn't going to pinpoint the location. He pondered the possibility a new werewolf pack had surfaced in the Midwest. It was true the vast majority of Guardian's clients were out-of-country. And if they were in-country, it was mainly cities with major ports.

If a pack had escaped Europe before the wars and laid low for the last century in some sparsely populated area of the US, there existed a slim chance the New World Pack had missed them.

Slim, but possible.

Why would they come looking for other werewolves now?

Breeding partners? The mere thought sent a spike of adrenaline to his groin. Any man, werewolf or not, would find her attractive. Was she meant to lure some virile males back to her pack?

She tugged her ponytail rubber band out of her mussed hair, smoothed the platinum strands and whipped it back up.

The motion pulled her top tighter against her torso and the firm roundness of her breasts rose high. Trey felt his already swollen dick push against his briefs. He had refrained from any sexual activity with his kind since Lazlo had announced the breeding plan and he had been too busy to court a human woman. His hardening cock proved his lust was not at all blunted by the mystery she presented. Her arms came down and her chest returned to its natural fall. He itched to rub his palm across the smooth mounds.

The sound of her throat clearing brought his attention back to her face.

The upturn of her lips indicated she was amused by his interest, but he chose to ignore it. If she was here to lure him into breeding with her, he refused to make it easy. He wasn't a stud bull for hire. "And you were going to tell me why you broke into my office."

"I'm here because I believe you have information concerning someone I'm trying to find."

Someone. Not him. The pressure in his pants eased while that thought settled with him.

Mario's instinct was right the other night. She had been after him.

He could possibly furnish the data she demanded, but he wanted something in return. Mario's grounding by Lazlo had delayed their search for her. She had fallen into his lap, he would not allow her to leave easily. "That's all you want from me? Information?"

"Correct. I need to know about the kid from the other night and his family. Trust me, I mean them no harm."

"And what about me? Do you mean me any harm?"

Her hands went to her hips and she smiled. She raked his body with the same lingering appraisal he had given her moments before. "No...harm."

What game was she playing? What could Mario and his family give her he couldn't? Unless, she knew Mario's brother, Lazlo, was the pack Alpha.

A picture of her pale skin entwined with Lazlo's dark limbs flashed through his mind. His stomach clenched tight at the image.

For now he'd go along with her game. "Maybe what you say is true, but you can't blame a man for wondering about a woman who broke into his office." He sauntered over to his desk and leaned against the edge, crossing his legs. He didn't want her to sense the anger that had flared as he thought of her and Lazlo.

She didn't move any closer, but her eyes never left him. "First I'd like to know the kid's name and if his father is around here."

Trey licked his lips. She didn't waste time. That was the wolf in her. She was direct and to the point. In bed she'd probably tell him what she wanted, where she wanted it and when she wanted it.

He repositioned his bear to face his fearsome intruder. The fuzzy guy's bow was askew where she must have read the tag. *She didn't want Lazlo.* She wanted Mario's father. He smiled as he straightened out the ribbon on his special little friend. "The boy's name is Mario Le Croix."

"And the father?"

Trey didn't reply. It was time to change the rules of the game. She wasn't going to get her answer until she agreed to help him. Then he would arrange a meeting for her.

"And his father?" she asked again.

"Before we talk about Mario's father, let's talk about us." He put his bear back in its place where it reminded him of simpler times. A time when he still called Lazlo friend. A time when he didn't feel the weight of the pack's survival on his shoulders.

He listened carefully to her breathing. Watched for signs of alarm at his change in topic. She stood perfectly still. A warrior waiting for the first strike.

Her slender throat moved as she swallowed before she spoke. "You want something before you'll tell me about Mario's father?"

Trey arose from the desk and closed the distance between them. Would she retreat at his advance? She slipped her left foot back a few inches. A clear sign she was putting herself on the defense, should he attack.

He smiled. "You are very perceptive."

"I'm *not* going to sleep with you." She didn't look at him when she spoke.

He wasn't sure if she said it for his benefit or hers.

She lowered her head and a few strands of hair slipped loose and covered her left eye.

Trey didn't think. He reached out. The silk locks glided through fingers. Such softness from a werewolf.

She jerked her head back.

The blonde hair fell from his fingers. He lowered his mouth close to her exposed ear. "Fascinating. Sex was the first thing which came to your mind. But I don't have to barter for sex. And as intriguing as the idea of mating with you is..." He paused as her cheeks darkened. "You have something else that fascinates me more at the moment."

He watched her chest rise and fall with one deep breath.

She firmly placed the palm of her hand on his bare chest. Her skin was satin on his flesh. Heat spread from her hand and jolted to his groin. He strained to not push against the heat, because her eyes made it clear. He wasn't getting any closer than this.

"What do I have that interests you, Mr. Nolan?" CJ asked.

"It's not exactly what you have, it's what you *are*."

"You need a private investigator?"

"CJ, let's drop the act. We both know who we are dealing with. As surprising as this may seem to you...according to my pack, you shouldn't even exist. If you agree to appear with me in front of my Alpha Leader and the Elders Council—"

"Alpha Elder what?" Her brow furrowed as if she didn't understand.

Trey lifted his lips in a sly smile and shook his head, "You don't have to keep it a secret from me. Obviously, I know what you are."

"What am I?"

Trey stopped smiling as he registered the confusion on her face. He laid his hand overtop hers. "You're a werewolf."

Chapter Three

Trey's hand was warm and large as he held hers to his chest. She could feel the rumble of his voice when he spoke.

"I'm a werewolf, too, and so is Mario. That is why you were following him?"

CJ peered into the golden eyes of the man, hoping to see a glimmer of humor in them.

He had to be joking.

Unless he was just playing with her mind. Unless he had no intention of helping her find her brother.

Or he was crazy.

She snatched her hand from under his and stepped back two paces. The carpet grabbed at her rubber-soled shoes, almost tripping her in her speed to get some distance between herself and Trey. "This isn't a game. I don't know the kid's name. I think he may be..."

Trey cocked his head and stared.

Did she want to tell this man she might be related to Mario? Would it matter? She hadn't thought of a cover story for something like this.

Werewolves? This was crazy.

"You think Mario may be what?" His voice rumbled low.

CJ couldn't find a reason not to tell him. It wasn't like she wanted to hurt the kid. "He may be related to me somehow. That's the only reason I'm here. You helped him slip past me the other night. I got your license plate number." No need to tell him how she really tracked him. "And now I'm looking for information. Simple investigative work." She lifted her hands, palms facing outward. No need to provoke him if he was mentally unstable.

She was prepared to hear another rant about werewolves, but he only answered with a raised eyebrow. Not knowing what to think, she breathed in Trey's essence.

She'd smell the truth from him.

Musk entered her mind. Heat. Spice. Wildness. As she opened her sense to his full aroma, his scent was overpowering. She had been forcing herself to block his odor by concentrating on the sweet candle smell permeating the air. Now she was unprotected.

Smelling him. Feeling his scent. Separating it into threads she could understand. Searching for the smell of salt. Fear. Discovery. *Was he lying?*

As her mind whirled with his scent, CJ drank him in with her eyes as well.

He was no average businessman. In his office, in his territory, he was a portrait of intimidation.

His white shirt hung off broad shoulders, open and untucked. The defined edge of his chest led to a narrow span of ridged abs. A dusting of hair blazed down his taut belly disappearing at his waistband.

In the bright overhead lights his hair appeared a deep sable. Shiny highlights from time in the sun streaked across his wavy, short hair.

She trusted her nose more than anything, but the look of Trey Nolan influenced her ability to think straight.

Her body was betraying her.

She focused on the salty scent of fear that always accompanied a liar. Her brain flooded with other ideas. At the first sniff of his handkerchief, Trey's aroma had sent her body into sexual readiness. With his utter maleness overwhelming her smell and sight senses, her body seemed to think it was time for the real thing. Her nipples strained against her sheer bra as she surveyed his long, lean body.

Her lips went dry. Her panties went damp. She squeezed tight internally trying to quell the distracting sensation. The motion only made her legs more unsteady.

The worst was the look on his face. He knew exactly what was happening to her.

"Having trouble standing, CJ?"

"I'm perfectly fine." *Liar.*

"You'll never be able to sniff the truth out of me. Most of the mature werewolves in my pack, such as myself, have learned to control our endorphin levels in this form."

CJ took his challenge and closed her eyes. His scent swirled in her mind. Ignoring her own body's reaction, she felt for the threads that existed in every person's scent trail.

He was a meat eater. Preferred spicy foods. His soap choice, a heady mix of musk and exotic floral. But his salty, sweat thread registered weakly. No evidence of undue anxiety or nervousness.

His base perspiration scent thread was steady, unmoving. Unnatural and inhuman.

It wasn't right.

A measured anxiety took hold. CJ feared he was much more dangerous than she first thought, werewolf or not.

"Okay, so you don't sweat much. Doesn't mean you're not crazy." Never taking her eyes off Trey, she walked backward until the broken glass of the picture frame crunched beneath her feet. She grabbed her small flashlight from the shards and slipped it in her pocket. She stole a glance to the side. The door to the bathroom was only a few feet away. She could easily be out the open window in seconds.

But she had some unfinished business with Trey Nolan, even if he was delusional. "Where is the kid? What have you done with him? If you've hurt him—"

"Mario is fine." Trey stepped closer, impervious to the glass shards around her feet. "Lazlo, our Alpha, has him confined to our compound on the outskirts of town. Mario has been mingling a bit too much with humans for the others' comfort and the night at the club left too strong of a scent to hide it."

Mingling too much with humans? With dismay, CJ looked at the prime specimen of a man in front of her. To think his mind was gone. It made her visions seem harmless.

And this man had taken her brother.

"Mr. Nolan. We both know there is no such thing as a werewolf. So let's just talk about Mario, okay? First, is Mario Le Croix his real name or did you make that up, too?"

He didn't seem to be listening to her.

"No such thing as a werewolf? The only way you could have found me was following my scent." Trey walked to a window. He pulled back the drape, revealing a starless night. "This is a fifteen-story building you just climbed. I assume you think Mario is related to you because you have the same primary scent thread. Am I right?"

"Ah...I...well, yes." Cold ran down her spine. This man may be insane, but he knew too much about her and her secrets. "I'll admit I can smell better than the average person. I used it to discover Mario, used it to find you, but that's it. I don't know what you believe, but I'm just a PI from Minnesota with a good nose."

"Minnesota? You're slipping. You didn't want to tell me the state before. But it doesn't matter. Just knowing your pack existed somewhere in the Midwest, we would have tracked them down."

"There is no pack. I'm not a werewolf." Last words she ever thought would come out of her mouth.

He ran his hand through his hair, but he made no move closer. CJ considered the window where he stood. One exit cut off. That left her two. The office door and the bathroom door.

The bathroom was closer.

Trey let the curtain slip back down and turned to face her. He put his hands in his pockets.

Could he have a weapon?

"So you're telling me you aren't a werewolf? You've never shape-shifted into a different form?" His voice was filled with disbelief.

CJ tried not to let her growing unease seep into her voice. "Last time I checked, I'm completely human, just like every other person on this earth."

He glanced down at the carpet and chuckled at her comment.

CJ didn't hesitate.

She made a run for the bathroom door. Her hand was on the open bathroom windowsill before she felt his iron grip on her arm.

Her response was automatic. Shifting her weight to one side, she recoiled her arm and swung.

Trey's body hit the mirror hanging above his vanity with a crack. He slid to the floor like a rag doll.

Had she killed him?

CJ looked out the open window to the alley below. Her rope was still in place. Two, three minutes tops and she'd be on the ground running. Could she abandon someone so obviously hurt? He might be crazy, but had he really meant her bodily harm? Guilt at hitting him with her full force tugged at her conscience.

Even a lunatic deserved help. She couldn't leave him without medical attention.

She turned back to the sight of his injured body. His eyes fluttered open. He pressed an open hand against his ribcage where she had landed her fist.

"Damn, that hurts." He pushed against the tile floor and labored to move. "I'm not going to ask how many men you've put in the hospital with your left hook."

"I know how to defend myself." She let go of the windowsill.

"Yeah well, hope I'm not around when you decide to go on the offensive. I've—"

A high, digital beep sounded.

Trey reached into his pants pocket and brought a cell phone to his ear. He made no mention of his pain to the person on the other end of the call. Trey talked very little. His brows knitted tight as he listened.

CJ walked toward him, ready to help him to his feet.

"—I understand." He held his hand out for her to wait. "I know. It's an order." He flipped the phone shut and gingerly slid it into his pocket. Sweat ran down his face at the movement.

"You made your point. If you're going to go, just go. I won't"—he took in a breath and winced—"try to stop you."

CJ bent down and reached for his chest. She could get him to his feet. "Sorry. Didn't mean to hit you that hard."

"Don't apologize. I should have expected it. You are a werewolf, after all."

The creep. She let go of his torso. He dropped back the few inches to the floor. This time she didn't feel bad when he flinched.

Trey lowered his lashes. "Touché. You think I'm crazy and you aren't a werewolf." With obvious effort, he steadied his voice. "Now don't hit me, but here's the deal."

Unbelievable. *Fucking unbelievable.* On the floor, barely able to move and he still wanted to make some sort of deal. "I'm calling the ambulance then I'm out of here. I can't give you the help you need." She stood and dug for her cell phone.

Trey wrapped a hand around her calf.

She looked down. His long fingers actually touched. His hands were huge.

Trey withdrew his grip. "Hear me out. I take it you need to find Mario and his father pretty badly. Believe me, the only way you'll find either is if I help you. If you set foot anywhere on our compound, the rest of my pack will kill you first. Ask questions later."

The absurdity of this conversation wasn't lost on her. Unless some cult had brainwashed him into believing he was a werewolf. Then it'd just be sad. She had heard of crazier things. "I'm calling an ambulance. That's it."

His eyes glared with urgency. "No, I can take care of this later. Right now you need to listen." He paused and awkwardly lifted himself to a sitting position against the vanity cabinets.

She didn't move to help him. "Once again we're at the point where you tell me what you want. You're in no position to bargain with me...for anything."

Why sex was still on her mind, she couldn't fathom. He was attracted to her. So what. No man living could hide his sexual arousal from her. She had to make herself clear.

"CJ, you don't believe me, but I know you are some type of magical creature. Maybe not a werewolf, but something similar." He put a hand on his side. He labored to take a deep breath.

Looking at his coloring, she wondered if there was internal bleeding.

It wouldn't be the first time she almost killed someone.

Trey's voice grew weaker. "My pack is in trouble. The younger werewolves' strength is weaker than the generations before. Their shifting takes longer, harder to control." He stared and wouldn't let her look away. "Our new Alpha Leader and many of the Elders believe we've allowed our genes to weaken by not making sure the strong of our kind breed together. So, they've outlawed lifemating. We no longer have freedom to mate or to love as we choose. They've taken our last bit of humanity and destroyed it. We're no better than cattle now."

Alpha Leader. Elders. Taken our last bit of humanity and destroyed it. She had never heard such ramblings from someone so close to passing out from pain.

She wanted him to settle down so she could get him to the hospital. "I don't understand how I could help. Monster or not." She crouched beside him, ready to catch him if he slipped into unconsciousness.

His breathing grew more rasped. She should shut him up. Get him to a doctor, but some part of her couldn't stop listening to his story.

"Lazlo is the Alpha Leader of the New World Pack. All werewolves must obey what he commands unless the Elders Council overrides him. Many of the Elders agree with Lazlo's theory and support the breeding plan, but some feel outlawing lifemating goes too far. I think with you I can sway them to veto Lazlo." He pulled her hand into his. "This affects Mario. Do you want him forced into a marriage without love?"

CJ looked down at the man. He believed every word he spoke. Uneasiness crept over her as she realized her father and brother were likely trapped in some sort of cult.

But why did he think he needed her to stop this Lazlo guy? She left her hand in his. His breathing had improved. "So, if it's true what you say, and you're not crazy, what does me being a werewolf have to do with this breeding plan?"

Trey tapped his finger against her chest. "Your existence would throw doubt on Lazlo's weak gene pool theory. How could they ignore the importance of another pack of werewolves," he said with surprising firmness. "Possible mates, possible history and information our pack has lost. The Elders might debate for weeks, which would buy me time."

"Time for what?" CJ watched Trey's face darken with resolve.

"A more permanent answer to Lazlo's insidious ideas." He put his hand on the vanity and tried to lift himself to a standing position.

She rose with him to hold his shaking frame steady. "There's a problem here," she said, forcing a calmness in her voice she didn't feel. "Beside the fact I'm not a werewolf. But let's say you can convince the Elders I am, I don't belong to a pack. No new strong genes to add to the werewolf soup so to speak." She had to show him the holes in his far-out plan.

"Well, let's keep that particular fact between us for now. The Elders are not as easily led as Lazlo would like them to be. I think a demonstration of your left hook alone will put them in debate for a week or two." Trey gave her a half grin. "And tracking me down using nothing more than a handkerchief in a city you don't know. Impressive even for a werewolf."

"That's all you need?"

"Yes."

"Mario is part of this pack?" If Mario was her half-brother, didn't she owe it to him to use Trey and rescue the kid from these strange people?

"Yes. I can arrange a meeting with him and his father, but there's a snag." Trey took a careful step toward his office. He turned his head and spoke over his shoulder. "You might be interested in what Lazlo just told me on the phone. Mario's run away."

She studied Trey's back as he stood waiting for her to reply. Werewolf or not, he was unlike anyone she had met. He might need her help, but she would have stuck to him like glue whether he wanted her help or not.

Mario would lead her to her father and the answers she needed.

The last vision had been much stronger than any previous ones. It seemed logical that pattern would continue until she got rid of them once and for all. Unfortunately, it appeared Trey was the only way to find her half-brother and her father.

The coincidence of her wolf visions and his claim to be a werewolf wasn't something she wanted to dwell on. He held the key to finding her father and saving her sanity.

The screech of a cat echoed through the open window. CJ paused. Her instinct told her this was her last chance to turn back.

51

She followed Trey into his office.

঩঩ৎৎ

CJ leaned over to make sure she got the last digits of the home phone number of Mario's mini-skirted dance partner. The redhead in the sequined peasant top and ripped jeans was hard to hear above the teens gathered outside the club to smoke. "Was that last number a five or nine?"

"Five. You know, she carries her cell everywhere. Are you sure you don't want us to call her? She could come right down." She flicked her cigarette butt to the sidewalk and ground it under her suede boots.

"Like, she's going to die when she realizes she missed meeting a modeling agent just so some dweeby guy could cry on her shoulder," added the brunette wearing the four-inch heels.

The redhead squinched up her nose at the brunette. "Save it, Ash. Mario's got a killer bod. You're just jealous 'cause he's crushing on Kaitlyn instead of you."

"Whatever," the brunette responded.

CJ didn't want to waste any more time with these two, so she wrapped up her story. "Well, like I said. When my photo crew is in town in the next few weeks we'll give you girls a call." After keying in Kaitlyn's phone number, CJ slipped her cell into her jacket.

She left them bickering over who thought who had a "killer bod."

Once she made it clear she wasn't going to be left behind while he went to find Mario, Trey had called his night security guard to escort her to the below-ground parking garage. Ten minutes later, dressed in a pair of straight leg Levi's and a black

Henley, he had joined her. A dark brown leather bomber jacket swung from his shoulders. He held her duffle bag from the alley in his hand.

He appeared completely healthy and fit. All signs his ribs had been used as her punching bag were gone.

She resisted the urge to rip away his shirt and check for bruises. She studied his limber movements. *Painkillers.* Guardian probably stocked them for their agents. After she made him recite the alphabet backward, she released her iron hold on the stick shift and let him drive.

Presently Trey was waiting in his Jeep two blocks from the teen club. CJ had convinced him the girl from the other night would be their best lead. Thanks to her talkative friends, CJ discovered the girl was a Kaitlyn Roberts. And she had a secret crush on Mario.

With Kaitlyn's parents' phone number in hand, they'd find her address and hopefully one missing teenage werewolf.

Teenage werewolf. She sounded like she believed this crap.

She skipped the cracks in the sidewalk as she walked back to the Jeep. The childish game contrasted with her dark thoughts. She had started this quest when Roz suggested unanswered questions about her father were the cause of the damn vision. Made sense to CJ. She watched Oprah.

A missing brother complicated her mission. Plus Roz's warning from earlier tonight flashed in her mind like an unwanted neon sign.

She was tempted to call Roz and ask if the tarot's "big, bad evil" didn't happen to be six-feet-four, with mesmerizing gold eyes and six-pack abs. Oh yeah, and was it a werewolf?

She thought about the white wolf of her visions. Her wolf, as she had come to think of it. It would have been easier to flee out the bathroom window if Trey had claimed to be a vampire.

She stood outside the Jeep, her hand poised on the car handle, settling her nerves before facing Trey. The city's night air was familiar. She just had to think of this as any other missing person's case.

"Any luck?" Trey revved the engine as CJ swung her long legs into the vehicle.

As the car left the curb, she dialed her mobile search engine. "As soon as I google the phone number I got for Kaitlyn, I'll have her address."

Trey peered over at her phone. "Kaitlyn who?"

"Kaitlyn Roberts, the girl Mario likes." She held the phone up so he could see the screen where she had entered the girl's number. "See. In a few seconds Google will text message me her home address. If we don't find Mario there now, I bet he's at least been sneaking around her window. We can find his trail. Track him down."

Trey turned left on a four-lane road and increased his speed. "We're only fifteen minutes from the lake where we used to go fishing. I say check there first, then go to this Kaitlyn's house."

"The lake? You've got to be kidding me. How old is Mario?" At the club, she had watched the teen long enough to realize he had some serious teenage angst concerning girls.

"What does his age have to do with anything?" Trey slowed and waited for her answer. Traffic zoomed by.

"Just answer the question. Sixteen?"

"He turned seventeen last month."

"And you think a seventeen-year-old ran away from home knowing there are going to be some wicked consequences." CJ shook her head in disbelief. "What? He's just going to some lake and wait to be found?"

"He loved it there."

"Do you remember what it was like to be a teenager? Believe me, if they aren't brooding about what's wrong with them, they're obsessing about the opposite sex."

Trey absorbed her words and shrugged. "Okay, you have a point, but this is a wild goose chase. He told me she didn't like him."

"According to the two girls she arrived with that night, she's crazy for him."

Trey shook his head. "Doesn't make sense. He's a werewolf. He could smell her attraction. Why would he think she doesn't like him?"

"From my observations, Mario has a bad case of low self-esteem. She could give him every signal in the book and he wouldn't notice."

"Shit. I didn't realize he had gotten so down."

Before CJ could respond to Trey's comment, the ring of her cell phone filled the Jeep's cabin. CJ flipped it open to find Kaitlyn's address. "Bingo, I got it. Four five one Maynard Avenue." She saw Trey suck in his lower lip. "Well, are you going to trust my instinct?"

"That's out by his high school." Trey slowed and pulled a fast u-turn. "We can be there in twenty minutes."

Seventeen minutes and twenty-five seconds later, they pulled quietly into the alley behind Kaitlyn's house.

CJ rolled down her window and smelled the air. "He's been this way."

Trey let the Jeep coast to a stop and put it in neutral. "But is he still here?"

CJ opened her car door. "Only one way to find out."

They crept along the dark alley lined by high security fences on both sides. Mario's scent ended at the gate of a beautiful ten-foot-tall, white vinyl fence.

Before entering, she covered her hand with her jacket sleeve. With one simple push, the gate swung open. "Fences kind of lose their effectiveness when you leave the gate unlocked."

She started to go in, but Trey held her back. "Mario might run if he sees you first."

"True," CJ had to concede.

She let Trey move in front of her. Her gaze went to his ass hugged by his jeans.

The yard was shadowed by a large tree and there were no outside lights. Mario's scent hung close to the fence, then darted across the lawn to the back of the house.

The windows were dark except for a faint glow from an upstairs window. If only it was open, she could verify by smell if Mario and Kaitlyn were there. She looked at the porch's roofline just to the right of the window.

It would be a stretch, but a tall teenage boy could grab it and swing himself up. She could.

Trey reached with a long arm to test its strength.

"I wouldn't do that if I were you." He was too heavy for the porch's trim to support.

"You want to go through the front door?"

"I was thinking more of sitting tight. Grab Mario when he decides to come out. He can't hide in her room forever."

"But what are they doing in there."

"You know him, what do you think he'd be doing?" She watched carefully for Trey's reaction. From what she had seen the night before, she doubted very much Mario was putting any moves on the girl.

"Mario would talk your ear off if you let him." He stepped away from the gingerbread trim.

"Good. As long as your friend Lazlo doesn't come tearing down the street, I vote we let him finish his conversation with Kaitlyn."

Trey peered up at the window, then at CJ. She saw sadness in his eyes. "Lazlo will make sure it's the last one he spends with her." He looked around at the expanse of lawn. "Do you see some patio chairs we could crash in?"

"This way." CJ headed toward an old sprawling oak in the corner. "I spied some place much better for surveillance."

After a few head bumps and bruised knees, they settled down for their wait in the tree house she had spotted. CJ against the wall. Trey pressed next to her. A cool night breeze blew in from the door next to him. Cozy was an understatement. There was just enough room for them to sit side-by-side.

Trey bent his legs and brought an arm above his head to lean against. "I think we're both about two feet too tall to be up here."

"I've holed up in worse." CJ attempted to shrug, but only succeeded in bunching the sleeve of her jacket against Trey's arm.

"Do lots of surveillance as a PI back in Minneapolis?" he asked with honest curiosity in his voice.

"There. Chicago. Kansas City. I've spent time in most major Midwest cities. Had a girl run all the way to New York last winter."

"What did the girl do? Steal her daddy's car?"

"Actually, her high school drama teacher convinced her with 'private' lessons she'd be a star. When he and his wife reconciled, he dumped the girl. Threatened to flunk her if she told anyone about their relationship. She figured she'd go to New York, make it on stage and get her revenge." That had been one of her recent cases, before the visions ruined her life. She didn't reveal the girl had been forced to work the streets for a few weeks before CJ found her.

"Bastard. I hope you put your left hook to good use."

"Didn't have to. Her father got to him first. He's in the slammer and the girl's in a new school. Last I heard, she was doing great."

"Is that what you do? Find runaways?" He shifted his position, trying to unbend his legs, and his hip pushed against her.

The fabric of her pants was thin enough the pointy rivets of his jeans poked her.

She didn't complain. It had been her idea to come up here. "Yeah. I figure since I got this super nose, I might as well do some good with it."

Trey laughed at her answer. He had a nice laugh. It was deep and came from his stomach, not one of those smart-ass chuckles men usually gave her. Being pressed so close, the sound reverberated the whole length of her body.

"Well, Miss Super Nose, I've got to tell the truth. I'd have probably written off the girl from the club and I'd still be looking for him."

"Wow. Almost sounds like admitting you were wrong."

He twisted his torso, to face her. "Actually, it's not so much I was wrong. I just underestimated you."

She smiled at his compliment. Being underestimated was one of her secret advantages. "I have a feeling you're a fast learner."

"It's a skill I mastered early." He stared out the tree house door toward the glow of the suburban night sky.

They sat in silence.

She watched him as he was lost in thought. Her eyes had adjusted to the darkness of the tree house enough to see the contours of his face. The devilish dimple in his chin. The straight nose. The narrow eyes with their thick eyelashes.

She had seen handsome men before. Even ones with the same dimpled chins and straight noses.

She had past lovers as handsome as Trey. Bodies as perfect. Lovers who left her unsatisfied. Left her wanting more.

Trey wasn't like them. He made her heart race and her belly heat. His scent was different.

He didn't smell like other men. Human men.

Was Trey a werewolf?

Even now, stuck in a wood box like a pair of sardines, she wondered what having those long legs wrapped around her would feel like. His large hand on her waist. His long fingers between her legs. Insane or a werewolf...she wanted him.

CJ inwardly cursed herself.

She was on one of the most important surveillance missions of her life. Still, she got lost in Trey's scent.

She was being an idiot.

After the second elbow to her ribs, CJ wanted him gone. Not only for her body's comfort, but also for her peace of mind. "Go wait in the Jeep. I can watch for Mario and make sure he leaves by the alley."

"No, he'd smell you. He'd run again."

Mario did have her ability. "So this strong sense of smell is a dominant trait in my family. Does my dad have it, too?" She waited for Trey to give her a clue about her old man.

He scrunched his eyebrows and snorted. "Of course he does, they...we all have it. It's a werewolf thing."

The werewolves. Again. CJ's tolerance for his fairytale was at its end.

So he smelled a little off. There had to be a rational reason for his strange scent. CJ had dealt with real monsters. They weren't werewolves. They were sick, perverted human beings.

She had to call his bluff. See if this story was insanity or his sick sense of humor. "Okay, I've decided. You're really a werewolf? Show me some proof."

Calling his bluff should make him sweat. She analyzed the smells floating across the night air.

Nothing. No anxiety spike. No salty sweat thread. Just like in the office.

"I told you. You're not going to catch me lying with your nose." He actually sounded annoyed with her.

The nerve of him. She wasn't the one talking nonsense. She glanced past Trey at the night sky. A half moon peeked out in the gray suburban night. "Let me guess, no full moon, right?"

Trey crossed his arms and bored into her with his glowing gold eyes. "Actually, the moon has nothing to do with shape-shifting. If it once meant something to us, we've forgotten."

"Forgotten? Doesn't seem a proper *werewolf* thing to do." She couldn't keep the sarcasm out of her voice. This stuff just couldn't be true. He was too damn normal. He had to be pulling some kind of twisted joke on her.

Trey's tongue came out and licked his full lower lip. He looked out the window, his brows furrowed in thought.

CJ's heart skipped a beat when he turned his stare on her.

With a surprising speed, his face came down inches away from hers. "As for a proper *werewolf* thing to do, I could change form for you, but"—Trey paused and spoke the words over her lips—"the space is fairly cramped. Plus, I'd have to get naked first. I think it's too early in our relationship for that step, don't you?"

She stopped listening after the word naked fell from his lips.

CJ couldn't answer him. She was too overwhelmed by his breath pouring over her face. Her resistance to his smell seeped away in his moist warm essence. She wanted to be in it, touch it, though it had no form. Lick it up and take it into her body. Her womb ached in physical pain from the desire she felt, even if he was a lunatic.

She couldn't take his scent, but she could take him.

CJ was never coy with men. Since they usually turned out to be disappointments, she had found it better to get her sexual curiosity out of the way.

How could Trey be different? His scent was new, but take that oddity away and he was still just a man. A distraction.

In one awkward movement, she tumbled over him until she straddled his legs, pinning his shoulders to the rough board wall of the tree house. Her breasts pressed flat against his arms crossed in front of his chest.

Trey's brows arched in surprise, but she gave him no chance to ruin this moment with any more talk of werewolves.

She pressed his lips hard with her own. Digging her fingers around his solid shoulders she ground against his jeans, the rigid zipper rough against her crotch.

Damn. He tasted like he smelled. Musky and spicy. His flavor poured across her tongue and she pushed it between his lips to savor more. He groaned under her assault, opening his lips to her penetration.

Her palms kept him pinned but he uncrossed his arms and grabbed onto her waist. His thumbs dug under her ribcage as he pulled her closer during the kiss.

She let go of his shoulders. Pushed her hands under his jacket across the thin cotton of his Henley. She could feel the heat of him. He was blazing. Heat for her. Heat from her.

He pulled away from her lips. "I want your hair down." The gravelly tone was low and urgent.

She did as he asked, reaching back to remove the black band holding her hair at the nape of her neck.

Trey moved his hands from her waist, then across the slick fabric over her breasts, weaving around her neck and finally entwining his fingers in her hair.

He grabbed it hard and yanked her face down to him, claiming her mouth. He captured her tongue. Sucked it. Stinging desire lit up her clit. She tilted her hips, driven to appease the need with the friction of their hips.

All this fabric and hard wood maddened her. The silence of the tree house was broken by the rip of the Henley's buttons being torn apart. Warning bells rang in her head, but the promise of sexual satisfaction in Trey's kiss kept her going.

Trey let her tongue slide back into her mouth. His hands slipped away from her hair. She jerked away from his embrace. "What—"

She smelled another.

They weren't alone anymore.

Chapter Four

Silently, Trey cursed Mario's timing.

Trey lifted CJ off his lap and placed her on the other side of him. *Away* from Mario sitting in the tree house doorway. Trey turned to the confused young werewolf.

"It's all right. She's doesn't want to harm you." Mario's wary expression didn't waver. "Or me. She doesn't want to hurt either of us."

CJ's face softened as she tucked her loose hair behind her ears. "Mario." She held out her hand. "I'm CJ Duncan. I'm a missing person's investigator. I thought you could help me find someone."

The warmth of her smile wasn't lost on Trey.

Mario didn't take her hand. He looked at Trey. "Oh. So...ah, are you aren't a, ah—"

"She is, or something close. You've got good instincts, kid. I've had the broken ribs to prove it, too." He didn't care what CJ thought of his statement. He'd show her the truth soon enough. "But she's okay. She's not here to make dog food out of anyone."

Mario narrowly eyed CJ's outstretched hand. His eyebrows arched as he looked to Trey for assurance. When Trey nodded, Mario took it.

Mario squeezed her hand with his supernatural strength.

"Strong grip you've got there." If she was surprised at the boy's strength, she didn't show it.

Mario let out a quiet whistle. "Wow. You're for real. I can't wait to shove this in Lazlo's face."

Trey touched CJ's leg. "This stays our secret. I don't trust Lazlo. We're going to wait till the Elders are convened before anyone knows about CJ." He eyed Mario to make sure he understood. "Now let's get you back to the compound. You ready for what you have to face?" Trey imagined Mario's escape had Lazlo furious. Everyone underestimated Mario.

"Yeah, I'm ready. He told me he was yanking me from school, so I figured I had nothing to lose. I had some unfinished business." A shitty grin came across the young werewolf's face.

CJ leaned in front across Trey's bent legs, her hair sweeping forward. "Was it worth it?"

Mario looked away toward the house. He lifted his eyebrows. "Definitely worth it." The teen made the ten-foot drop to the ground without another word.

Trey sneaked a glance at CJ, her lips flushed red. He didn't feel much like talking about his woman either.

His woman. She'd probably break him in two if she knew he had just thought of her in those terms. He shouldn't, yet he couldn't lie to himself. She was different. Beautiful, no question, but the inner strength she possessed awed him. Never shaking under pressure. He found her damn near irresistible.

And if her move in the tree house was any indication, she wanted him, too. He hoped she didn't react with such fervor to every male werewolf in his pack. He wanted to think the man in him, not the animal, attracted her.

Trey's blood surged remembering how she marked his lips with her kisses. She didn't know it yet, but they were going to finish what they had started. Until they did, no other man, werewolf or human, dare interfere.

They followed Mario down the tree and headed out the gate. Whatever had happened in Kaitlyn's bedroom put an energetic bounce to Mario's gait. He waited at the Jeep for them to catch up.

Trey grabbed CJ's elbow, his voice a low whisper. "We can't let the others know if Mario just had sex with Kaitlyn."

CJ pulled her elbow free and lifted one eyebrow. "Don't worry, I'd smell it on him if they did. Didn't you ever have a crush on someone and then find out they like you, too? He probably feels invincible right now."

"Invincible? We wish." Trey jogged the last few steps to the Jeep. He opened the door for Mario to climb in.

The kid still grinned like an idiot.

Trey debated whether to leave CJ in his office or take her to her hotel room. He decided she'd be safer under his watch. Another pack member might catch her scent in the city.

He didn't give her an option. He drove straight to the garage under his office building. Mario and CJ remained silent throughout the drive, lost in their own thoughts, leaving Trey plenty of time to think about how to keep CJ at the office.

He doubted she'd like his idea.

He made good time on the deserted night streets, but before he put the Jeep in park, Mario leaned forward from the back. "Trey, I think we have company."

From across the deserted garage, the blue headlights of a silver Lexus made a beeline for them.

Lazlo.

He laid a hand across CJ's chest as she cocked her head to look at the oncoming car. "Stay in here. I don't know what he'll do if he finds you. With a little luck, he may be distracted enough with Mario not to detect your scent." He motioned Mario to go out the door on his side.

The Lexus parked perpendicular to Trey's Jeep, effectively blocking him in.

Trey got out and Mario quickly followed behind. He slammed the door shut fast.

The tall, sleek form of the Alpha Leader stepped from the idling car. Even at three in the morning, Lazlo dressed in an Armani suit. His long ebony hair pulled back into a sleek ponytail. Always the perfect picture of power. Always in perfect control.

He stood eye to eye with Trey.

Lazlo didn't say a word to his younger half-brother who shifted from foot to foot beside Trey. He simply bent his head toward the Lexus and Mario obeyed.

Always the same. Lazlo in charge. Mario obeying. It was one of the reasons Mario and Trey had hit it off. Trey actually listened when Mario talked.

Trey had nothing but silence for his old friend, though it had been over a decade since he thought of Lazlo with any of those fond feelings. Trey stopped mourning their lost friendship long ago.

"I'm pulling Mario out of the school you convinced the Elders he should attend." Lazlo's voice carried a hint of a Spanish accent inherited from his parents.

"I know. He told me. You think that's wise? He excels in their prep courses."

Lazlo's nostrils quivered, the only outward sign of his anger. "Don't tell the Alpha what to do with a disobedient whelp. You forget your place. You are only CEO for Guardian. I lead the pack. You must do what I say."

Trey held out a hand toward the Lexus. "I've returned your brother as you ordered."

"Brother or not, I won't tolerate his bad behavior. He will be treated like any other werewolf."

"Be careful, Lazlo. Mario may not be the werewolf everyone expects him to be, but he has strengths." Just because Mario couldn't control his shape-shifting long enough to participate in the youth training challenges, he had been labeled as weak. "Your belief in this bizarre superiority of strong genes will be your downfall. I'll promise you it."

Lazlo moved to within an inch of Trey's face, his steps echoing in the empty garage. "Are you threatening me to a Challenge? Because I can have the Elders convened in a day."

Trey cursed his tongue. Why did Lazlo always make him lose control? Of all nights, he did not need to provoke the Alpha this night. Not with CJ a few feet away and he still unable to guarantee her safety.

He prayed Lazlo was too angry to notice CJ's scent.

The Alpha's hand shot out and circled Trey's throat. His fingers able to grasp Trey's thick neck easily. "Who else is in the Jeep? What other werewolf are you poisoning with your rebellious ways?"

Lazlo always went for the throat. Trey gasped for air to talk. "It's just a human...a woman...good time."

"Don't take me for a fool." Lazlo released Trey with a shove.

Trey hit the pavement hard. The ribs, only freshly healed from CJ's assault, screamed out in pain.

ಬಿಇಬಿಅ

"Things in the mirror are closer than they appear" was written in the sideview mirror where CJ watched Lazlo throw Trey to the ground. They were about to get a lot closer. She didn't care what Trey said. She couldn't sit on her butt and do nothing while the tall, slick dude beat him to a pulp.

She had hung back when Lazlo gripped Trey's throat, respecting Trey's wish that Lazlo not discover her. She thought Trey would fight back.

He didn't.

When Trey's face hit the pavement, her innate sense of fair play overrode self-preservation. Painkillers or not, Trey was already injured, thanks to her assault earlier.

She sprung her door and whipped around the back end of the Jeep, her rubber shoes silent on the pavement. With a strong grip on the smooth fabric of Lazlo's jacket, she swung the stunned man around to meet her fist.

The sound of cracking bone echoed through the empty parking garage.

The tall man didn't let his own broken nose slow him down for a second. He pivoted on his feet and let out a long kick, easily catching her on the right side. Pain shot down her legs, making her stumble, but she stayed upright.

She regained her balance quickly enough to dodge another hit. CJ wasn't in the mood for a dance. Without hesitation she ripped the spare tire hanging off of Trey's Jeep and flung it toward Lazlo's stomach.

His ass hit the ground with a thud. She took the second he stayed down to reach Trey's side.

"Can you get up?"

"Eventually."

"Okay, hang on to me, I'll get you out of here." She bent down to throw him over her shoulder, praying she didn't damage his ribs more. CJ looked over at Lazlo to see if he was still out of commission. Disbelief shocked her. "What the hell?"

The dude stripped his jacket off and tossed it on the car. His shirt followed.

Trey frowned up at Lazlo. "Oh, shit. Lazlo, don't. She doesn't know who you are."

"Shut up, Trey. She attacked without warning while I was in human form and she used a weapon." He kicked the tire with his shoe while he unhooked his belt.

Trey raised himself to his elbows and pushed CJ's hands away. She fell back on her heels amazed he could breathe enough to speak. He had to have several broken ribs.

"Just stop for a second. I can explain," Trey said.

"Okay, start explaining, but if she so much as twitches a muscle, I'm taking her out," Lazlo threatened.

"She doesn't know our rules. She fights by the rules of her own. I didn't tell her who you are. She was trying to protect me."

Lazlo whipped out his belt. The thin leather snapped like a whip. "Stupid move on her part. Now get your pathetic self out of the way and let me finish this."

The sound of a car door slamming startled all three of them.

"I'll tell the Elders if you kill her now." Mario stood tall as he challenged the Alpha Leader. "I don't think they'll be too pleased. A new werewolf is a big deal."

Lazlo stood quiet at Mario's threat. The blood flowed from his nose, spilling down his face and naked chest. His injury, enough to make a typical man cower, hardly seemed to faze him. His hands fisted at his sides.

She readied herself to jump between him and her brother if he made another move. Trey must have felt her body tense, because he laid a hand on her arm and shook his head, no.

The Lexus hummed in the silence of the garage.

Some part of CJ knew she should be afraid. Apparently Trey and Mario thought their leader meant to kill her. And they had no question he could.

CJ knew better.

This guy might be one hell of a fighter. The one kick he got in had been hard, but no one had taken her down. Ever.

Not one man. Not even three. A few gang members had once tried to stop her from grabbing their latest initiate. During that fight, she had learned what she was truly capable of doing.

When they had surrounded her, she had gone into automatic. She didn't realize what she had done until too late. Their three broken bodies lay bleeding on the street. The stop sign she had ripped from the concrete curb vibrating in her hand.

The three men survived. The police believed she had "found" the sign broken off. She had taken every effort not to lose control since.

But tonight her strength was vital to defeating this Lazlo bastard.

Trey interrupted her thoughts. "Mario's right. With two of us to confirm her existence, they'll be very unhappy you destroyed her before they could interview her. Even as Alpha, you may not escape their punishment."

Lazlo ran the back of his hand across his mouth. His blood splattered onto the pavement. "Where did you find this female?"

No one talked about her as if she wasn't there. CJ answered before Trey could. "I found him. I'm a private investigator."

"Your Alpha allows you to work alone? Who sent you?" demanded Lazlo.

Trey didn't want any of his pack to know she was a loner, so she chose not to enlighten Lazlo. "Well, I don't really feel like talking right now." She stood to her full height and lifted her fists in front of her. She knew how to block a blow just as well as throw them. "You were saying something about a fight before Mario interrupted."

The asshole smiled at her. Bloodied and half naked in a parking garage and he still had the nerve to condescend to her. Arrogance even permeated his scent marker. Anger roiled inside her as they faced off.

Lazlo waited, eyes revealing nothing.

CJ smelled the air, trying to determine if he'd attack. Her muscles twitched in anticipation, but she didn't make a move when he bent to retrieve his shirt and coat from his car hood.

He slipped them on, not bothering with the buttons. "Maybe another day." He glanced at Trey. "I'll accept any challenge to my honor."

Lazlo walked over to CJ and stood within hitting distance, his hands nonchalantly in his pockets. "Apparently your pack has different customs concerning the rules of engagement with another werewolf. I'll forgive you your earlier attack. To defend a fellow werewolf is honorable, but the next time I will not be so understanding."

Trey struggled to stand, but he would not take CJ's arm for support as he stumbled to get his legs beneath him. "So what

71

now, Lazlo. Will you call home the Elders to discuss the existence of another pack?"

"You would like the Elders to vote against my plan wouldn't you." Lazlo lowered his voice to a whisper. "You talk of downfalls...your ego is more important to you than our pack. Now I ask you, do you still honor the pledge of obedience you swore to me as Alpha Leader?"

"As much as I ever have, Lazlo." Trey didn't blink at his answer.

"You try me."

"And the Elders?" Trey asked.

"I will convene them when I find it necessary." Lazlo glanced at the gold watch on his wrist. "It's getting close to morning. It is time for us to return to the compound. Follow in your Jeep."

"Of course."

"Good, I'd hate to turn the Guards after you, Trey." Lazlo twisted the words out with a sarcastic snarl.

Trey waved a hand to Lazlo's car. "Well, let's get moving. I'm sure neither of us is enjoying our present condition." With that, Trey spat a glob of blood on the pavement.

Knowing the uselessness of suggesting both men stop at the ER before going home, CJ simply followed Trey to the Jeep. Lazlo motioned Mario back into the Lexus.

Before Trey could climb into the driver's seat, CJ stopped him with a gentle touch. "I can follow his car. You have no business driving."

Trey headed to the passenger side door. "Truthfully, I hurt too damn bad to *try* to argue. Go ahead."

After Trey painfully crawled into his seat, CJ shifted the Jeep into reverse and waited for the Lexus to move. "I know how to tail a car. You should rest."

She waited for Trey's reply, but heard only his heavy breathing as he slumped asleep in his seat.

ಬಿ෴ඏಏ

The gurgle of Trey coughing blood turned CJ's attention from the taillights of the Lexus to the man crouched over in the seat next to her. He had only slept for ten minutes.

Trey ran a hand over his ribs, wincing as he came in contact with the most severe breaks. "Man, Lazlo didn't hold back, and they were still healing from *your* attack."

CJ shifted down. "Enough bullshit. I don't care what fucking Lazlo ordered. I'm taking you to a hospital."

The car in front of them hit its brakes as the Jeep fell behind.

Trey covered her hand on the stick shift and feebly tried to make her change gears. "Don't be crazy. I'm not going to die. I just need to shift to my wolf form, but I don't think I can wait till we're to the compound."

She watched the Lexus slow in front of them. The stupidity of going anywhere but a hospital right now pissed her off. Trey needed help. She pushed her knee under the wheel to steer and pulled her cell phone from her pocket. "What's Lazlo's number. I'll call him. Promise to bring you back to the compound after a doctor has examined you."

"Put the phone away and speed up. I don't want to piss Lazlo off"—he took another ragged breath—"more than I already have tonight. I'm pushing my luck."

73

The Jeep lurched forward when she shifted. Her peripheral vision caught Trey's wince of pain. "Sorry."

"CJ, for the next couple of minutes I suggest you keep your eyes straight ahead."

"Why?" She looked directly at him in the dark confines of the car.

"Well, you know how you said you needed proof I was a werewolf? You're gonna get it." He rested a large hand on the dash and paused, "But it's not the prettiest sight. Not when I'm hurt and squashed in here." He leaned forward, tugging the leather jacket off, then tossing it in the space behind the seats.

"You're going to become a werewolf? Here? In the Jeep?"

"Shifting is the only way to heal these wounds. And I'm going to have to stay a wolf for awhile so when we get back to the compound try to keep your mouth shut till I'm human again."

"Aren't you going to stay with me?" She didn't need him, but for some reason being in *the compound*, whatever the place was, without him didn't sit right with her.

"No, now I'm hurting damn bad. Promise me. Don't talk to Lazlo till I'm there. Don't trust him, CJ, no matter what he says about me."

"Well—"

"I really don't want you to die." He yanked the Henley over his head. His entire torso was marked with black and blue bruises.

Next she heard the swish of the zipper and saw him pushing his jeans down his long legs. Those clothes, too, were swung behind his seat.

"Why are you taking your clothes off?" CJ asked.

"I get tired of buying new clothes." Trey turned the radio to a rock song and cranked the volume.

She fought to keep her eye on the road and off Trey.

They exited the main street. A series of turns forced her to pay attention to the Lexus. Luckily the traffic was light for this time of night, but some early shift workers were already on the road.

"CJ, I didn't want to do this like...well in a car, but I think I've got some major internal bleeding. I hurt like hell. Promise you won't freak out when you see me as a wolf." Trey's tone turned urgent. "Promise?"

"Sure, whatever—"

The muffled sound of cracking sent a shiver up her spine. She couldn't tell for sure what had made it. The damn radio blared so loud. She lowered the volume as she checked on Trey.

He seemed bent over, as if he had curled his head down between his knees. Oh, shit. He was puking. Probably blood. She had to get him to the hospital.

She returned her gaze to the increasing traffic of the road. Her hand went across the seat to touch his head. Give him some comfort. Guilt racked her. She shouldn't have let Lazlo intimidate her into going against her own instincts.

Her hand made contact with Trey's hair...

She snatched her hand back.

No, fucking way could his hair feel so bristly. *No way.*

She ran her fingers over Trey's hair again. Her sensitive palms revealed tufts coarser and thicker than Trey's wavy brown hair. The utter wrongness of its texture unsettled her more than anything she had witnessed tonight.

Fur.

Shit.

She peeked at the passenger seat and the bile rose in her throat. Where Trey had been something else sat, a creature covered with fur. She glimpsed dark thatches of hair emerging from deep brown skin. But the skin wasn't just skin. It undulated, as if the something beneath it churned. Shifted.

Like a moving mass of road kill right next to her.

CJ focused on the street and fought the urge to vomit. Once her stomach settled, she glanced again at the thing.

She saw what she thought were Trey's arms, but in his crouched position she couldn't make out where his legs began. The Jeep's interior hid most of him in shadows.

The sound of a car horn brought her back to the road and she had to swerve to miss an oncoming car. The jerk of the wheel sent the creature careening into the passenger door.

The high-pitched whimper made every hair on her neck rise on end. One more look to the side confirmed her fear.

Oh, fuck. *Fuck. Fuck. Fuck.*

Large golden eyes stared back at her. She recognized them. She could never forget them. Trey's eyes.

But no human sat next to her.

In the passenger seat sat a very large, very real wolf. If she thought her eyes fooled her, her nose couldn't. It carried Trey's scent. A scent engraved in her mind and the something different she had always sensed but never been able to identify. Wolf.

Big and bad. God she prayed he wasn't evil.

The Lexus in front of her hit its brakes and made a sharp right into a small drive overgrown with brush.

It took effort to shift the Jeep down and turn the wheel. Her hands shook and hell if she could make them stop. A soft sound escaped the wolf's throat. With a slow gentleness she would have never believed possible, it nuzzled its head beneath her arm and laid it down across her legs.

She moved her gaze from the road to her lap. Golden eyes regarded her with an unblinking stare. Saying what? She didn't know. This was Trey, wasn't it? He wouldn't hurt her.

CJ lifted her hand from the wheel and warily put her fingers into the thick fur between the wolf's ears. His warmth radiated under her touch. And though the fur was coarse, it caressed her hand. Lush and full.

With a soft whimper, the wolf closed its eyes.

Chapter Five

The shaded drive led into a wooded hill. Since they had left the parking garage, she had kept an eye on the odometer. They had gone about fifteen miles and were well away from the congestion of Seattle proper. They had driven through twelve lights and passed a seedy-looking bar when they turned onto the last road. Following the leader of a pack of werewolves into the wilds of Washington wasn't the smartest thing she had ever done, but at least there were signs of civilization to lead her back to the city.

Though the small road was well maintained, its weaving curves forced her to drive a slow speed.

The wolf continued sleeping on her lap, its hot breath damp against her thin shirt.

The Lexus in front of her braked and she observed two small guardhouses flanking the drive. A tall woman dressed in a black paramilitary outfit stepped out of a building and leaned over to talk to Lazlo.

The woman's gaze went to CJ in the Jeep, but Lazlo must have given her more instructions because it quickly jerked back to him. CJ could just make out his face in the Lexus's side mirror.

Lazlo and Mario pulled ahead and the guard simply waved CJ through. In the rearview mirror CJ saw another guard appear to talk to the woman. The whole set-up made it clear how this compound place handled unwelcome company.

Trey had told her he was the only way to get to her father. It sure as hell looked like he had told the truth.

As the Jeep tailed the car, the narrow road opened into a large paved parking area surrounded by deep overgrown brush and trees. Twenty or so vehicles were parked beneath the canopy of the border trees. Not a junker in the lot. Most of the autos were large, dark-colored SUVs. CJ saw a few 4X4 pickups and a pair of gleaming chrome Harleys down at the end.

The Lexus stopped near an empty parking spot. Mario got out and motioned for her to pull in. Lazlo drove off down another small driveway into the forest.

CJ relaxed her grip on the steering wheel as she eased the Jeep next to Mario. She wasn't sure how long she'd have a reprieve from Lazlo, but she was glad to have a moment with Mario and Trey without the Alpha.

Mario opened the passenger door and the wolf roused himself from his slumber. She hadn't realized how heavy its head had become until he lifted it off her legs.

It scratched a great paw across its ear. Drowsy eyes blinked up at CJ. Before she could open her door and get away from the wolf, a large rough tongue gave her a messy slurp upside her cheek.

Wet wolf saliva ran down her face. "Gross." She wiped it away with her shirtsleeve.

The wolf pulled its jaw back in a manner almost resembling a smile before it turned tail and vaulted out the open door. Its dark chocolate form disappeared quickly into the shadowed trees.

"Well, he looks a lot better than when we left. Lazlo never holds back when he fights." Mario reached around the empty passenger seat and retrieved Trey's clothes and her duffle. "It might take him several hours to fully heal. We probably won't see him till tonight."

CJ sat back in the seat and smelled the air. Wilderness. Moss. Earth. And wolf. There were others nearby. Others who weren't Trey. She couldn't tell how close, but close enough.

Werewolves of Seattle. Not in her wildest dreams did she think her visions would lead here. She stared down at her hands resting on her legs. Still steady. She hadn't gone crazy yet.

The kid leaned into the Jeep and covered her hand with his.

His touch held warmth. His fingers long like hers. Long like Trey's. "Are you okay?" He whispered the question.

"Mario, do you do that, too?" She found it difficult to imagine the youthful face changing into a creature of the wild. Her own reflection caught her eye in the rearview mirror. Did she hold that secret in her blood as well?

The teenager shrugged his shoulders. "Sort of." He leaned back out of the Jeep and took a look around the woods. He made an exaggerated movement with his eyes to convey they were being watched. "You're supposed to go with me. You can hang out at Trey's cabin until he gets back."

She got out of the truck and tried not to think about what lay in the woods a few feet away. Were these werewolves she sensed or regular wild wolves that would kill without thought? She didn't doubt her strength, but she had never defended herself against someone with claws and two rows of fangs.

Just the thought of fighting exhausted her. It had been over twenty-four hours since she'd slept. Hopefully Lazlo would give her a few hours' rest before her interrogation. "Trey's cabin got a couch to sleep on?"

Mario smiled at her question. A real smile. "You lucked out. It's pretty comfortable. I crash there when shit at the dorm gets too crazy." With Trey's clothes and her duffle, he walked into the trees and followed a small footpath. His long legs covered the ground fast.

CJ found herself dragging. Pulling an all-nighter wasn't her favorite activity, but she urged her tired body on. She didn't want to pass up this chance to ask Mario about his father. There wasn't room for both of them on the path, but she walked as close as she could behind him. She attempted to find recognizable markers if she had to make a run for the vehicles, but the forest grew so thick every inch looked the same to her. She hoped her scent trail would remain there long enough to follow.

Too bad she had never done the girl-scout thing.

She sniffed the air and the wolf smell had dissipated some. She'd take the chance they weren't being listened to and ask some questions.

"You mentioned a dorm. Don't you live with your mom and dad? Or isn't having a family allowed in your pack?"

He looked over his shoulder. "We live with our parents until we're twelve. Then we move into the dorms so we can start training, our version of high school."

"But you didn't have to train because you were so smart?"

Mario snorted. "Yeah, something like that. But school's all done with now. I blew it, sneaking out to the club the other night, so it's back to digging my nose in the dirt with the other dogs."

The tone of his voice when he said *dogs* was unmistakable—typical teenager sarcasm. She doubted the other werewolves appreciated being called dogs. She had always assumed her independent, nonconformist streak came from her

81

mother. Maybe her father had passed that one to both her and her brother. "What do your parents think of Lazlo pulling you out of school?"

"Doesn't matter. Lazlo is the Alpha. What he says goes."

CJ bumped into Mario's back when he stopped abruptly. Ahead of them, almost hidden in the trees, sat a rustic cabin. The dark wood siding blended with the shadows and no lights shone through the two windows on either side of the door.

Three steps led to a covered porch along the front length of the cabin. A few bundles of wood lay stacked on one side, on the other a pair of muddy hiking boots.

Mario marched up and swung the door open. "Here we are. They don't look like much from the outside, but we've remodeled them on the inside. All the money Trey's been earning for the pack is being put to good use."

CJ entered Trey's home and found Mario wasn't lying.

Before joining her inside, she caught him scanning the woods. He frowned, then closed the door with a slam. He set her duffle down in an open hall and motioned her toward the kitchen off to the left. "I'll show you the layout, then let you get some sleep. Lazlo will send someone to get your bags from the hotel. Do you have the key?"

"How thoughtful of him," she said with a sarcastic smile. She retrieved the key card from a pocket and dropped it into Mario's hand. He gave her an odd look as she did. He put the card into his pocket and moved to the granite-topped counter.

He yanked a drawer open. He pulled out a paper and pen, while he continued to explain some nonsense about running the dishwasher. Hastily he scribbled words on the paper and handed it to her.

They're listening outside the windows. You'll be guarded until Trey returns.

It didn't surprise her. She glanced up from the pad and realized the aloof teenage expression he had worn since their arrival at the compound had vanished.

In its place was a questioning gaze. He stood there and studied her face, her body, her hair.

He knew. He knew she was his sister, but the bewilderment on his face revealed he couldn't quite believe it.

She held her hand out for the pen. "Why don't you show me the bathroom. I'd like to take a shower before I crash."

He gave it to her, touching her hand as he did. "It's right down this hall." He pulled her hand against his and they stood in the kitchen, palm to palm.

His fingers were longer, but their shape the same. Hers light, his dark. His nostrils quivered, no doubt finding the same scent threads that had revealed him to her.

He dropped his hand and motioned for her to follow.

Was he angry? Confused? Did he think his father had cheated on his mother?

She followed Mario down a short hallway off the kitchen and kept an eye out for someone watching through the windows. She scribbled on the pad. When they stepped into the bathroom she handed him her note.

I might be your half-sister. That's why I followed you at the club. I don't know for sure. I need to talk to your father. Where can I find him?

Mario took the note, double-checked the window and shoved the paper in his pocket. He mouthed the word, "Impossible."

"Is there anything else you can help me with?" CJ looked the kid straight in the eye. He seemed so confused; she didn't want him to think she intended to tear apart his family. She took a chance and whispered, "I'm not here to cause problems. I just need some help."

The kid stood there in the middle of the small bathroom. Looking out the window, then at her. CJ waited to see what her younger half-brother would do. Would he call in the others and reveal her secret? Maybe they already knew.

A lopsided grin appeared on his face. He leaned forward and whispered, "Hate to tell you this, but you being you is a problem."

CJ sighed in relief. Cocky kid. She liked Mario. She didn't want him to be her enemy. "Do the others know I might be related to you?"

Mario went over, turned the sink on and made a scene of washing his hands. The water poured out full blast making it impossible for anyone outside the room to hear their whispers. "You've reminded me of someone since I saw you. I didn't realize who until I talked to you about my parents on the path. You've got Dad's dimples."

She had always wondered about those dimples on her face. "Couldn't you smell it on me right away?"

Mario shrugged. "Only a little and only when I knew what to look for. Those scents are deep in our odor markers. I don't know any werewolves who can smell well enough—" Mario jerked his head to the window. He turned off the water and wiped his hands on his jeans.

He walked past CJ out into the hall. "I've got to go *now*."

She followed him, thinking about what he had said about being unable to smell those threads. Perhaps these werewolves weren't as powerful as she feared.

He put his hand on the door handle. "Trey will be back in a few hours. Just hang out." He lifted his fingers to his lips. Before he turned to leave, he held out his hand.

She grasped it in her own. *A little brother.* One gentle squeeze and he pulled back to open the door.

Mario smiled and left, closing the door quickly behind him.

A little brother. And hopefully an ally in this strange world she had entered. After witnessing the brutal strength of Lazlo, she needed a friend in the pack. Doubts about Trey nagged at the edge of her mind. Figuring him out would have to come later.

She leaned down and grabbed her duffle. Not much in it, but she had stuck in a T-shirt. She headed back to the bathroom, the only room with one window and a sturdy blind. No reason to give the werewolves outside a peep show.

Throwing the bag to the floor, she stared at her reflection in the mirror. Deep dimples appeared on either side of her forced smile. She didn't picture a werewolf having dimples.

Werewolves should look like Trey and Lazlo, all muscles, glaring eyes and chiseled faces.

She closed her eyes and recalled Trey in his wolf form. The long, menacing snout covered with sleek hair. Thick fur running down the heavily muscled shoulders of the wolf. The impossible had happened in the seat of that Jeep, yet she couldn't deny it *had happened.*

Trey had become a wolf.

Could she do what Trey had done? Change form? She tried to imagine what if felt like to shift. Painful probably.

What would she look like? The image of her white wolf flashed in her mind.

She opened her eyes in shock. Could she be the white wolf?

CJ grabbed a comb Trey had left on his sink and pulled it through her long, pale hair. She had never thought of it as unusual coloring, probably because there were so many people of Nordic descent in Minnesota. But in the summer when she went to the lake, the sun bleached it almost white.

She slammed the comb back down. She couldn't let herself think she was a werewolf, just because it appeared that Trey, Mario and her father were. Her mom was completely human. If Karen Duncan had been anything other than a desperate, hardworking single mother they wouldn't have spent so many years struggling to keep a roof over their heads.

She caught a movement past the bathroom window. Lazlo's goons. She was seriously not liking that dude. Men with power trips were her personal least favorite.

She glanced down at her watch. Six-thirty a.m. The last few hours had flown.

The large, tiled shower beckoned. Mario had said Trey wouldn't be back till nightfall and it didn't look like Lazlo would be letting her go anywhere soon. After pulling the blind tightly shut, she stripped off her clothes, tossing them in a pile on the floor.

Something in her pants clinked against the hard tiles.

Of course, her cell phone. How could she have forgotten?

That phone could be her only tie to the real world, if she could use it without being heard. *Mario's water trick.*

She grabbed it from her pants pocket and stepped inside the shower stall. Turning on the water full blast, she backed into the corner and dialed Roz's number.

After three rings the call went to voice mail.

"Hello, friends. You've reached Rozlynn Royal's Psychic Life Coaching. You are important to me. Please leave your name, number and short message after the beep. Peace out."

CJ watched with dismay as the bars faded on her phone. All these trees were shit for getting a connection. "Roz, it's me.

I'm close to meeting my father, but there's some weird stuff going on. Um, I'm losing signal, so if you don't hear from me by..." She had to pause and figure out it was Saturday morning. "If you don't hear from me by Monday night. Let my Mom know I'm with a man named Trey Nolan and—"

The signal went dead.

She finished her thought anyway. "And let her know I love her." Stupid box of buttons and circuits would run out of battery life by Monday night anyway.

Better than nothing, though. If she got her bags from the hotel, she could recharge it. CJ stuck her head out of the shower and made sure the window blind hadn't moved. She tucked the phone into the pocket of her pants.

Stepping back in to the shower, the warm water eased down her tired muscles. She lathered Trey's loofa with a minty shower gel and stroked it down her long arms. She had given them quite a work out. First on Trey's ribs, then on Lazlo's face.

That last hit had been quite satisfying. No, she wasn't sure what she had stumbled into with this werewolf pack, but at least one thing had gone her way.

She hadn't had a vision in front of Lazlo.

ʚ৪ৎ೮ৎ

Trey stayed in the shadow of the trees provided by the setting sun until he had identified all three of the werewolves guarding the house. Sebastian and Bruno were in human form. Like Trey, Gracie stalked the woods in wolf form, lingering upwind and farther from the cabin than the males.

They were three of his top operatives at Guardian. But they were also loyal to Lazlo, especially Bruno and Gracie. Until Trey could beat Lazlo in a Challenge, the others would follow Lazlo's orders first. Not his.

Trey didn't hold it against them. The werewolves had to stay a united pack or they would become vulnerable, like their ancestors in Europe who had been decimated a half a century before.

Pack loyalty was the most important trait to the New World werewolves. Personal feelings aside, Trey would not disobey Lazlo either.

At least while Lazlo remained Alpha. No one had ever issued a Succession Challenge in the short history of the pack. When Trey was ready, he would be the first. Until then, he had to obey.

Lazlo's orders concerning CJ had been made crystal clear when he had cornered Trey out in the hunting grounds a few hours earlier. Like Trey, he had been in wolf form and hunting for the sustenance to heal the wounds from CJ's blows. Trey had gotten the deer first, but in deference to his Alpha, he waited until Lazlo had eaten his fill. After the Alpha devoured most of the tender parts of the kill, he had lain back in the tall grass and shifted into his human form.

Even his shifts were controlled and elegant, though not nearly as fast as Trey's. Trey had always bested him in speed.

So as Trey finished the scraps, Lazlo detailed how Trey would be CJ's keeper until he and the Elders decided what to do with her. Several of the Elders were out of the country on missions, Mario's father Rupert included. If Lazlo wanted Trey to be CJ's jailor, so be it. Trey understood he was her protector.

CJ would not understand the danger of provoking the werewolves. She hadn't seen the worst they could do in all their forms.

The fact she seemed to have no knowledge of werewolves made him wonder if she'd be able to shift at all. He had to have the answer before thrusting her in front of the Elders.

Not wanting to surprise his fellow werewolves, he sent up a quiet howl announcing his presence. With a bounding leap, he came out of the trees. Tucking his wolf snout under his furry chest he rolled in the air and hit the ground in a ball of motion. He let the momentum of his leap carry him through his shift. Without a misstep, he rolled to his feet and walked as a man once again. His wounds fully healed from twelve hours in wolf form, his unmatched speed at shifting had returned.

Bruno waited for him near the door, while Sebastian came running around the corner of the cabin. Gracie soon appeared at Bruno's side, her soft tail brushed against the back of the man's legs.

Bruno and Gracie were two of the lucky ones. They had already chosen each other as lifemates when Lazlo's breeding plan identified them as suitable breeding partners.

They waited for him to speak. He still outranked them in the hierarchy of the pack. None of them had ever challenged him. "You know your orders. Lazlo has instructed me to watch the prisoner from here on out."

The glance between Bruno and Gracie was almost undetectable, but Trey caught it. Lazlo wanted Trey to think only he guarded CJ, but obviously those two had received orders to make sure Trey did as he was told. Nonetheless, all three nodded in agreement and faded away down the dark path leading to the compound's main camp.

Trey's bare feet made little noise as he entered the cabin. CJ's bags from her hotel sat in his hallway.

CJ's soft breathing came from the cabin's small living room to the right of the door. Twilight settled over the forest, with the spring sun disappearing quickly. He would have liked to take a quick shower, but he didn't want to risk her waking and trying to leave the cabin without him. Returned to full health by his wolf form, his shift left him energized.

A cold shower would have helped with the full erection he sported thanks to the beautiful female only a few feet away.

Instead he closed his eyes and forced himself to think about how to use CJ to upset Lazlo's plans. Any sexual encounter would complicate matters too much.

After retrieving a pair of sweats from the laundry room, he walked into the living room and lit the fireplace. Trey watched as she twisted on the couch, snuggling deeper into the oversized cushions.

Satisfied she slept, he circled the room closing blinds and lit several small votives artfully arranged near the windows. His mother had picked them out during her last mission to Brazil. Their labels identified them as "Rainforest", but Trey didn't much care what they smelled like. He only cared that they pissed off the other werewolves because they interfered with their ability to smell clearly.

Once enough candles were lit to mask his activities inside the cabin, but hopefully not too many to offend CJ's nose, he crashed in the soft suede recliner next to his couch and lifted the remote to kick in his surround sound stereo. With the push of a button the music of the Stones softly filled his cabin. Rock served his purpose best.

He long ago mastered the art of distracting the werewolves living around him.

CJ's sleeping form filled the couch, the black leather sofa barely long enough for her shapely legs. She had grabbed the fake fur blanket his mother had arranged across the back. CJ rested on her side with one arm under her head and a mass of blonde hair swept across the sofa's arm.

The blanket remained securely in place over her, except for one leg thrown tantalizingly over the top. Her pale skin contrasted sharply with the dark throw.

His gaze followed her leg down to her slender foot. Its arch high and graceful. Her calves were slender, too, without the bunched muscles of the female werewolves. Yet she had used those legs to climb fifteen stories to his office.

Who was she really? She had come looking for her father, but why? She must have had some clue her father wasn't a normal man. Could she really have gone through life being able to track a scent the way she could and not question it?

There had to be more to the woman. She had to know her strength wasn't normal. It had been many years since someone even got close to touching Lazlo with a blow, let alone breaking a bone.

The sunlight faded behind the slotted blinds. Soon the only light in his cabin would be the glow of the fireplace and the faint flicker of his candles.

He wondered how she smelled. The scent of the magical candles were the only thing he could associate with smell and for some reason imagining CJ with their sweet, strong odor felt right.

So far everything about her proved to be strong, body and spirit.

Her hand went to her nose and she rubbed it. She squirmed, pushing the cover to the floor. Arching her back, she stretched her legs over the end of the couch and yawned.

A second later her eyelids flew open. "Blow out those damned candles." Her face scrunched in disgust and she sat up. Her bare feet hit the hardwood floor with a soft thud.

"You could've slept in my bed in the loft." An image of CJ curled in his sheets sprang up and he found himself with another uncomfortable erection. He shifted in his chair, hoping she wouldn't notice.

CJ yawned again and rolled her neck in a stretch. "The couch was fine. What time is it?"

Trey had left his watch in his jacket pocket. "Not sure. According to the light I'd say around a quarter after seven or so." He noticed the T-shirt she wore barely covered her hips. Dark pink boy-cut briefs peeked out over the top of her thighs. "They brought in your bags from your hotel. They're by the door."

She jerked her head around and saw the bags sitting in the front hall. "I suppose it's safe to assume they've been searched?"

Trey didn't bother replying. They both knew the answer.

He stood and walked to the kitchen to grab himself a beer. Halfway there he called over his shoulder, "Hungry?"

"Famished, but you don't have anything but sour milk and some nasty looking ham sandwiches."

Trey reached the kitchen and opened the fridge. As expected, it held a six pack of Heineken, a bag of apples, two gallons of milk, orange juice, eggs, bacon and several days' worth of pre-made sandwiches. The freezer would contain two frozen pizzas, a dozen hamburgers and a gallon of mint chip ice cream.

The teens who were on cafeteria circulation stocked his fridge every Saturday. Most of the werewolves enjoyed hunting the wildlife on the compound to slake their hunger, but few had time to hunt daily. The pack found that supplying food to each cabin was the most efficient way to feed everyone.

He grabbed two beers, an apple and a sandwich. Then he thought about CJ's powerful punch. He grabbed another sandwich for her. Chances are she had the werewolf appetite, too.

When he walked back into the living room, CJ was zipping up a pair of jeans she had pulled from her bags. She eyed him.

He set the beer and food down on the coffee table in front of the couch.

"Where did the grub come from?" She reached for the sandwich first and took a bite.

"Part of the training for our young werewolves is to maintain the compound. It builds pride in the pack. Most of the adults don't have time for shopping and cooking, so they prepare it in the cafeteria and stock the cabin fridges as necessary."

She finished the sandwich and followed it with a long gulp of beer. She sat the bottle down half-empty. "Didn't realize I was sleeping that heavy, but I won't knock the food. Quite the efficient little cult you have going here."

"Cult? We're nothing of the kind. You saw for yourself. Or don't you believe yet?" He had been waiting for this. He wanted to see how she explained his wolf shift.

She stared straight ahead and didn't make eye contact. "Oh, I'll admit you're a werewolf. I don't how or why, but you're right. I saw it. Believe me I lay here for I don't know how long racking my brain. Trying to figure out how you might have faked what I saw in the Jeep." She faced him square on. "I had one answer. You're the real deal."

"We all are. Lazlo, Mario, me and, I suspect, you." She had agreed too readily. Trey leaned forward, resting his elbows on his knees. "You *are* like us."

"No, you're wrong. I've concluded you guys are nothing more than a cult with some weird supernatural stuff thrown in," she declared, her blue eyes challenging him to prove her wrong.

Trey sat his bottle down on his coffee table with a clink, his vexation at her denial increasing. "Are you saying that with your nose and your strength that you aren't one of us?"

"Right now, I don't know if I'm a werewolf. If I accept that you are, logically I can believe my dad's one, too. Maybe I inherited some of this stuff, but I am not *one of you*." She leaned toward Trey. Face to face, they sat. "I am my own person. My mother raised me by herself, with no lifemate or Alpha or Elders to help her out. She raised me to be completely self-sufficient. Watching the way you and Mario groveled to Lazlo was nothing more than observing the power of a cult leader."

Great going Trey. He had finally convinced her werewolves were real and she had lumped them in with a bunch of crazies. They were always the others. The crazies. The monsters.

He got up and stretched his legs. He walked to a window and swiveled the blinds open. Outside the fading sun speckled the emerging leaves with a soft glow. How could he explain what the nature of the pack was? Why it meant so much to him? Why he needed her, so he could save the pack from Lazlo? She thought they were a cult.

"Are the guards still out there?" CJ asked.

Trey couldn't see them, but he knew they spied. He closed the blinds again. "Lazlo should have known he couldn't keep the secret from you. They're not close to the cabin, but two of them are in wolf form and keeping watch on the perimeter about a hundred feet out. If I leave, they'll report it to Lazlo. If you leave, they'll stop you."

"They'll *try* and stop me," CJ corrected him.

"Don't underestimate us. You caught Lazlo by surprise, and believe me, my strength is not an accurate measure of our power."

"Why does Lazlo want me to be a prisoner?"

"I suspect because he must discover who you are and your intentions before the Elders return home." Trey came back to the couch. He dropped down on a soft cushion, lifted his feet to the table and grabbed the apple she hadn't touched. "I'm curious. What did lead you to Seattle? You hardly seem the type who would want to reconnect with an absent father." He took a bite of the juicy apple, searching CJ's face for a clue.

CJ ignored his question. She eyed the room instead. "What if they have your place bugged?"

"Don't worry, they don't. I'm the one in charge of Guardian. Lazlo has never dirtied his hands with making money. He's a bit of a purist about those things. He has exceptional hearing and expects all werewolves to hone their skills rather than become dependent on technology." Trey pointed to the remote. "That's why I've learned to play music softly at all times. It helps with the eavesdropping."

CJ's brow furrowed. "What music? I don't hear anything."

"You don't?" He reached for the remote and pushed the volume a degree louder. She gave him a blank look. After three more volume increments, she nodded.

He lowered the volume back down to a less noticeable level. "Interesting. You don't hear like a werewolf."

"Never claimed I had great hearing."

"What about your vision?" he asked.

"Used to wear contacts, but had that laser surgery a few years ago. See great now."

Trey couldn't believe what she said. He had never heard of a werewolf without superb hearing and vision. Of course, he had never heard of a werewolf who couldn't smell either.

As far as he knew, he was the only one.

Chapter Six

"Trey, I think someone is coming." She didn't so much smell them, as sense the person, or werewolf she supposed, with a tingle of awareness shooting up her spine. A vision of Lazlo entered her mind.

Trey sprang from the couch and ran to the door. He placed an ear to the door. A smile spread across his face. He pulled the door open.

An older man stood in the opening, his fist raised to knock. Trey moved out of his way and let the man through. He carried an old-fashioned doctor's bag.

"Trey. Good to see you. You haven't been over to visit me in awhile."

"Been busy at work. Trouble near your old village in the Ukraine. Some locals disrupting the work on Herr Braun's new factory. I had to prep a second team."

The man with steel gray hair clasped a hand on Trey's arm and shook his head. "Probably the stupid grandchildren of the same ignorant peasants who killed my family. If I believed in the old ways, I'd curse them for a millennium." There was undisguised anger in his voice.

The older man frowned as he regarded Trey. "And you staying away, it has nothing do with my work for Lazlo on the breeding plan?"

"I've been busy. I understand what he did with your research isn't your fault."

"You may not agree with Lazlo, but his intent is honorable, Trey. He is the Alpha. We need to follow him. We must make the pack strong again." The man brought his heavy, white eyebrows together.

Trey paused, then moved out of the older man's grasp and motioned over to where CJ had risen from the couch. His expression revealed no reaction to what the man had just said. "Doc Vogel, this is CJ Duncan. I presume she's the one Lazlo sent you to see."

The man came closer and reached out a hand, so CJ took it. She wondered what the hell he had in his doctor's bag. His firm handshake surprised her. According to his face, he looked close to sixty. He stood only a few inches shorter than Trey, but still a clear six-foot. His designer polo shirt hung off shoulders that retained a well-muscled shape.

She inwardly squirmed as his gaze skimmed down her long blonde hair. Grinning, he put down his bag, grabbed her other hand in his, then very blatantly inspected every inch of her, smiling the entire time.

"Lazlo didn't tell me she carried Nordic blood. We thought the Nordic Pack was slaughtered centuries ago. This is wonderful, Trey. Wonderful."

She pulled her hands from his grasp. Talk of slaughtering and blood struck her as an odd introduction. "I'm not—"

"She's not supposed to talk about why she is here until Lazlo has had a chance to discuss it with her. You know how he is about gossip around the pack." Trey caught CJ's eye, his intent clear.

Keep quiet.

The older man nodded in understanding, then patted the cushions for CJ and Trey to sit.

"Okay, I'll let you off the hook this time, but he did give me instructions to run a DNA analysis on her, so if you'll just sit for a moment I'll get my things ready." He reached into the bag and pulled out a needle, which looked much larger than necessary to get a sample of blood.

"I don't remember giving the okay on this." CJ tried to keep her eyes from giving away her fear.

"What? Afraid of a little blood?" Vogel asked. He reached into the bag again and pulled out a rubber band to tie off around her arm. "Your pack doesn't teach you to control your fear endorphins very well, do they?"

She silently cursed her anxiety, but needles were not her favorite thing. Watching the druggies shooting up heroin around the streets where she had grown up left her with a strong dislike for the things. "Why do you need to do a DNA analysis on me?" It seemed strange a doctor out in the middle of the woods could do that procedure. She was certain such lab work took lots of big, expensive equipment.

Trey put a hand on her thigh. She supposed he was trying to reassure her. "Doc Vogel is our resident researcher. He held a professorship at the University of Kiev before the remaining European packs united and migrated here in the late forties. He's been trying to preserve our genetic makeup, since so many of our kind were slaughtered before and during World War Two."

Disbelief struck CJ. If he was professor in the forties, he had to be at least ninety, maybe older. And they still allowed him to poke people with big, sharp needles?

Doc Vogel seemed to know what she thought, because he wiggled his white eyebrows when he lifted her arm to tie the tourniquet. "Aged well, haven't I? I am the only one left who remembers living in the old country and the way it used to be for the European packs. You'll have to come and see me after Lazlo is through with you. I'm sure we'd have lots to talk about."

"Will do." She dug a hand into Trey's thigh. An impulse to leap over the back of the couch and get the hell away from his needle flashed in her mind. If only so much wasn't at stake.

Her father. Her life back to normal. One needle poke couldn't scare her from her mission.

Trey's hand moved from her thigh to go around her waist. He pulled her next to his large thigh, reached up with his other hand and turned her face toward her. "It's okay. It looks worse than it feels. He's been doing this a long time, he's got a gentle touch."

She closed her eyes and opened herself to Trey's warmth. She let herself get lost in his musky fragrance to overshadow the pain of the needle. He didn't let her down. His scent was like a security blanket she needed to wrap around herself. Once in his warmth, her body relaxed.

His smell, more real than half the crap she had seen today, comforted her. It was sure as hell a lot better than remembering what he had done in the Jeep the night before.

The sensation of the rubber tourniquet releasing drew her from the safety of Trey's aura. She opened her eyes to find Doc Vogel putting his tools back into his bag. The man *was* good.

A few minutes later Doc Vogel left, making her promise to visit him after her interview with Lazlo. Trey didn't seem to have a problem with it so she told him she would.

It wouldn't hurt to find out a few facts about Mario's family from someone other than Trey.

Trey didn't protest when CJ excused herself to brush her teeth with her own toothbrush. In truth, she wanted to see if they had confiscated her cell phone charger.

She shut the bathroom door and checked the pocket. Empty. The cell phone useless without its charger, she went to retrieve it from the toilet bowl tank where she had wrapped it in Ziploc bags and sunk it. Before she fished it out, she thought about the last call she had made. Did she want Lazlo to find Roz's number or her mother's? She retreated from the tank and left it hidden, hoping if the worst happened to her, that Trey wouldn't have plumbing troubles for a long, long time.

A sinking dread took hold of her. Though her visions struck her many times during the daylight hours, the bad ones were always late at night. If she had one tonight in front of Trey, he would demand an answer.

Of course, having visions involving a wolf and a city she had never been to didn't sound that crazy considering she'd be confessing to a werewolf.

A damn werewolf. And a whole living, breathing pack of werewolves.

A week ago, she would have been on her ass laughing at the idea. But she couldn't deny what had happened in the Jeep. Fuck, was she out of her element on this one.

If only Roz were with her. Roz would know how to handle all this magic junk.

Were they just freaks of nature? Poor humans whose genetics twisted a million years ago and made them the creatures they were today. Doc Vogel and Lazlo seemed to think the answers were in their DNA. It made some sort of sense. It would explain how she inherited these strange abilities from her father.

Trey rapped on the bathroom door. "Everything okay in there? You need something?"

She shook her head and tried to breathe normally. She felt like an open book around these people with their super perceptive senses.

His question sent a wave of goose bumps up her arm. He had a great voice when she took the time to listen to it. Deep, with a rough edge that sounded like he could growl as well as talk.

An involuntary giggle burst forth when she realized that he actually could growl. Once she regained her composure, she grabbed her luggage and reached for the door.

She opened it to find Trey leaning against the doorframe, his arm raised above his head. She wondered how long he had stood there and what he had heard.

"How much stuff are you missing?" Trey asked as she walked past him and laid her bags next to the couch where she presumed she'd be sleeping.

She sat on the couch. "Not much." She chose to keep quiet about the cell. "So what's the plan? I just sit here and be caged until the almighty Lazlo calls for me?"

Trey crashed in his recliner and grabbed his remote. The large plasma screen TV mounted next to the fireplace flickered on. A high-speed car chase zoomed across the screen.

"Yeah, that's it in a nutshell." He lifted one corner of his lips and raised an eyebrow. "But I'm guessing since you're still here and not trying to kick my ass to escape, you'd like to dig more info from me about your father?"

CJ felt an unwanted stirring when he looked at her with his mischievous grin. Damn, he confused her. It didn't take her this long to get a good read on most men. "And you're going to help me?"

"I will, if you let me know why you want to find him. I need to make sure you mean him no harm."

"I only hurt when attacked." She thought back to the way he had held her in his office.

"Or when someone else is being hurt." Trey lost the teasing smile. "By the way, I never thanked you for coming to my defense with Lazlo. Hope you don't have to pay for it."

"You don't need to thank me. I have a feeling you would have done the same. Can I venture to say Lazlo is not one of your favorite people?"

Trey's arched eyebrow and sardonic grin answered her question.

Heat pooled between her legs. He still had on his sweats, but he had thrown on a T-shirt while she was in the bathroom. His scent came to her strong and musky, with a bare trace of soap. He hadn't taken a shower for hours and she liked it.

She had dated athletic, outdoorsy men before, but none of them emitted the natural earthiness of Trey. There had always been disappointment on an intimate level with those other men. As if their outdoorsy personas promised more than they could deliver.

Her imagination flared with images of a werewolf like Trey Nolan in her bed. Could he deliver those fantasies?

Trey clicked the remote in his hand and switched to a channel with some lady hocking diamond earrings. "Are you going to tell Lazlo why you are here?"

"Will he punish Mario if he discovers I followed him and that he led me to you and the pack?"

Trey leaned back in the recliner and put arms behind his head. The sleeves of the T-shirt stretched tight around his biceps. "That's hard saying. He's done the worst he can by taking Mario out of school, but Lazlo has a temper."

CJ tried not to stare at the way his muscles bunched. She forced herself to look at his face. "What's the worst he can do?"

"An Alpha can order any type of punishment from solitary confinement to a whipping."

"Sounds like the fucking dark ages." She turned her head to the window when she caught the scent of a wolf outside. "Or a cult."

"The guard werewolves are moving closer to hear over the TV." He raised the volume.

"Well, I don't want to subject Mario to Lazlo's wrath again. I'll just tell Lazlo I was sent to investigate a possible pack by my Alpha."

"That might work. If you can lie without Lazlo sensing it." Trey challenged her with his eyes. "Can you?"

CJ doubted it. Scrap that plan. "Here's another option. You could tell me who Mario's father is, you arrange a meeting for me tonight, and then I'll sneak out of here."

Trey snorted. "Well, first you won't be able to 'sneak' out of here. They'll be on you before you're over the gate. Second, Mario's father is out of the country and the soonest he can be back is Monday night. Third, I still need you to distract Lazlo."

CJ couldn't believe his nerve. "Monday night. When were you going to tell me I was stuck here for at least two more days? Am I supposed to avoid Lazlo that entire time?"

"No. We just need to create a story for you that is plausible. An explanation you can use that isn't an all-out lie."

"If I tell him what he wants to hear, he'll be much more likely to believe. An interesting truth I've learned about human nature over the years." She sent Trey a scathing look. "That is, if he's human enough."

Trey took a second to reply. "At one time he was, but he's changed. We'll have to be careful."

"It seems like I'm risking quite a bit just to be a distraction for you. What are you up to?" She watched him pause. He wasn't the only one with questions. "I'd like some answers, too."

Trey blew out a deep breath and leaned in closer to her. His voice was quiet. "In our pack, since we united in the fifties, we have had three Alpha Leaders, my grandfather, my father and Lazlo. To appoint an Alpha, first the Council of Elders, who are all male werewolves over the age of fifty, choose eight werewolves between the age of twenty-five and thirty-five—"

"Also male werewolves, I'm guessing." Typical chauvinists.

"Yes, *male* werewolves. Those eight participate in the Succession Challenges. The four winners of the first four fights move on to round two, and so on until one werewolf is declared the winner and assumes the position of Alpha Leader."

CJ saw the tension rise in Trey's face.

"Naturally, because of my size and heritage, I was one of the eight chosen. Lazlo defeated me in the first round." He paused and held his hand in a fist. "It should have never happened. No one cares about this pack the way I do. Now the only way I can unseat him is if the Elders allow me to confront him."

He put his hand on her knee. "I think how he handles your appearance will give me their vote to proceed with the Challenge, and it will give me time to"—he glanced down as if searching for the right words—"strengthen my powers enough to defeat him."

"What do you mean strengthen your powers? You're a werewolf. How much more strength do you need? Can't you just accept he won?"

Trey's eyes darkened. His hand gripped her knee harder. "He's destroying us. Yes, we need to stop this diminishing of our werewolf abilities, but his way is not the way. He would rip apart the threads of family. Threads that give us our humanity. Otherwise we are nothing but animals. We have to be free to choose our own mates and to love our children for more than the caliber of their werewolf abilities. We're not monsters."

CJ thought about the children she came into contact with on the street. The ones nobody searched for. So many of them lost from broken homes, kids lost in juvenile detection systems and foster care. Without the love of families, so many became hardened. Mean. Dangerous.

If those kids were given super human powers, she couldn't imagine the havoc they'd create.

"Think about it, CJ. Our families, our loved ones, that's what keeps us together. That's what makes us obey the laws of the pack. We don't harm humans, because that would endanger our family. Endanger our children. Lazlo would replace love with science. Do you know what that could lead to? We already must obey a hierarchy of strength, but it's balanced by our humanity. Lazlo would create a pack of animals who exist only for power."

"You think the pack would start harming humans?"

"Very likely. Weaker werewolves would be denied lifemates. We're not meant to be loners. Who knows what damage that could do? They could become dangerous to humans, like rogue animals."

Trey swallowed and lowered his voice again, his agitation easily visible.

"And many of us have strengths completely unrelated to our werewolf abilities. I know it's not my werewolf abilities that built Guardian into the company it has become, and Mario, he's a computer genius. Lazlo would have him scrubbing toilets for the rest of his life."

"You won't let this happen?"

"Not if you help me. I can't tell you why I want just a few more days, but I'm close to gaining the advantage to overthrow Lazlo. CJ, I need you. Mario needs you."

She watched the passion in his face as he spoke. His gold eyes flared brighter as he described the effects of Lazlo's breeding plan.

He required more time to stop Lazlo. Time she could give him. It wasn't like he asked her to fight for him or to give up trying to contact her dad. Her brother was part of this pack. From what she had seen, Trey would be a lot better leader than Lazlo. "I'll help you."

She laid her hand over his. Her fingers seemed dainty next to his. His heat touched her core. She wanted to deny it, but his aura broke through her usual defenses.

"Well, then if you're ready to help me, we've got to find a story for you to tell Lazlo. Do you think you can shift? Have you ever tried?"

She shrugged. "Shouldn't I just know how to do it?"

"Not necessarily. We don't learn to shift until we hit puberty. It can be very painful at first. It takes control and concentration to do it right. If a child tries too young, he may become scared halfway through and be stuck in a half human, half wolf form."

"Like the thing I saw in the car." She shuddered inwardly at the memory.

"Hey, be careful. I was that *thing* in the car. But I'll forgive you. I know it wasn't pretty. I'm not usually a slow shifter. You hurt me pretty bad last night."

"You seriously think I can do that? Shift?" She couldn't keep the skepticism out of her voice.

"And I think if I can show you that you'll be much more able to fool Lazlo, because up here"—Trey took a finger and pointed to his head—"you'll be confident you are a werewolf. You're strong enough, believe me, that broken nose was a first for him. I think if you face him head on, he'll believe whatever comes out of your mouth."

Knowing that she could defend herself against Lazlo offered some comfort. "Okay. Let's do it."

Trey grabbed the remote. He switched off the TV and cranked the radio to a news talk program. Some of the candles were already burning, but he made sure every votive was lit. She scrunched her nose at the assault of heavy fragrance that masked them from the others. When he finished the distractions for the guards, he grasped her wrist and led her over to the fireplace.

His hand sent a wave of sexual awareness through her body. His every touch forced her to stamp down long-dormant urges. CJ maintained control, but it was a struggle.

Once they stood on the fur rug in front of the fireplace, he stretched his arms behind his head and grabbed the neck of his T-shirt. He pulled it up and she leered at his arm muscles flexed rock hard.

The hem of the shirt rose over his tanned muscles inch by inch. CJ tightened her fists so she didn't reach out and stroke them. Her aggressive nature urged her to make a move on him. Still, she overrode her desires.

Trey's hands went to the waistband of his sweats. He hooked his thumbs in the band and pulled them down. Stepping out of them, he threw them to the side.

He stood naked before her, the firelight reflecting off his tan and chiseled body. Every inch of Trey was covered in lean muscle, defined and taut. *Every inch.*

This wasn't foreplay. This was serious business, but the sight of Trey's nude body and his rather large penis, full and firmly aimed upward, tempted her restraint. She sucked in her breath, as she eyed the shaft from its velvet hood to the dark mass nestled behind it. The air buzzed with sexual energy. A rush of moisture coursed between her legs reminding her, werewolf or not, she wanted Trey Nolan the man.

Trey lifted her chin with the tip of his finger. "CJ, we need to be naked to shift. I'm waiting."

She peered into bright gold eyes. She swallowed hard trying to hide her need. "You need an erection to shift?" Her voice cracked as she attempted her best to sound sarcastic.

Trey wasn't fooled. The finger moved along her jaw, then tapped her on her upturned nose. "You're a beautiful woman. I'll try to keep my attention on helping you. I've only helped one other person shift, so believe me, I won't let my mind wander even if my body has other ideas."

"Well, here goes nothing." She gripped her own shirt and pulled it over her head. CJ put her hands on her jeans and slid them down her legs. The air was warm near the fire, but a shiver traveled up her spine. "Tell me how this is gonna go down."

Their bodies were inches apart.

Only her cotton briefs between them.

And she was supposed to concentrate on turning into a wolf?

She fought the temptation to peek at Trey's body again. Her eyes looked straight ahead at his lush, moist lips. Not a good idea. CJ settled for staring at his warm, tan neck. She didn't have to see herself to know her nipples were hard and primed. A part of her wanted to take Trey's hand and put it on her chest. She wanted him to squeeze and lick. Kiss and nuzzle.

She bit her lower lip instead. She nudged down her panties and let them fall to her ankles. Her gaze lowered and she saw Trey's penis jump with excitement. She had performed a strip tease or two in her younger days, but never had she felt this self-conscious of her body.

Trey cleared his throat. "Let's get down on our knees. It's safer closer to the ground for a beginner."

Her legs were shaky as she lowered herself. Her body tipped forward.

Trey caught her against his broad chest. He gently pushed her back, as she used her arms to steady herself. "Hey, don't worry. If you're meant to shift, you'll do it."

Her balance returned, she steeled herself for what lay ahead. "And if I can't shift?"

He shrugged his broad shoulders. "Well, you get to watch me again and I promise I do it better when I'm not crammed into the passenger seat of the Jeep." He pushed a strand of hair behind her ear. "Don't be scared, I believe you can do this."

His hand felt so good against her face where his fingers brushed against her sensitized skin. "I wouldn't exactly say I feel scared." *More like horny.* "Just anxious."

His hand fell from her face and brushed down the length of her arm. He reached to the coffee table and brought over a small brown leather book she hadn't noticed.

"What's that for?" It wasn't much larger than his hand, and the cover was dark with age.

"It's an old collection of spells I found a few years ago in Spain. The not-so-smart antiques dealer said it was a medieval dictionary." He carefully flipped the thin pages until he came to a page with a small poem printed neatly in the center of the sheet. "It's actually a witch's spell book." He smiled and looked at her with a mischievous twinkle in his eyes. "If you believe in such nonsense."

He turned the book so she could see the fine print. She didn't want to read the spell, afraid of what might happen, but she saw a few words before she pushed it back toward him. "I'd rather you do the spells. It doesn't look like any language I know."

"It's several languages actually, Spanish, French, Latin and several more I can find no record of. Probably this witch's attempt to write an oral language that had never been recorded."

"Wouldn't that have been dangerous in Spain? I mean, isn't that where they burned witches at the stake?" Terrible images of women bound to stakes, flames at their feet, flashed in her mind.

"That's what I thought, but think about it. Witches, real and otherwise, burning at the stake in record numbers. If their knowledge and traditions had been handed down orally through the centuries there was a very good chance that these spells"— he lifted the book—"could have been lost forever. The woman who wrote this probably thought she had no choice."

"Why do we need the spell of a dead Spanish witch?"

"Magic." Trey said the word with dead seriousness.

"Do you need to say one to shift?" She didn't remember him reciting a chant in the Jeep.

Trey shook his head. "No, but that doesn't mean werewolf shifting isn't magical. It's a magic that I carry within me." He

111

traced a fingertip across the old writing. "I've come to think of it as my supernatural soul, something that exists outside of the physical world, but yet is very much a part of me."

CJ wondered if this special soul Trey spoke of was a part of her as well. "You don't think it's just a trait you inherited? Like the salamander that changes color, or like a caterpillar metamorphosing into a butterfly?"

"I think part of it is in my DNA, but the power I've glimpsed using this book, and other magic objects, tells me there is more to me than some coding in my genes. And no matter what the modern world insists, or Doc Vogel, or Lazlo...werewolves are magical creatures. I know it. I feel it in here." Trey placed her hand on his chest. "I may be flesh and bones, but there is another force at play. This unknown, this *magic* lets me ignore the usual rules of nature. And the same goes for you. You are magical, too, CJ. You know it in your heart."

He was right. She had never set foot in a gym, yet could send a full-grown man to the ground with one punch. She took physics in high school. Energy didn't work that way. Her strength couldn't be explained by a simple genetic quirk.

She was either magical or on one hell of a delusional trip.

Years of denial fell away. Her mother had never let her ask the questions she needed to ask. Maybe her visions were her own mind crying for answers. Maybe magic had led her to Seattle. To the werewolves. To Trey.

CJ felt soft, salty tears reach her lips. She swiped them away from her face before Trey could comfort her. He looked down at the book for a few heartbeats, not commenting on her momentary lapse of self-control.

Fear danced on the edge of her control, but she was ready.

He took one more glance around the room. She knew he listened for wolves outside. "It's time to start. I think casting this spell over you will help. I have some candles that would help, but they're at the office, so we'll have to do without." He moved closer. Only an inch separated them.

Somehow he kept his engorged penis from touching her belly, but CJ had to concentrate on not pulling closer. Every fiber of her being yearned for the contact.

He leaned his face forward and placed a gentle kiss on her forehead. "We're strong enough to do this together. Ready?"

CJ peered into his steady stare. As she looked into his strange golden eyes, it hit her. She did trust him. She could do this. "Ready."

He read the words aloud. "*Los vientos de vandering. Spirtos van shifinger. Relanchent dies korper. Zu indre animalia.*"

She kept her gaze trained on Trey. Watching for his shift. Looking for his strength to help her. His deep voice didn't waver. She sniffed the air around them. He wasn't nervous. He was one with this strange ritual. He continued to chant the words.

His heavy wolf aroma slowly emerged dominant in his scent thread.

His skin darkened around his eyes, which themselves stretched longer and receded deeper. The bridge of his nose widened and pressed out. Time seemed to slow.

"*Los vientos de vandering.*"

CJ became aware that her peripheral vision had blurred into a foggy haze.

Just like her visions. A sliver of dread pricked at her mind. Would she lose control?

She squeezed her eyes closed, afraid of what she might see. Afraid Trey would disappear. She concentrated on his soft, firm voice instead.

113

"Spirtos van shifinger. Relanchent dies korper."

Slowly she became aware of a tingling sensation on her face. Her skin stretched tight across her cheeks. Pain shot through her ears as she felt them move across her head, pulling at her skull. She squeezed her hands into a fist to stop herself from covering her head in fear.

Sound. It exploded in her mind as never before. Trey's voice trembled along her bones until she swore she felt the vibrations of it through to her feet. Just as she did with a scent thread, she focused on the sounds entering her mind.

She heard her heart pounding like thunder. Or was it Trey's? They were beating as one.

The soft hum of air through their lungs.

The endless pop and crackle of bones moving, realigning, rejoining.

She yearned to open her eyes, but she had learned to distrust what she saw. Part of her wanted to see if she mirrored Trey's shift. She laid her hands against her thighs trying to feel for fur, but the flood of sound and smell overwhelmed. She couldn't tell what she caressed beneath her palms. Perhaps her hands were gone and the sleek wolf paws were in their place?

"Relanchent dies—" He paused in the spell and the next sound she heard was the deep low growl of his wolf.

Somehow the noise lessened or her fragile mind finally decided to ignore the new overpowering sense. Her focus returned and she realized something else loomed before her.

A choice.

As clear as two roads, she felt the pull of two different powers calling to her. With just a thought she could turn either way. One power oozed with brute strength, she turned her mind toward the path and became aware of a mighty supernatural energy pulsing through her limbs.

"Not that way."

Trey's command was in her mind without his voice saying the words.

So she went toward the other road. Instead of a physical flood of power, this path enclosed upon her like a new skin of perfect perception. The sensory overload from her initial shift settled into a calm river of information that her mind easily placed and prioritized.

The sounds of Trey's body, of the werewolves on guard a few hundred feet away, and of the other creatures in the woods were all clear and unique. She found them no more overwhelming than the usual aromas of the world that she had lived with all her life.

Was this it? Was it over?

When she opened her eyes, would her sight be this enhanced? Would she see the world with new color and light she had never experienced before?

Her body had shifted. She grasped the truth without opening her eyes. Though the soft fog of her visions still clouded her mind's eye, she was confident this had been no illusion.

Her feelings were real.

She was the white wolf. It all made sense to her now. The wolf inside her supernatural soul had called her here to the pack. To Trey. Her wolf wanted to be freed.

She tried to open her eyes to see her new form. To revel in the oneness with the world she felt.

She commanded her eyes to open. She felt them. This was her body, but it wouldn't obey her.

The fog grew stronger, growing into blackness in her head. She screamed for Trey, but she had no voice. No growl. Nothing.

She screamed silently, trapped inside her mind.

ಣಞಣಚಚ

"CJ, wake up. Can you hear me? Come back."

Trey called to her. She wanted to go to him. She struggled against the swirling black fog. *Wait, this was a vision.* She knew how to leave a vision. Walk away from the wolf.

But no wolf stood before her. There was nothing. Panic flooded her. What had she done? Where had his spell sent her?

"Damn it, woman, come back. Wake up." Trey's plea grew louder.

One thing penetrated the blackness. Trey's voice. She pictured him. The image of him kneeling in front of her, dark and confident, came to her. She concentrated on the details. His thick sable hair. The veined muscles of his arms. His face etched with determination.

She counted. "Ten, nine, eight." With each number she traveled one step closer. "Seven, six, five, four." She could smell him. His fragrance wrapped around her and pulled her forward. "Three, two."

She dropped into his arms. "One." The whispered word fell from her lips.

His warm, hard arms were around her body. She felt him nestle her head under his chin and a broad hand smoothed her long hair.

A soft, deep fur rug brushed her legs.

She opened her eyes and he was there. In his cabin, in front of his fireplace, she lay curled on the floor held up only by the strength of his embrace.

"But I thought I did it? I felt it. I felt myself change." Her throat ached with a sob she refused to let loose. She had been so confident it was real.

"No, CJ, you didn't change, it went wrong. I don't know what happened. I felt something different this time, too." He stroked her arm as he talked to her.

"I felt my skin stretch. My hearing, it was incredible. And the power, Trey. I sensed a strong power and you told me not to take it so I didn't, and then..." She pulled out of his arms and pressed her hands against his chest. "...then total peace. I was a wolf. I was an animal." She pounded her chest with the palm of her hand. "I knew it here."

"CJ, I think you *were* a wolf, but not in your body. Because as soon as I realized the spell wasn't helping you shift form I tried to stop shifting myself. I couldn't. You wouldn't let me."

"You mean I controlled you?"

"It seemed like we were both in my body shifting into the wolf. I've never heard of anything like co-shifting, but I don't think there has been anyone like you before either."

"So that's it. I'm not a werewolf."

Trey pulled her close again and crushed his lips to her hair. "You are a werewolf. This wasn't the spell. This wasn't the time, but I was with you when we became the wolf. You are meant to be one of us."

"If this spell didn't work, what will?"

"I don't know. We'll find another spell. Make it happen. If there is one certainty I've learned in my quest for"—he paused and moved his hand to her trembling shoulder—"my search for what I need. Is that in the world of magic our physical bodies are only a small part of the equation."

"Trey, I think I'm going crazy. Two days ago I didn't even believe in werewolves and tonight my heart is breaking because I can't shift and go running through the night with you. My emotions are taking over. I'm not like this." She wasn't. Not even when she was on the worst case, with the worst outcome. She never broke down.

A strange pulse still beat within her. An aftershock of energy. She sensed a new aura around Trey. She definitely smelled it.

"Well, considering you scaled a fifteen-story building when you didn't know you had supernatural strength, you might be crazy." His arm tightened around her. "Don't think you're crazy for wanting to be who you really are. Sometimes we have to take that leap and act on what we believe in our hearts. Our minds play tricks on us, but our hearts reveal to us what we want. That belief has carried me through dark times. Lonely times."

The firelight danced across his dark face. His eyes were distant. Thinking about somewhere else. Some other time.

She didn't want Trey distancing himself from her. She wanted him here. With her. Now.

She wanted to lose herself in Trey. It felt good to finally admit it. She needed to be with him tonight. Her body demanded it. Her heart ached for it.

She touched her lips to the skin of his shoulder. The taste of the wolf clung to him, the smell. Her tongue lapped up more of his intoxicating saltiness.

He arched away from her kiss. "I don't know if we should—"

"I'm tired of should and shouldn't. I want you more than I've wanted any man." She licked the side of his neck following the tense cord of muscle to his ear. His soft earlobe found itself caught between her teeth. "I don't care if it's magic or not." She really didn't.

He pulled away again and pushed his finger to her lips. "Are you sure you want this? Now?" He moved his finger and waited for her answer.

Why was he still talking? She buried her hands in his lush hair and pulled him closer. His eyes held their questions. To answer him, she pushed his mouth down to her breast and pressed her nipple against his lips.

Trey opened his lips and licked the pebble with his warm tongue. She lowered her gaze and watched mesmerized as he brought her nipple deep into his mouth and sucked hard.

Her womb buzzed with pleasure at his rough kiss. His large hand brushed across her chest and he did the same with her other breast. Her skin so pale against his tanned hands. A foolish part of her just wanted to throw him on his back and climb astride. The lust was so strong, her lower lips swelled with blood at the thought.

She struggled hard to control herself. She had never felt this need to bring a man into her before. *Never.*

Instead of forcing him, she brushed her legs up and down his firm buttocks, digging her heels in the tender dips of his hips. He seemed able to take her demanding friction.

He leaned in and kissed the arch of her neck and shoulder. Her hands moved to his sculpted shoulders and she let her fingers feel every curve and ridge of muscle.

His sexual fragrance shook her self-control. It intoxicated her mind. She pulled herself off the rug and buried her nose in his soft warm hair. She tugged him closer with her hands.

She wanted the aroma. All over her.

She wanted to be in it. Surrounded by it.

She couldn't get close enough. Trey's scent threads wove around her, enticing her with their nearness.

"Slow down, CJ. You don't realize what you're doing." He tried to pull his hips out of her locked legs. She wouldn't let him go. "This arousal, it might be from the shift."

She didn't want to think about the shift. She wanted to think about this. "I don't care. It's not magic. You don't understand. Since I discovered your scent. I can't get you out of my mind. And now, with you in my arms." She kissed his lips and pulled them between her own. "It's like I want to devour you. Not just your werewolf smell. I've smelled the others; they don't make me feel this way. Only you." She licked at his rough neck, loving the pulsing strength of his thick veins. "Don't tell me you don't feel it?"

He drew away from her embrace and studied her with a strange look. He restrained his urges, too. CJ wrapped her long fingers around his arm to pull him back. "I don't play games. I want you."

He sat back on his haunches and pushed her down on the fur rug on her back. "I can satisfy your desire. Trust me."

Trey's dark head went to the spot crying for attention between her legs. He brushed aside her pale curls and rested between her lips, his actions spiking her lust. Anxiety followed. CJ clamped her fingers around his shoulders. She didn't let men go down on her. "No, don't."

He raised his face. "You could make me stop. Do you really want me to?"

CJ let go and lay back on the silky fur. If she trusted anyone, it was Trey.

And the rough brush of his fingers against the side of her lips drove her to want more, not less of this intimate attention.

His gentle touch did not prepare her for the heated softness of his kiss.

Her lips turned to cream under his. He kissed her harder, pulling at her lips and delving with his tongue to places she never knew were connected to her pleasure center. Tingles of electricity crawled up her belly with sensual strokes.

Her body wanted more. Demanded it. She laid her hands on his back, ready to pull him level with her. To bend him to her will.

The barrier of her lips opened. With distracting timing, Trey slid his long finger into her, causing her to squeeze tight around him. He withdrew and reentered her in a mind-numbing rhythm. The motion sent pleasure through her entire body.

His penetration became larger. She realized he had placed two fingers inside her core. He grew slower in his strokes. "Don't stop."

He didn't. He curled his fingers and found the soft spot in her womb. The patch of yearning nerves came to life under his gentle touch.

Never pushing too hard. Not too fast. He worked her body until she flooded with a plateau of pleasure she had never experienced. CJ tried to remember what she wanted. She wanted Trey. Wanted to mate with him. Mark him as his scent had marked her.

His hand wouldn't let her give action to her wants.

Instead she felt her body lifted in a wave of craving that would only be satisfied by more of Trey.

Her back arched high over the fur rug. Her heels rammed into his hips. The climax folded over her, taking her deeper into her body than she had ever been. She contracted around his fingers, around his body. Her pants of pleasure filling the cabin, until her bliss eased away into memory.

She gasped as he pulled his fingers from her. Her last sensation was hearing Trey's own heavy pants as he laid his head on her still quivering stomach.

Chapter Seven

The waxing moon hung high in the night sky. Trey found himself wide awake and in considerable discomfort. Just the feel of CJ's soft hair next to his face made his loins stir. It didn't help his arousal when, after her climax, she had fallen asleep like a kitten in his arms. She didn't protest when he carried her up the stairs to the loft.

It had about killed him to let her sleep. The urge to wake her, take her was unusually difficult to deny. He played with fire.

A werewolf's desires could be hard to control. His own lust reminded him of what he struggled for, what he wished to achieve using CJ. Lazlo would have the werewolves live like this forever, resisting their desire, curbing their passion to breed only with their appointed mates.

A snarl escaped his lips as he pictured CJ mated to some other male. Full werewolf or not, her strength was great and Lazlo would want it. He would never let Lazlo degenerate her into a breeding bitch. Never.

He brushed his hand along her smooth lean leg resting atop his thigh. His action didn't ease the dull throb of his cock. This might be the last night to be with CJ. Ever. She wouldn't stay unless forced. Her life wasn't here. It wasn't with him.

If only they had met somewhere else, under different circumstances...

But they weren't random strangers spending a night together.

CJ had entered his life at the worst time possible. She wanted her father. Instead, he had wedged himself between her and her family so he could use her for his own purpose.

He had thrown her as live bait to distract Lazlo and the Elders. Now he dragged her deeper into his problems.

He had no choice but to do everything he could to stop Lazlo. Yet regret dwelled in his heart.

The outcome of their experiment earlier didn't sit well with him, or her response. He had underestimated CJ's emotions. Her tough exterior hid fear and loneliness. He recognized it, because he had felt intense isolation, too.

It was hard to be different, when revealing your difference was impossible.

He shouldn't have forced her to make her shift. Because of her incredible strength, he had been certain she was a full werewolf. Now her interview with Lazlo would be trickier. CJ had to convince the Alpha she wouldn't threaten his power. That was Trey's job when he presented her to the Council. He made her walk a fine line.

For CJ, it was too late to go back. She stood more alone than ever, knowing she was neither human nor werewolf. His arrogance made him use magic to push her where she wasn't meant to go. He'd wanted to complicate Lazlo's breeding plan so badly, he hadn't thought about what it would do to CJ if the shift failed.

Then to take her with him on his shift. To have her experience what he did, to feel her joy at the shift. The sounds, the complete oneness with nature, the smells.

Trey's hand stopped on CJ's slender hipbone.

The smells. He closed his eyes and remembered the sensations. The candles, CJ's soap, those fragrant memories sharp and clear. Deeper, fuller scents that were like a blanket around them as they shifted. The essence of the fire, the richness of the surrounding woods. A new appreciation of what he missed of the world overcame him.

He opened his eyes in the darkness. CJ's sleeping form curled beside him. His werewolf eyes saw her clearly in the pale moonlight. He pushed closer to her glorious hair spread over the pillow until he felt the smooth silky strands against his cheek.

He knew her smell now. Embedded in his memory. He'd never let it go. He didn't know how it compared to the other females in the pack. Their fragrance remained a blank to him. He was certain CJ's scent was all her own. It had to be, she was a one and only.

Lacking a context to describe, he couldn't. Yet, when he reached into his mind and recalled the warm, strong sensation, it was undeniably her.

Part of him wanted to tell her of the gift she had given him, but then she'd know his secret. In those few moments of smelling, he saw the world fully for the first time. Unlike the spell he had cast with his amulet in the office, during this shift he had known a whole world of aromas, not just the heady mix of magical candles.

Yet, he had kept his weakness hidden from everyone, even his mother. Should he confess it to CJ, just to tie her closer to him? He had to remember, she had yet to face Lazlo. He doubted she would expose his secret willingly, but did he want to take the chance?

His thumb made lazy circles on her soft skin, as he thought about their joint shift. As if together, they made a perfect werewolf. Her supernatural strength and sense of smell completed his wolf's own abilities. Two halves making one complete magical being.

Two halves making one.

Horror slammed into Trey. His hand froze on her body.

CJ possessed the two abilities he lacked. He had been calling his powers to him for months, then as he almost reclaimed them that night in the office, presto, she was there.

All the air seemed to leave the room as the implication of what that meant crept into his mind. CJ hadn't come into his life at the wrong time. She had come because *he had called her.* Her powers were his.

When they shifted, she had kept the shift going, overpowering his own wishes. Could she know they were connected? Could she be here not to find her father, but to steal the rest of his powers? He couldn't deny her supernatural strength was greater than his. It wouldn't be a stretch to believe she could be his superior in the realm of magic either.

The thoughts tumbled in his mind, as he tried to prove his theory wrong. Mario. She was related to Mario, but did that prove her innocence? Her attraction for him. Was it real, or did she use it to overcome his defenses?

Trey removed his hand from her body, not wanting to let his carnal urges betray him. Until he knew for sure, he couldn't let her get close to him.

"Don't stop rubbing. I like it," she purred. Her eyes were still closed, still hidden from his probing. "Your bed is a lot more comfortable than the couch."

"Well, maybe it's the company." His gaze followed a path across her hipbone and down the low slung groove of her waist.

Heat rushed into his groin. He wanted so badly to touch, he groaned with desire. His cock throbbed to life, but he kept his hand clamped to his side.

Not sensing his reluctance, CJ inched her smooth leg higher until he felt her push against the sensitive sac beneath his penis. She nudged him suggestively. He moved his hand down to push her back.

"It's not morning yet, is it?" Her voice husky.

"No, it's"—Trey checked the clock on the far bedside table—"only three." He attempted to inch away from her.

"Gee, that's kind of early for such impressive morning wood." She opened her eyes, her lips in a provocative smile.

Trey moved his hand down to cover the hard-on in question. "Well, what can I say. I was having a good dream."

CJ moved quickly and, in one motion, she swung her body above him, straddling his hips. The moist heat of her own sex, smoothing his cock, sent tremors racing deep into his loins. Trey dug his fingers into the sheets.

Apparently her desire wasn't just an aftereffect of their earlier magic experiment. She wanted him. He wanted her, but doubt plagued him.

She leaned down, dragging her erect nipples across his sensitized chest. Her nibbling kisses on his neck heightened his arousal. He shuddered as she raked her nails gently down his stubbly cheeks. Moving her attention to his stomach she traced his six-pack abs with her tongue.

He opened his mouth to have her stop, but the words died on his tongue.

As a male werewolf, he was the aggressor with his human lovers. With female werewolves, couplings were often fast and hard, foreplay forgotten in their rush of supernatural passion.

CJ seemed to have the aggression of the werewolf, with the curiosity of his human lovers. A combination he was having a hard time denying.

Her heated velvet lips brushed the top of his penis. Trey moaned with reluctant ecstasy. His cock quivered under her kisses. He stretched his arms above his head and clasped them white-knuckled behind it. He denied the urge to throw her on her back and plunge into her.

CJ's long fingers wrapped around his sex and he could feel the gentle tug of her grasp on the tender organ. Spirals of pleasure shot to the base of his cock and he clenched his butt to stop from spilling his seed all over her hand.

She licked the length of his penis and swirled around the top, teasing the rigid cock with her wet tongue. He wasn't going to last long if she kept that up.

"I want you inside me, Trey," she said in a throaty voice. Like a female werewolf in heat. He recognized the tone. They didn't like to be refused. Perhaps this wasn't CJ; perhaps this was still the magic of the shift making her act in a way she'd regret in the morning. Or a distraction? Did she know more about magic and their connected souls than he did?

He didn't want to believe that of her, but could he trust his heart?

And what of his true intentions? He was using her. He had made her help him and now he must take her powers to complete his own werewolf soul.

He couldn't give in to his urges, his desires. One way or another he was going to have her powers. Making love to her didn't feel right. He couldn't let this go any further.

But damn, she was determined. He'd have to convince her she didn't want to have sex with him. That acting on their lust risked too much.

"Are you on birth control pills, CJ?" He somehow got the words out.

She shook her head, no, and entwined her silken hair around the base of his shaft. "They make me sick and, quite frankly, my boyfriends bailed long before it was an issue."

His hips bucked off the bed with this new soft friction up and down his shaft. "I don't..." CJ played with his cock, rubbing her hand over her hair twirled around it. He moaned involuntarily. "I don't have any condoms here."

The motion stopped, but her hand wrapped him, tightly keeping his erection hard and ready. "You're afraid I might get pregnant?"

He took a breath and peered into her eyes, darkened to a deep blue by lust. "It's been known to happen. I'm not ready for that. We should stop." He eased out from underneath her hot grasp, despite his body aching in resistance. He needed a cold shower and a few hours spent on the couch if he wanted to survive his vow not to make CJ regret this night more than she already would.

Or to protect himself, if her intentions were the same as his.

CJ didn't let him out of her hand. She lifted herself erect and held his shoulder to the bed with her other hand. "Trey, I don't play games when it comes to sex. I want this. I want you. Tonight. But you're right, the last thing we need to do is risk a pregnancy. With all the magic I feel swirling around us, who knows what would happen. You don't have any condoms?"

This Trey could answer honestly. "Not here. I don't bring my women back to the compound and I've been avoiding the female werewolves for quite some time." He went to move away again, but she held him down.

Her strength made her arms like steel. He couldn't get away until she wanted him to go. The first-time experience of being at the mercy of a woman in bed shook his resolve. His pulse quickened under her steady eye.

Drawing on every ounce of control, he whispered, "CJ, I need to leave this bed. I want you, too, but this isn't our time." A painful ache constricted his throat. He swallowed and waited for her to understand what he meant. "I'm going to take a shower and crash on the couch. I should have never let it get this far."

CJ removed her full weight from his shoulder and gave him a look he didn't understand. He glanced at her hand now resting on her own thigh. He could get up if he wanted, but a primal instinct kept him beneath her.

She leaned forward and softly took his lips in her own. The gentle offering crushed any resistance he could muster. "You didn't let anything happen. I'm not naïve. I, ah..." She moved her hand from his cock and used her hips to hold it between them. Her slender body moved slowly on top of him in a rhythm instinctive to women. "I'm greedy. I've just always been disappointed with my lovers. For once I wanted to feel this kind of passion."

She slid slowly down his hard body and retook him in her mouth. Her gentle kisses were replaced by stronger ones until he felt the growing pressure signaling his oncoming climax.

He reached to pull her lips from his cock. It had no effect. She moved out of his grasp easily. In his heart, he didn't want her to stop. She drew him to the edge in a way no other woman could.

The wave of his climax poured through his body and his legs bucked with the spasm of his release. CJ slid off his body as the final spasm of pleasure racked his body.

She climbed out of bed.

He lay alone as his orgasm ebbed.

Her feet pattered down the stairs from the loft. Seconds later the bathroom door opened and closed, and next he heard the rush of the shower. His own chest was sticky with his spent orgasm, but he doubted he'd be welcome to join her in the shower.

His rejection hurt her.

With regret at what he had to refuse and regret at losing a chance to make love with CJ, Trey got out of bed and went to the kitchen instead of the bathroom. A paper towel was a poor substitute for a shower, but he'd have to wait till morning. After he wiped himself down, he went to the fridge and grabbed a long neck.

Just before he slammed the door shut, he heard a wolf sprint off into the forest.

Lazlo's spies were listening. Lazlo would find it amusing Trey and CJ had not consummated their attraction. Well, it would be one less thing Lazlo could use against CJ.

Trey prayed they'd let her go. The worst-case scenario would be if Lazlo decided she could be of use in the breeding plan.

Unless he could overthrow Lazlo before the Council on Tuesday. If he took her powers before Lazlo got to her, before she was presented to the Elders Council then, she would be only a human. No werewolf could harm a human. She'd be protected.

He'd lose the chance to cast doubt on Lazlo and the breeding plan, but he'd have his full powers. He'd just have to find another way to persuade the Council to let him Challenge the Alpha.

CJ might hate him, but it was the only way he could protect her and his pack. He had to put the pack first.

And if his worst fears were true, if she came to Seattle to take his powers from him, well, he'd beat her at her own game. Though he prayed his paranoid suspicion wasn't true.

Trey swirled the beer in the dark bottle and thought about the guards posted outside. Hopefully he still had the freedom to come and go as he pleased. He had to get to his office either today, or Monday. Only the amulet would reveal the truth to him.

He heard the shower stop. She'd be out soon. The least he could do was give her his bed for a few hours. He downed the beer and left the bottle on the counter. He walked into the living room. Without the fire the cool April night made the room chilly. The throw CJ had used was balled up on the couch.

He wedged himself onto it and covered his large frame as best he could. The soft throw most likely held her scent. Trey sniffed the fabric. Nothing. It smelled like nothing to him. He closed his eyes and forced himself to put her out of his mind.

Maybe not being able to smell wasn't such a curse after all.

ಬಿ೭ಲಿಉ

CJ awoke to the sounds of a woodpecker tapping away on the tree outside the loft's only window. Her head pounded behind her eyes and her ears rang with an ungodly pressure. If she didn't know better, she would've sworn she had a hangover.

She covered her eyes. It had to be at least midmorning. The sun shone too bright. She lifted her head from the pillow and scanned the room for a clock. She found it on Trey's bedside table. The neon numbers showed clearly it was ten-thirty. Next to it sat a glass of water, two aspirin and a note.

I remember the morning after I tried my first spell. Felt like a truck hit me.

-T.

Trey. She had made a fool of herself last night. Almost crying like a baby when she found out she couldn't shift, then jumping Trey like a sex-starved teenager.

Who was she kidding? The desire she had felt for Trey wasn't new last night. She had wanted Trey Nolan from the moment she heard his voice at the club. Last night she had lost her fear and gone after him.

Idiot. He wasn't any different than a human man. Her assertiveness had turned him off, as it did every other man. She pulled down the sheets and climbed out of the rumpled bed. CJ reached for the aspirin and water.

Digging through her bags, she found a pair of jeans, a red T-shirt and her favorite set of matching lycra bra and panties. They were bright red, like her shirt. She wasn't always a boring girl.

As she dressed, she studied Trey's bedroom.

A simple space. The log walls were unfinished, their knotty pine giving the room a masculine warmth. The stairs from the first floor were centered in the fourth half-wall. To one side was a walk-in closet. The rustic pine railing on the other side overlooked Trey's living room. Raw beams crisscrossed the length of the cabin's ceiling and simple ceiling fans hung down to circulate air.

Against one wall stood a large bookcase stuffed with books. She lifted one gently and opened it. An old German bible. She put it back and chose another. This one a textbook on farming techniques. While the contents were hardly exciting, the engraved leather binding was an exquisite piece of artwork.

The next book, however, had symbols she recognized from Roz's tarot cards. She guessed it was another ancient spell book of some sort. She quickly reshelved it. This new world of werewolves was enough for her. She'd leave the magic spells to Trey.

Trey hid his magical collection right in the open, alongside bibles and farm books. To others, he simply collected antique books. The other werewolves would never guess what he was up to scouring antique stores.

The man *was* smart.

Beside the books were a few framed family pictures. Built with the same athletic frame, Trey's father stood level with him in their one photo together. The older man had wider features with a heavier brow. It was a picture of them on a boat with a large fish next to them. Trey's face burst with pride. His father smiled, but with a closed mouth that didn't seem to go to his eyes.

Trey had told her his father was Alpha before Lazlo. She studied the two men. Perhaps the worries of being the all-powerful leader meant Trey's father didn't have much of his own life. The man's eyes drew her in. She had seen that look before. When lost in thought, Trey carried the same brooding air. The survival of their kind weighed heavily on both men.

CJ eyed the next frame. Trey was a boy, maybe ten. A beautiful woman leaned over his shoulder. The similarities in their smile and high cheekbones were unmistakable. A formal photo, but the photographer had done an excellent job of catching a spirit of spontaneity in the woman. CJ bet she had given Trey his rebellious streak.

These werewolves were a strange group. So human in many ways, taking vacations, having families. Yet, so different than everyone around them.

"But not *my* problem," she said out loud as she turned her back on Trey's memorabilia. She went back to her bags to pull out her shoes, frowning at Trey's oversized bed that dominated the room. The fragrance of their aroused bodies entwined in its sheets. Reminding her this attraction to him was real, something beyond the supernatural. If lust could become love, she didn't know. But it seemed stronger than any attraction she had ever felt for a man.

Last night, the condoms were just an excuse. He had wanted her to stop. She had read it in his face, in his voice, in his body.

But why? Their sexual chemistry was undeniable. She had sensed it in his office and during the shift. In his smiles. His touch.

The shift must have changed his mind. It proved her not a full werewolf. Not one of them, but not entirely human either. CJ stalked over to her bags and threw her brush down. Finding a hair clip, she wound her hair into a loose knot behind her head.

So Trey didn't want her. It hurt, but she'd survive. That instinct she had inherited from her *mother.*

Finished dressing, she shoved on her well-worn pair of Nikes and headed down. The smell of frying bacon wafted upstairs. A welcome new odor to replace the fragrance of his room.

His smell, overwhelming in his bed, had given her disturbing dreams during the short night. Dreams filled with a black wolf and a white wolf, dreams of tangled limbs and erotic acts. Dreams closed in with the hazy fog that echoed her visions.

An unspoken relief had filled CJ since her hallucinations stopped. Maybe they were over. But truthfully, part of her still wanted those visions, clues that could lead her to her father and past this infatuation with Trey.

Their disappearance left her feeling lost in this strange world. They had led her to Seattle and Trey, and now they deserted her.

Visions or not, she couldn't let her lust for Trey distract her any longer. It was now her job to continue what *she* had set out to do when she left Minneapolis. This game between Lazlo and Trey wasn't her problem.

She needed to find her father. Figure out who he was and how she ended up being this strange werewolf half-breed. Mario was still the key to getting to her father. Trey had too many ulterior motives.

She couldn't trust him anymore.

In the kitchen CJ found Trey pouring two glasses of orange juice. He motioned over to the small table where he had placed a platter of bacon and a bowl of bananas.

He set two plates on the table. "I thought you'd be hungry."

She took a seat and grabbed a banana. She could use a cup of strong coffee but her nose told her Trey didn't have a coffee bean in the house.

He scooted the orange juice next to her plate and sat in the chair opposite her. He forked several pieces of very crisp bacon onto his plate and lifted his glass.

She didn't want to talk about last night. She wanted to move on. The silence made her skin crawl. Trey's piercing eyes drove her crazy. For once she missed Roz's endless chatter. The hyper redhead was a hell of a lot better than a surly werewolf across the table.

Let him think what he wanted. She had her own agenda. She picked a few less blackened pieces of bacon for her plate. "I need to talk to Mario. Do you know where I can find him?"

Fifteen minutes later Trey led CJ on an overgrown trail toward the dormitories where the teen werewolves lived and trained. She smelled the others not too far behind them, but their trackers kept off the path. She had learned their scents over the night. Trey had told her the female was named Gracie and the large male, Bruno.

At least there were only two.

Trey wanted her to stay at the cabin, but CJ had challenged his plan. He must have decided leading her straight to Mario would land him in less trouble than her taking on the two guard dogs.

"So are those two behind us close enough to hear what we say?" She hated not knowing if she could be overheard by the werewolves. Trey seemed to instinctively recognize the right volume.

He talked over his shoulder. "Not with the racket you're making on the trail."

CJ stuck her tongue out at his back. Desire or not, making a move on him had been a mistake. That truth hurt like a knife. Though she lingered over the thought he didn't have a problem going down on her after the shift. Perhaps he'd been as sexually charged as her after their strange experience.

Or perhaps he was just an asshole. If that was the case, she didn't want to let him off so easily. She had tried to ignore him this morning, but his glares pissed her off. She hadn't been the one to cause the problem. "Well, if they can't hear us, I say we talk about what happened last night. You could have

137

warned me about the hangover and the other side effect," CJ said quietly. She picked her way carefully, but the paths were covered with dead twigs and leaves that crunched under her sneakers.

He kept moving forward. "I should have remembered about the headache. I was so wrapped up in your shift, I forgot about some of the side effects." Trey paused on the path. "I shouldn't have forced you into a shift. You're so strong, I just figured you'd be able to," he said, regret in his voice.

"I suppose now it will be harder to derail Lazlo's plans." She held his gaze. "I know. I get it. I'm a distraction."

Trey grabbed her arm and pulled her close to him. He lowered his head and talked in a hushed tone. "You're not just a way to distract him. I need your help, but I want to help you, too, if you'll let me. My plan just didn't go like I wanted. I don't want you hurt." His breath was hot and heavy.

He fit perfectly in these woods. Even as a man, she imagined he could step into the trees and be lost to sight. His dark green T-shirt, black jeans and well-worn boots seemed to melt with the colors of the brush around them.

This Trey seemed the true Trey. Not the man in the business suit, not the inferior werewolf subject to Lazlo's abuse, but the woodland warrior. The werewolf. Part of nature and yet beyond it.

CJ didn't know what to think. Trey Nolan became more of a mystery the more she knew of him. One minute he was all over her, the next rejecting her advances, and then the next acting as if she was some sort of damsel to be rescued.

Her stomach clenched tight. She didn't need these complications. He had coerced her into helping him and she was no closer to her father than two days ago. Her visions had stopped, but for how long she didn't know.

Her life wasn't here. It was home with her mom and Roz. It was with the families who needed her. The families she could help only if the visions stopped for good.

Trey stood next to her, waiting for her response to his declaration of protection.

She stuck up her chin and made a fist with her hand. "I can take care of myself, if you remember. Now let's keep moving before Spot and Fido catch on to what we're talking about."

"I don't know why you need to talk to Mario. I told you his father—" He took a few side steps down the path.

"My father." After being with Mario in the cabin, she was certain of that truth.

"Well, it doesn't matter. He won't be here until Tuesday morning right before the Elders meet. Lazlo's called a Council meeting."

"Then I'll wake early and meet him Tuesday morning. Mario is still my brother and I'd like to talk to him. Find out what kind of man my father is." Find out if he knew she existed, if that would mean an end to the visions.

Trey slowed as the path curved steeply down a small hill. A few crude steps were carved out of the path. "I'm only guessing Mario's here. Lazlo may have ordered him to do maneuvers. He could be anywhere on the compound. It's over three hundred acres of woods."

CJ chose to ignore his warnings. She couldn't tell him that spending another day locked in the cabin with him would drive her mad. He might be convinced she just suffered some aftereffect of shifting, but she knew better.

His scent had her in an almost constant state of arousal. Her body seemed to be on a different wavelength than her mind, and getting away from him seemed her only answer.

She shoved aside the hand he held out to help her down the stairs. She didn't want to show weakness to Trey or any other wolf watching. "I do have one question about our shifting last night. I swore there was a point where you called to me. Like there was an alternative beside the path we took to become the wolf."

"I need to warn you about that. I was surprised at how fast the change moved last night. I planned to help you past that."

"Lots of things moved too fast for you last night." CJ leveled the insult at his broad back.

Trey turned to answer her, but the sound of cracking wood pierced the air, followed by a howl that made her heart jump with fear.

She stopped in her tracks. Trey took off at a dead run directly toward the source of the sound. She moved quickly to catch up, but before she could regain him in her sight, two sleek wolves passed her. The larger of the two followed Trey and the other blocked her path.

She almost tripped over the damn pale-eyed animal that stood growling at her. "Oh, no you don't. I'm following Trey and that's it." Her firm voice cut through the forest like steel.

CJ pushed it out of the way with her knee, but the wolf just rolled and returned to all fours to stand in her way again. Gracie. The wolf had the same mousy brown coat as the muscular woman's dull brown hair.

She looked the wolf square in the eyes. "Okay, here's the situation as I see it. I'm not trying to escape the compound. And I'm guessing Lazlo won't be too pleased to find you ripped my throat out just because I was trying to follow Trey. So either get out of my way or fight me. Wolf or woman, you make the choice."

She spread her stance and raised her arms. If she could take down Trey, she could handle this bitch.

The wolf stared for a few seconds. A second howl sounded from somewhere down the path. It sounded different than the wolves she had heard over the last day. In truth, she almost heard a roar in the ear-shattering sound. The wolf glanced at CJ one more time then simply turned and followed the same path as Trey and Bruno. CJ didn't hesitate to follow.

Another beastly scream ripped through the forest and this one sent every bird in the area squawking into the air. Finally she saw a building before her, a large, two-story log structure. *The dormitory.*

The others were nowhere in sight. Yelling came from the back of the building. She recognized Trey's voice among the chaos. She raced around the corner to find Trey and a transformed Bruno, naked and standing in front of a small concrete building. It had a steel door with a tiny window.

Her gut roiled with dread about what she'd find inside.

She caught Trey's eye and he motioned for her to stay put. She ignored him and kept walking toward them. Gracie didn't seem to be anywhere in sight.

The steel door shook like someone was driving into it with a catapult. When the lock held, the animal inside let out another furious howl.

Trey caught her by her arm before she got to the window. She jerked out of his grip.

"You need to return to the cabin. Bruno will take you. I need to go find Lazlo."

"What is in there? Why would you have to cage a wolf? It sounds like it's going freaking insane."

"Yes, it probably is. And I'm going to Lazlo to get an explanation of what happened." Splitting wood caused Trey to turn and check the concrete building. "He should have known better than to put Mario in there."

Mario? Her brother locked in a concrete box no bigger than a dumpster? Wolf or not, she had to help him. She'd rip the damn door off its hinges if she had too.

She ran around Trey and past a startled Bruno. She reached the steel door and peered into the darkness. She smelled Mario. But he reeked with a new repugnant odor. Evil. She smelled blood. Mario's. He had hurt himself in his struggle.

Bruno and Trey both yanked her away from the opening just as a black snout appeared from the darkness and clamped onto the thick bars. The grate of its teeth against steel killed her brazen courage in an instant.

Bruno's strong arms were able to hold her momentarily. "You can't let him out. We just have to pray the door holds until he's calmed down enough to realize what's going on." CJ was in such shock at finding Mario in the cell, she didn't try and fight the male werewolf. Bruno pulled her back a few more steps. "It's been so long since he shifted, I think we all forgot how powerful he can be."

CJ sensed real concern in his voice. "Mario's done this before?"

Trey's jaw clenched as he explained. "A few times, but he sounds more enraged than he's ever been. Remember when I told you that Lazlo's breeding plan was to stop the weakening of the pack? Well, Mario in there is a prime example of what he's fighting to stop."

"He doesn't sound weak. He sounds like he's about to tear the place apart." CJ brushed Bruno's hand off her arm. The man didn't seem concerned with her anymore. His eyes were locked on the door of the cell.

Trey started to speak, but Mario gave the door another hit. The hinges creaked under the assault. "Bruno, did Gracie go to get Lazlo?"

"Yes, we thought it best he was here." He winced as a strange squeal came from the door's window.

Trey frowned. "We're going to need Doc Vogel and his tranquilizer gun in case Mario breaks free."

Bruno fell to his knees and began shifting to a large tan wolf with gray tufted ears. His size matched Trey's wolf.

Once Bruno bounded off into the woods, Trey pulled her farther from the cage. "He's not that kind of weak. Each werewolf's weakness is different. Most of the younger ones just have a weaker sense or two. They can't smell or see as well as the older ones. Some shift so slow it can take them an hour to go through the change. But Mario's curse is different." He paused as the door strained from the Mario's assault. "He can't consciously shift. Only his rage causes the change."

Chapter Eight

The animal inside the cell went silent. CJ felt Trey brace for another howl, but instead the large jaw snapped around the steel bars. The long yellow teeth scrapped the metal causing a shrill screech to reverberate in its prison.

CJ involuntarily moved closer to Trey. "You mean he becomes a wolf whenever he's angry?"

"Not exactly. He doesn't shift into wolf form at all." Trey's eyes watched the trees surrounding the dormitory. "Remember you asked about the other path, the one I wouldn't let you follow."

CJ followed his gaze, wondering if the others waited in the woods, called by Mario's howls. She thought about the power she had felt in her body last night. Its enticing strength. "I've never felt such power. Almost impossible to resist."

CJ watched Trey closely. He nodded to the right. She caught the sun reflecting off of a pair of shining eyes just beyond the first tree.

Trey put his hand on her arm. "It's Sebastian. He'll help if Mario gets through the door."

Alarm crept into CJ's gut thinking how close she had come to accepting that power the other night. "What does that part of the shift have to do with what's happened to Mario?"

His grim expression cemented her anxiety. "Accepting the pull of the other path during a shift changes you into what we call our Beast form."

"You mean like some type of huge super wolf?" Images from a few recent horror movies raced through her mind.

"More monster than a wolf."

As if on cue, the pounding of the door resumed.

CJ couldn't imagine what her brother had become. The endless shaking of the cell door rattled her thoughts. "You didn't tell me about this before you tried to shift me?"

Mario let loose an ear-splitting howl. Somewhere far away a dog barked in return.

Trey pulled her closer and left his hand on her back. "It isn't an easy path to follow. The power is strong, but you would have sensed the chaos that comes with it and turned back to the wolf. Our Beast is dangerous. Though fear and rage can summon it, we don't choose that form unless we must. We've learned to use it. I took a chance not telling you. I didn't want to scare you away from becoming what I wanted you to be."

"Are you telling me Mario can only become this Beast wolf?"

"Yes, he couldn't transform to wolf during his first guided shift at puberty. Unfortunately Lazlo guided him and being the older brother he taunted Mario. Lazlo's arrogance pushed him over the edge. Mario shifted into the Beast and almost killed Lazlo before the others pulled him off."

The pounding stopped and the Beast tried once again to break the door with its teeth. CJ watched the gruesome jaw and wondered at Trey's judgment. "Yet you let Mario go to public school? What if he hurt someone?" Didn't he have a clue how cruel teenagers could be?

"You don't understand. He was much happier there than here. He got along with the kids." Trey glanced over his shoulder as if he heard something or someone coming. "We discovered right away only one thing set Mario off into a rage strong enough to bring on the Beast."

The answer came to CJ immediately. "Lazlo."

Trey nodded. "Lazlo doesn't tolerate weaknesses in others. He's continually held up Mario as the example of what is wrong with our pack. He seems clueless to the harm he has done his brother."

"If only Lazlo angers him, can't someone else settle him down. Can't you do something? He trusts you, doesn't he?"

Trey kicked at the ground with his boot. "He used to. He's upset with me. I didn't tell him you were his sister right away. He doesn't think I should have got you involved with the pack. He doesn't want Lazlo anywhere near you." Trey's eyes met hers. CJ couldn't read his expression.

The sounds had stopped from the cell. She smelled the air, checking for a change inside. Mario's strong odor still clung to the breeze but the repugnant thread she had sensed earlier had lessened.

CJ shook off Trey's hand. "Wait here," she ordered.

"He could hurt you. He's not himself."

"You keep underestimating me." She marched the ten feet back to the concrete building. "Mario? Can you smell me? It's CJ."

She wished she could hear better, though she did catch the murmur of a whimper as she neared the door. She stopped a few inches short of the door, but didn't put her face anywhere near the bars this time. "It's all right. We'll get you out of here. You're not alone. Remember that. You've got Trey and now you've got me."

She stopped for a second and smelled the air. Mario was changing inside the cell. As if the evil she smelled before had drifted away.

She heard vomit splatter inside. "Mario, are you okay?" She waited a second longer. His ragged breathing unnerved her. He didn't sound good. "Mario?" She went to the barred window and peered inside. Only a small beam of light from that window hit the floor. The rest was hidden in shadows too dark for her to see her brother.

Quiet as a whisper, she heard his voice. "I'm back. I can't stay here."

What had Lazlo done to him? "Trey's here, too. We'll make them get you out."

"CJ I want out of *here*, the compound, the pack. They make me crazy. I don't want to live like this."

He sounded so broken it scared her. She had seen kids pushed to the edge. Sometimes they didn't come back. "Mario, these people are your family. They love you. Lazlo is only one werewolf. The others care. Believe me, I've met kids with absolutely no one. They'd think you were the lucky one." CJ heard the sound of a four-wheeler crash through the brush. Her time with her brother was running out.

A motion at the back of the cell caught her eye. A bare foot slid into the light, bloody scratches raked across it. CJ grabbed at the steel bars, wanting to get to him.

Mario slowly crawled into the small patch of light. His face streaked from tears and sweat. Matted hair pressed against his gaunt face. "Promise me if you escape you'll take me with you."

Her palms hit the doors with a thud. This sucked. They would kill him keeping him here, but she felt so damn powerless against these werewolves. "Mario, I can try. I can't promise—"

147

CJ stopped. The hot, sharp scent of Lazlo came from behind her. She prayed he hadn't heard their conversation. Another four-wheeler came down another path much slower than Lazlo's.

She glanced over her shoulder to see Doc Vogel climb off his ATV with a large gun slung over his shoulder. Apparently her brother wasn't anyone to mess with when he shifted.

For some sick reason she felt proud her little brother made these three grown werewolves nervous. Maybe together she and Mario could escape them.

"Get away from there." Lazlo gripped her by the shoulder and pulled her from the door. "You don't know what he can do."

Mario struggled to stand in the small square of light. "She's safe, Lazlo. I'm back to human."

Lazlo checked the small window. Satisfied at what he saw, he pulled a set of keys from his pants pocket.

CJ observed Trey and Vogel whispering in hushed tones. She couldn't believe Trey wasn't laying Lazlo flat on his ass for locking up Mario like some animal.

Fine. If he wouldn't come to Mario's defense, she would. "Just what kind of crazy place are you running? Imprisoning kids in concrete cells."

Black eyes met her own. Their menacing intent clear. "This is none of your concern." He leaned over his shoulder and shouted. "Trey, get her back to your cabin. And keep her there this time."

He stepped between CJ and the door and turned the key in the lock. The heavy steel door opened with a thud as the abused hinges clattered to the concrete floor. Mario's strength proven by the piece of wood embedded in the six-inch deep door. Lazlo hunched to fit through the opening and went inside.

CJ took a step to do the same, but Trey grabbed her hand to stop her.

"Best let Lazlo do this. He needs to see what his *discipline* does to Mario." He glared at the tall Alpha's back with hatred.

She wasn't letting the other werewolves off so easily. Mario needed someone to come to his defense, not just hate Lazlo. "Our father lets Lazlo treat him like a dog?"

"Your father isn't the Alpha Leader. This is the way business works around here. The Elders have power, but not on a day-to-day basis."

Lazlo emerged from the prison with Mario hanging on his shoulders. He had wrapped the boy in his own white linen jacket, now stained with filth and blood. The boy looked exhausted and paler than when CJ had seen him on Friday night. He had several wounds from tearing apart the contents of his cell. She wondered if he had spent the entire last twenty-four hours in that barbaric cage.

Doc Vogel came forward and helped Lazlo walk Mario to his four-wheeler. He glanced at Trey and CJ, his expression dour.

CJ wanted to go to her brother. She wanted to jump on a four-wheeler and take him off this freak-show compound. Her feelings for her father soured, seeing how he let his son be treated by the pack.

Trey's hand clamped tight on her arm. "Let him go. There is nothing you can do for him now."

Lazlo carefully helped his brother climb behind Doc Vogel on his four-wheeler. The teen glanced at CJ one more time before they drove off down the path. Lazlo stood and watched them go.

Trey removed his hand. "Don't worry about Mario. Doc Vogel will make sure he gets fixed up and fed. Mario is the only werewolf who can't shift to heal himself, so Vogel's made sure

149

he keeps enough antibiotics on hand. Mario does have friends in the compound."

CJ wanted to climb in Mario's head and comfort him. Let him know he wasn't alone. That being different could be good. "He doesn't belong with the pack, Trey. He's too different from the rest of the werewolves. You don't know what he's going through."

Trey gave her an odd look. "Believe me, I know."

The roar of an engine jarred CJ's hearing. A second later Lazlo gunned it straight for them. The dust the damn machine stirred up made her cough as he skidded to a stop in front of them.

His face was a cool mask of disdain. "Not that it matters what you think, but I didn't order him put in solitary. The training units went north to our Luna Peak Compound for exercises this weekend. I instructed Major Slavonsky that Mario should not be included because I believed he might try to escape. Apparently the major interpreted my instructions to mean putting Mario in solitary for the weekend."

Trey put a hand on Lazlo's vibrating bike and leaned down to make his point. "You're pushing him too hard. Mario feels like a loser locked in here with the others. They can shift and fight like full werewolves. You're going to kill him if you keep him here and try to make him someone he isn't. How many times does shit like this have to happen before you realize *you* can't help him." He turned his back on Lazlo and motioned his arm for CJ to go back to the path to his cabin. "Let's go. There's nothing more we can do here."

CJ didn't glance over her shoulder as they moved into the forest, but she could feel the burning glare of Lazlo's stare.

ഇരുന്നു

Trey could see CJ pacing the living room floor through the cabin's sliding glass doors. She worried about Mario. She had insisted on seeing her brother, so he had taken her over to Doc Vogel's lab. Mario had been asleep when they arrived, sedated by the Doc because of the many wounds he had to clean and stitch.

He wondered about her thoughts as she watched her brother sleeping. Her fingers had grazed the old scars scattered along Mario's arms and legs. Scars from past Beast shifts that had left him bruised and battered.

Satisfied the Doc was doing everything he could, she had been grim when they left. Ever since getting back to the cabin, she had pressed him for answers about Mario's future. Answers he didn't have.

He explained he wasn't the Alpha. He couldn't control what happened to Mario. What he didn't tell her was, with her help, Mario might have a very different future. Too risky yet.

Trey watched the smoke drifting from his grill and thought about CJ and Mario. They had an obvious connection. Mario had never calmed so quickly for anyone else.

Yes, things would be very different when he had his full powers restored. Then he could challenge Lazlo for the Alpha position. As Alpha he could take care of Mario. Trey couldn't think of anyone better for him than CJ Duncan. Perhaps the kid could go with her to Minneapolis and start over.

He expected CJ would jump at the chance to take Mario with her.

All he had to do was tell her the truth about his own weaknesses. Reveal his quest for his own powers, and broach the possibility she may have come to Seattle because of his magic spell.

151

But maybe she knew all those things. Maybe she was planning to take his shifting ability and escape with Mario on her own.

He had to find out how much she understood about her unusual strengths and exactly what brought her to his city.

He had to find out what made her come seek her father.

He lifted the lid of the grill and checked the eight burgers he had prepared. Perfection in a bun. He placed four on a plate for CJ and him to eat and launched the four remaining ones off the deck into the forest below.

Sebastian caught one before it hit the ground.

Show-off. Trey lifted his beer in a silent toast toward the wolf and left his friend to his guard duty.

Oh, Sebastian would do what Lazlo told him and make sure Trey and CJ didn't leave the compound, but he doubted Sebastian would listen as carefully to what went on inside the cabin as Bruno and Gracie.

He, like Trey, had yet to be paired with a female. But because of Lazlo's plan, Sebastian had to watch the woman he loved get paired off with another male. Trey had sent him on a grueling mission in Sri Lanka to prevent him from tearing apart the other male. A story that would be played out again and again during Lazlo's reign as Alpha.

Lazlo was obeyed, but hardly popular.

He put together the burgers and buns, grabbed some ketchup and a beer for CJ and went to the living room.

She had changed from her earlier clothes. She said they smelled too much like Mario's Beast. She had quizzed him about the Beast.

He couldn't tell her much she didn't already know. The werewolves, including himself, didn't use the form as frequently as their wolf form. But occasions arose when the agility and strength of the Beast was the only option. The super strength of the Beast could leave them drained and vulnerable for hours after shifting back. They were taught young about the difficulty in controlling the Beast, training hours both summoning it and suppressing it. The only way he could describe it was like driving a car with too much power when you couldn't always be sure the brakes would work. Even his Beast could do serious damage.

His explanation had seemed to satisfy her.

"Here, I made you two burgers. There's fruit in the fridge if you want it."

He put the food down on the coffee table, the beer clinking with the glass top.

She eyed the food, but stayed standing. He watched as she strode to the fireplace and placed a leg on the stone mantel. She wore a different pair of blue jeans. These were faded, with a few rips at the knees. They hung low on her waist and fit her like a second skin. He approved. She also must have run out of T-shirts. Instead, she wore a pale blue cotton top with tiny pearl buttons and a blue ribbon woven around the large neckline leaving her shoulders almost bare.

The fluttering sleeves accentuated her long lean arms. An utterly female shirt and one he couldn't picture her buying. She wore a loose braid and wisps had worked loose to frame her face.

She caught him staring.

What the hell. He might as well tell the truth. "Nice shirt. You look pretty in blue."

"I'll tell my mother you like it. She bought if for herself and decided it was too youthful." She strode over and grabbed a hamburger. "I don't get much time to shop."

He settled back into his recliner, his plate balanced on his knee. "CJ, sit down and eat. You can't get Mario out of here tonight anyway. He's exhausted."

She choked on her hamburger. She glared at him and motioned with her head to the door.

"Sebastian's on duty. I just fed him four burgers, so I imagine he's more interested in taking a light nap than eavesdropping on us for Lazlo."

"Well, I guess we can finally really talk." She sat and put the burger on her plate. "Tell me right now. Are you going to let me see my father or not?"

Trey didn't know what to tell her. "I can't guarantee it. Lazlo doesn't want you meeting any of the Elders before he informs them about you. He wants to make sure you don't jeopardize their support of the breeding plan."

"I still don't see the big deal. So my father had an illegitimate daughter without any of the others knowing. Does it matter if I'm a full werewolf or not?"

"The problem is you are *part* werewolf. You have powers, CJ. And with Lazlo's great genetic theories, our genes should be so different from humans we can't make babies, at least not babies with any of our powers. Second, your human genes should make your werewolf powers weak. Theoretically, according to Lazlo, only two strong parents can make a strong werewolf." He took a swig of beer. "Believe me breaking Lazlo's nose proved you are anything but weak, yet you definitely didn't have two strong werewolf parents."

CJ paced back and forth. She frowned as she hit the floor with her boots. "Damn. This whole fiasco is a lot more complicated than it was supposed to be." She stopped and planted her fists on her hips. "It's your fault. My father. He was all I wanted. You could have sent me to him and Lazlo never needed to know about me."

She had hit the nail on the head. It was his fault Lazlo kept her prisoner. His hunch told him he had more to do with her being in Seattle than her father. He had to find out more about her trances he had witnessed.

When they had shifted the other night, they'd moved together as one. Perfect complements to each other. All senses united and strong, and full werewolf strength coursed through them.

Perfect complements. Too perfect for coincidence.

He had worn his amulet the night he touched her at the club and she went into her strange trance.

He had been casting his spell the night she passed out in his office. The truth just waited to be found. "I don't think finding your father will solve your problem."

CJ finished her first burger. "No, not anymore it isn't. My brother is being treated like a freak by a bunch of werewolves with an insane mentality that compels them to follow a crazy leader. No, I have two problems to solve now." She snatched up the second burger and continued standing, staring down at him, "Oh, wait. I still have to think of some story when the almighty Lazlo decides it's time to interrogate me. That makes three."

Trey had thought about Lazlo, too. He doubted very much Lazlo would harm CJ before the Council met. Too many werewolves had seen her. The Elders would ask uncomfortable questions if she suddenly disappeared. "I think you should just tell him the truth. Tell him about being part human, tell him about being unable to shift. Tell him why you came here."

"Don't you think that will make him mad? I mean you just said it yourself, I could blow his precious breeding theory out of the water."

Trey ran his hand up and down his jeans. "I know Lazlo about as well as I know myself. Our best hope is he'll be so confident with his breeding plan he'll dismiss you as unimportant. He has a tendency to overestimate his power."

A chancy idea at best. Revealing his trump card to Lazlo before the Elders met didn't sit well, but if his theory about his missing powers was right, it wouldn't matter. He'd have his full abilities by the time the Elders Council met. CJ would simply be a human, and he'd have to find a way to convince the Elders to let him challenge Lazlo.

Yet, one question remained in his mind. No matter the hurt it might cause, the truth had to be found. "What made you decide to find your father? I mean, it sounds like you liked your life. Why come looking for him now?" There he asked her. His palms sweated, waiting to find out if his worst fear was true.

CJ finally stopped pacing. She stared out of the window before dropping to the couch. She ran her hands over her face.

"Because I couldn't do my job anymore." She leaned back in the couch, a dark look in her eye. "Because one night the runaway I tracked was in my sights. An asshole pimp hassling her to turn tricks for him. He pulled her into his car. I couldn't let him move her. I remember running for her, but I went into a trance, like you saw at the club and your office. When I finally came to, she was gone. They found her body two days later."

A cold lump formed in his stomach. Had he caused a girl to die because of his spell?

He never thought he'd affect anyone else when he went searching for his powers. "CJ, what happens when you go into those trances? Do you see things? Feel things?"

"It's going to sound crazy." She grabbed a tasseled throw pillow and hugged it to her body.

Trey leaned forward. "Hey, remember I'm the guy who believes in magic and turns into a wolf. Try me."

Her voice grew quiet. "Well, at first it's just like fog rolls over me. I don't always realize I'm entering a trance at first. The fog will clear and I'm looking at something else. I mean I'm not seeing what's actually there."

"You have a wolf in this vision, don't you?"

She slanted her eyes at him. "Why yes, Mr. Werewolf, I do. But not always. Sometimes I just see buildings. I always thought they were random buildings. Until I saw the Space Needle. Then I knew. My visions were of Seattle. Where my mom came from." She swallowed. "That's how I found Mario. I had seen a big complex with lots of teenagers coming out the doors. A mall, maybe a high school. I went to the Seattle school district web page and found a building that looked strangely the same."

"But why did you think your visions were about your dad?" Trey asked.

CJ smiled. He hadn't seen those dimples all day. "You see my friend, my roommate, Roz is a psychic." She rolled her eyes. "Well she says she's a psychic. I didn't believe her before, but I'm having second thoughts. After the girl died because I zoned out, I finally let Roz do a reading on me. She said the hallucinations had to do with my father. She thought they were my subconscious telling me I needed to find my father. The Space Needle was a symbol for Seattle and the wolf was my mother trying to protect me from the truth." She sighed. "Well, she got that part wrong, but pretty much...I agree with her."

"You think finding your father, Rupert, will settle your subconscious mind and your visions will end?"

"Yep, sounds simple, doesn't it? Truth is, I haven't had one since the werewolves entered my life. Maybe this was all I was meant to find out."

Trey hated to ask because, in his heart, he knew the answer. "When did your visions begin?"

CJ hugged the pillow tighter and leaned back on the leather couch. She tilted her head and stared at the ceiling. "Around midnight, six months ago. The top twenty countdown played on the radio during a stakeout and I lost numbers ten through four. I thought I had fallen asleep and dreamed the whole thing. The first vision wasn't as defined as the rest. The animal could've been a dog or a wolf. They've gotten worse each time."

His darkest fear was true. Six months ago, he had found the amulet in a museum in Kiev. He had left a bag of gold coins in its place when he'd stolen it. He had no idea he could harm anyone else with his power-summoning spell.

He brushed a hand through his hair. On one hand relief washed over him. CJ wasn't hiding some plan to take his powers. A girl had died. She wouldn't lie about death. The pain was etched on her face for him to see.

Now he had to tell her these visions weren't random. They were his fault. Guilt constricted his chest, but it was time to tell her the truth. He owed her. "CJ, your father isn't the cause of these visions."

She jerked her head down and glared. "How can you know?"

"I know." He licked his lips and took a breath. "Because I'm the one causing your visions."

Chapter Nine

Trey had left fifteen minutes ago and already CJ tired of the Sunday afternoon television programming. He had told Sebastian he had to go back to the office and get some paperwork for the Elders. Not wanting to risk Lazlo's wrath, Sebastian had insisted CJ be secured in the cabin.

Watching Trey argue with a completely nude man had looked absurd, but she was beginning to realize nudity and werewolves just went together. Trey had caught her checking out Sebastian's impressive physique.

He hadn't seemed amused.

Now she sat tied to a long chain with a pair of fuzzy handcuffs, which came from who knew where, obsessing over their last conversation.

She thought over his confession. Trey had told her, *"I know, because I'm the one causing your visions."*

He seemed absolutely certain of his guilt. He had mentioned another spell and an amulet, but nothing else. He insisted he had to go back to Guardian and retrieve the amulet. He swore it was the key. He said he had been wearing it both times she had gone into a trance.

Despite his obvious turmoil, she pressed him for an explanation. His mouth set in a grim frown, he had simply ignored her.

That pissed her off. She had trusted him with her secrets.

She had been truthful with him from their first night. Admitting she thought Mario was her brother, admitting she searched for her father. Eventually, she had even told him about her visions and yet, he couldn't do the same for her.

He had a secret and he deliberately kept it from her.

CJ hit the remote and watched the cars speeding around some Midwest speedway. She cranked the volume higher. The roar of racing engines filled the room.

The fur-covered handcuffs sat firmly around her wrists. She found it hard to believe Trey honestly thought these flimsy cuffs would hold her. She focused her attention on Sebastian's scent.

She definitely smelled wolf, but couldn't get a reading on his exact location. Just her luck. He was doing laps around the cabin to work off the hamburgers Trey had fed him earlier.

Instead of worrying about how to get around Lazlo's guard, she concentrated on removing the annoying handcuffs. She grabbed the crumpled throw from the couch and clumsily wrapped it around the cuffs to muffle the sound when she tore them from the chain.

Satisfied the fabric could absorb the noise, she brought her wrists together. In one quick burst of power she pulled the cheap metal apart. Perfect. They fell loose from the chain and dropped to the floor in a loud clink.

She froze. And waited.

Sebastian didn't burst through the door so she figured she was safe.

She eased herself from the couch and scanned the area outside the window for any sign of the wolf. The late afternoon forest remained quiet. The other wildlife must avoid the werewolves. She thought about retrieving her cell phone, but decided she didn't want to risk it being found if they caught her before she made it over the fence.

It sucked she didn't have a plan to get Mario out of here. But she'd be back for him. Somehow.

She bolted up the loft stairs to grab what she could from her bags, but stopped on the first step. A strong wolf smell seeped into the cabin.

Doc Vogel. His scent was almost as unique as Trey's and it held strange undertones she couldn't place. It held a thread she hadn't picked up on any of the other werewolves, yet to her it was impossible not to notice. Of course, maybe as werewolves aged their scents changed.

CJ jumped over the back of the couch and hid her broken cuffs under the blanket. She snuggled on the couch appearing to be engrossed in NASCAR.

Vogel didn't bother knocking, but instead shouted a command in a foreign language to Sebastian and barged right into the cabin. He marched over and stopped at the end of the couch. His gaze followed the chain that ran from beneath her blanket to the stairway.

"Trey thought this would hold you?" He sat at the other end from CJ. He plopped the old medical bag between them and cocked an eyebrow. "You are the one who broke Lazlo's nose?"

She wasn't incriminating herself. "Don't know what you are talking about."

"Don't worry. The guards on duty saw his nose when he pulled in on Friday night. It was all over the compound before he had a chance to shift. Of course, everyone else thinks Trey let him have it. But I believe differently? Am I right?"

"Don't you think Trey can take down Lazlo?" She wondered why Vogel would think it was she who hit the Alpha.

"Well, he couldn't defeat Lazlo during the Succession Challenges. Don't see why it would be any different now. And quite frankly, Trey is too clever to take on Lazlo directly. I have my suspicions Trey has other ideas."

A cold knot formed in CJ's stomach. Was Vogel here to get her to squeal out Trey? She wouldn't put it past Lazlo to try that route.

She guessed Trey had plans to overthrow Lazlo. But if Vogel knew, Trey could be in danger. If Sebastian overheard their conversation, Lazlo could get wind of it.

Vogel placed a large hand on CJ's leg. She automatically tried to pull it away but he held tight. The smile on his face didn't match his grip on her leg.

Vogel leaned closer and talked in a low voice. "Don't worry. Quite frankly, it doesn't matter who is Alpha Leader to me. Lazlo, Trey. They're young men. Ambitious men. They may lead the pack down different paths, but all in all I think both men want what is best for the pack." He lifted his hand and straightened the blanket he had mussed, much as if he was her grandfather tucking her in. "Don't worry, I won't tell a soul about Trey's plans. Don't really know what they are, I just know Lazlo underestimates Trey. Everyone does."

CJ watched the man as he lifted his bag to his lap. His face revealed little, his scent less. Trey had trusted him, but she wasn't ready to make that call. "Hate to break it to you, but I'm the last person Trey'd tell anything. He is simply my keeper because Lazlo doesn't want to deal with me."

"Ah, well, you've hit on the reason I'm here. Lazlo did send me, but not to pump you for information. He'd simply like the pleasure of your company for a few hours, but he wasn't certain you'd cooperate." He patted the black bag. "He gave me permission to sedate you if necessary." He leaned over the bag

162

and lowered his voice. "Another clue, I believe, that your strength might be a bit too much for the typical werewolf to handle."

He moved his gaze about the room, "Now where did Trey leave the key to the handcuffs Sebastian said you were wearing."

What the hell, he seemed to know she wasn't a weakling anyway. Kicking off the blanket, she lifted her two arms. "Don't need it."

He chuckled. "I hope, since you haven't made a run for it yet, you'll be agreeable and simply walk with me to Lazlo's. I'd love a chance to chat with you for a bit."

CJ glanced at the old man, then toward the stairs. Sebastian or Vogel alone, she could have probably handled, but fighting two werewolves might be more than she could manage.

Sooner or later she had to face Lazlo again, and it looked like the time was now. "I'd much prefer to walk."

"Good, then we shall." Vogel held the door open for her and Sebastian waited on the other side. "Sebastian, Miss Duncan has agreed to meet Lazlo without a fuss, so we won't need your assistance to take her to his cabin."

Sebastian didn't step out of the way. "Trey ordered me to keep an eye on CJ."

Vogel lifted his finger and pushed against the younger man's chest, "*Lazlo* instructed me to bring her to his cabin. I suggest you curl up and take a nap until I bring her back."

With a look to CJ, Sebastian moved out of the way and let them pass. He didn't look pleased the older man insisted he stay behind. CJ was certain that Trey would be informed of her whereabouts as soon as Sebastian could reach him.

Whether Trey would be happy that Lazlo wanted to talk to her, she wasn't sure. If Lazlo meant to get rid of her before the Elders met, surely he would have done it by now, and he wouldn't have sent Vogel. Perhaps sending the older man was Lazlo's way of telling her she had nothing to fear.

She hoped she was right.

They followed the path Trey had led her down when they first arrived. This time she noticed the many small paths that intersected with it. The whole compound seemed a web meant to confuse.

"I am surprised to find you alone. Trey seemed, shall we say, a bit protective of you the other night." He walked leisurely and CJ had to force herself to take smaller steps. She bristled with eagerness to get this face-off with Lazlo finished.

Mario was first on her list to discuss. Next, she'd bring up her father. She was ready to offer to disappear when the Elders came if he could guarantee she could meet with her father.

Trey seemed to have his own agenda, but she saw no reason to share it with Vogel. "He has something he needed to get at the office."

"I see. Well, Trey takes pride in Guardian. It's been a good project for a young man raised to be Alpha."

CJ didn't respond. She didn't want to become embroiled any more than she was in the pack's inner power struggles.

They turned onto another path before they reached the parking lot. The thick foliage prevented her from seeing the exact location of the sun. She wasn't sure in what direction they walked.

Vogel stopped and pointed to a narrow trail. "Mario's family cabin is that way."

The doctor wasn't lying. The scent threads told her the same. She shrugged. "So?"

He resumed strolling forward. "I just thought you'd want to know where your father lived. You might have a chance to visit him after the Elders meet."

CJ wasn't surprised. He had taken a blood sample from her after all. "When did you figure it out?"

"Only this morning, after I saw you with Mario. Your concern was quite touching, really. It will take some time to do the DNA match with Rupert's sample, but I'm confident I'm correct."

"Will my father be in trouble for having a daughter outside the pack?" She had never asked Trey if she would endanger her father. She had been so concerned about finding him and Mario she hadn't thought about that until now.

Doc Vogel shook his head. "Oh, he might be reprimanded, but I think there will be such shock you exist at all. They'll overlook Rupert's dalliance." He slowed his pace more. "It's rather amazing, really. I don't believe there is any record of a human and a werewolf producing a baby. My research into our genes led me to believe it was impossible. Yet here you are." He glanced over his shoulder and smiled at her. "You're a bit of miracle in my book."

"Are you saying werewolves and humans have never intermingled?" Trey had talked openly about human lovers. It didn't seem likely he would flagrantly break werewolf law.

"Oh no, it's happened, but most of us prefer our own kind. Trey's a bit of an exception, but his affairs never lasted long. Though there are many in the pack who frown upon it. Recently Lazlo has been petitioning the Elders to outlaw it."

CJ found it hard to believe that she was the first product of these unions. "How do you know for certain a baby was never born between a human and a werewolf?"

"Truthfully, I can't say it *never* happened, since the old scattered packs of Europe were awful record keepers. After the wars we didn't find much use for humans. If the rare werewolf strayed, a pregnancy was never noted." He stopped in his tracks. "Except for you. And you seem to have inherited some werewolf powers as well."

CJ wasn't sure why he stopped. But she had a feeling she wouldn't like his next question.

"Who *is* your mother?"

She was right. No way in hell she was bringing her mother into this. "She's a human. Nothing more."

He gave her one more sidelong glance, then continued. "How old are you, CJ?"

"Thirty-three."

"Trey's thirty-three. Born in 1973. I assume you were, too." He pursed his lips and narrowed his eyes.

"December of '73. Is that important?"

Her question seemed to startle him from his thoughts. "What? Well, not really. Nothing of importance." His pace increased as the path grew wider and more open.

If he had any more questions, he didn't have time to ask them, because the trees suddenly thinned and they emerged into a small clearing in front of another cabin.

₠₠₠₠

Lazlo's cabin wasn't at all like Trey's. His walls were finished with wallboard and painted a cool gray. His loft was enclosed and instead of a warm wood railing, the staircase was a dizzying steel contraption. The furnishings in the living room consisted of black leather, chrome, glass or electronics.

Doc Vogel had left her at the door with a reassuring smile and a feeling he might be one of the few werewolves who would be strong enough to defy Lazlo.

She felt oddly underdressed in her old blue jeans and wished she had at least put on her black cargo pants. She wouldn't have felt so out of place in the cold room. She was positive Lazlo would make another appearance in Armani.

The strange smell of gas seeped into the room. The fireplace glass moved open and a false flame leapt to life. Apparently cutting wood wasn't Lazlo's style.

She stood, staring at the black leather couch. Its back was to the rest of the cabin and she didn't want to have Lazlo sneak up on her. She decided to stay standing and wait. She sniffed at the air. His scent covered the cabin. She wasn't sure from which room he'd come.

She didn't have to wait long before she heard him clear his throat at the top of the stairs. "Sit and make yourself comfortable. I have some wine chilling for us." He made little noise in his bare feet as he came down the steel staircase. Black jeans rode low on his hips and he wore an unbuttoned white shirt. The view the open shirt offered was impressive. He had a long, lean torso with a light covering of dark hair. Tight abs disappeared into a trim waist accentuated by his low jeans.

His glistening long hair hung loose around his shoulders. His exotic look, so intimidating in the designer suits, was breathtaking in this simple ensemble. CJ couldn't deny the man was beautiful.

He went into the open kitchen at the back of the cabin and returned with two glasses of rosé. The aroma of the wine proved a pleasant distraction from Lazlo's strong presence in the room.

She sat on a metal and leather chair that reminded her of a doctor's waiting room. He handed her a glass, then reclined into the large leather couch. With an arm thrown over the back and his legs crossed, he looked like a model for some fancy cologne.

How deceiving looks could be.

Lazlo took a slow slip of wine, watching her over the rim. "Miss Duncan, it's a pleasure to finally have a chance to talk without Trey breathing down my neck."

CJ kept her mouth shut. She wanted to stay out of their personal battle. She wanted to tell him he seemed to be as much in Trey's face as Trey was in his.

He placed his wine glass down on a steel coffee table. He bent forward, one finger tracing a circle around the glass's edge. "From what I gather, Trey seems to think you will upset the Elders enough that they will halt the breeding plan. Which is a possibility, but I doubt it." He slowly lifted the glass and took another sip. His eyes gleamed with dark determination. "Our pack is in trouble. You saw firsthand Mario's difficulties. As each new child reaches puberty we experience new and different manifestations of this epidemic. Trey doesn't have a plan to stop it. I do."

CJ sat her wine on the table next to her. This was no social visit. She wanted to keep her mind sharp. "You think breeding the strong with the strong will stop this 'epidemic'?"

"We won't know until the new offspring reach puberty. But yes. I think it's the best chance this pack has to survive. I will not see the werewolf simply evolve out of existence. I will do everything in my power to save our kind." He cocked his head toward her and raked her with his gaze. "Everything."

CJ couldn't believe he would be looking at her with anything other than suspicion. She suddenly wished she hadn't been quite so willing to meet him alone.

Lazlo swirled the wine in his glass. "We're a noble species, CJ. Powerful and intelligent. We've always remained hidden, hunted, but this is a new millennium. Perhaps if we protect our bloodline, it will flourish. Then in time we could bring in outside scientists, researchers. Why, we may even find a gene in our strange DNA which could help the world." He stretched his long legs before him. "What do you think of that?"

"Sounds like you've got it all figured out. I'm curious, have you told the Elders about your grand plans?"

His eyes flashed with anger. "The Elders are stuck in the last century. It took me years to convince them that we had to enact a systematic breeding plan to save the best of our genes. No, they can't think beyond old traditions and superstitions."

"Superstitions? You mean like magic." CJ wondered why Lazlo was so certain science held the key to their problem. "Has it occurred to you, maybe the werewolf is a magical creature?"

"I realize our mere existence has you doubting the limits of reality. I assure you the laws of nature apply to us as well as to anyone. We are born, we live, and"—his voice went quiet—"we die." He tapped his fingers along the stem of the dainty goblet. "The dark ages are over. Magic is nothing but ignorant people trying to explain things they don't understand."

He seemed convinced humans and werewolves were two different species. She wondered how he would explain her parentage. "What about me. Has Doctor Vogel told you? I'm Rupert's daughter. My mother is human." She grew uneasy when Lazlo didn't act surprised at her announcement.

"I don't know what Trey has been telling you, but I'm not the idiot he supposes. I sensed you were related to Mario that first night. Your reaction to Mario's confinement only reinforced my suspicion."

So Lazlo had known about her origins this entire time. She wondered why he had waited so long to bring her here. "Did you know I was Rupert's child?"

He shrugged as if her question was unimportant. "I alone have access to the Alpha Leader's records. So I perused the entries Trey's grandfather had made concerning discipline about thirty years ago and found an entry on Rupert. Do you know what happened?"

Her temper rose hot in her gut at his arrogant tone. He knew she'd want to know the truth. "Enlighten me," she scoffed.

"Well, apparently my rascally stepfather was chasing tail outside the werewolf compound. Of course, seeing you, I imagine your mother was quite a tempting beauty herself." His teeth flashed white between his dark lips.

His smile left CJ cold. Part of her wished Trey would come pounding on Lazlo's door. Soon.

He continued his tale. "The records note Rupert had developed a strong attachment to a human girl and he was ordered to break it off. Shortly thereafter, Rupert was taken in front of the Elders Council for the death of three humans. Once Rupert was sent overseas on an extended mission he calmed down, to say the least. He's been the perfect pack member ever since."

His story prompted more questions than answers. How much did her mother know of this and who had her father killed? Did she know that her young lover was a werewolf? Had he known she was pregnant with his child?

Done with playing the polite guest, she frowned at him in defiance. "Well, obviously the all-powerful Alpha didn't catch them soon enough." She raised her eyebrows in mock surprise.

"Because here I am. So how does your grand theory explain me? You say humans and werewolves are different species. Vogel says a baby from their union has never been recorded."

Lazlo snorted in derision. "You think your conception was magic. No, Doc Vogel sometimes gets a little mired in the past. I'm sure he neglected to tell you few written records of our kind exist from our centuries in Europe. The two World Wars disrupted the packs and with the communist takeover in what were our most populated countries...records were destroyed to protect our kind from detection. I highly doubt you are the first mix."

She was no closer to making contact with her father by arguing with Lazlo. Irritation nagged her patience, but she had to finish what she came for. Right now Lazlo seemed the only way to get to her father. "It seems you have it all figured out. Well, when the Elders are done I'd like a chance to talk with Rupert and then leave."

"I'll consider it." He stared straight ahead and sipped his wine.

"Letting me meet my father or letting me leave?"

He didn't answer, but instead stood, with his wine dangling from one hand, and went to a bookshelf next to the fireplace. He brought a large leather book over and handed it to her. "Open it. It's a photo album my mother made for me."

She turned to the first page and saw a black and white picture of a dark man who bore a striking resemblance to Lazlo. The man was pushing a young black-haired boy on a bike along a gravel path.

He knelt down on one knee, setting his wine glass next to her untouched one. "That is my father. Enrico Medina. He was killed when I was ten."

CJ wondered what this had to do with her. "I thought werewolves could heal themselves from any wounds."

"Not a head wound. He took a shot just above his right ear, protecting a Soviet scientist who defected to France. If a werewolf is unconscious he cannot make the shift. He lost too much blood and died before the rest of the squad could move him to safety." Lazlo traced a finger across his father's face then quickly flipped a few more pages in the album. "Doesn't sound very magical, does it?"

The anger in his voice was clear.

The next picture was a formal color portrait. The young man in the center was a younger Lazlo. As a teen he had the same gauntness as Mario. A small boy, perhaps one or two, was sitting on his knee, obviously Mario. Over one shoulder stood a dark woman with cascading black hair. And above them all was a tall brown-haired man with a dazzling smile and deep dimples. His broad features were not as refined as the woman and her sons', but he was undeniably handsome.

CJ sucked in her breath. She had dimples, her mother didn't.

"Your father, Rupert. The pack was shocked when my mother married him a few years after my father's death. Rupert had never lifemated with any female werewolf and was known as a bit of a loner. A good fighter when needed, but not strong enough to be a squad leader like my father."

"So you resented him and you take it out on Mario."

"I love Mario. And I do not resent Rupert. My mother was lonely. Our heritage is a passionate one. We do not like to be alone."

He traced a smooth finger down her arm holding the album. An involuntary shiver snaked along her spine.

The way he was looking at her arm almost made her think he might bend over and take a bite of it. Instead, he flipped a few pages more until she saw a picture of him and Trey. Together. Smiling.

They appeared young, perhaps twenty. Lazlo was no longer a gaunt teenager and looked much the same as he did now except his hair only brushed his shoulders. They posed on a beach, both wet and holding a beer. Three surfboards stood anchored in the sand behind them.

Trey seemed completely changed to CJ. His hair in the photo hung inches below his shoulders. It fell in wet waves around his broad grin. Leather strands encircled his neck and a large Celtic rope tattoo encircled his bulging left bicep.

Lazlo pointed to the tattoo. "The Elders were furious when Trey returned with this tattoo from our trip to Cancun. To them anything with ties to the spiritual or mystical was dangerous. Many of them had lost their packs to Hitler's death squads and the communist purges. But Trey didn't care. He rubbed it in their faces. All he cared about was impressing the girls. He was the son of the Alpha Leader after all." The venom in Lazlo's voice was undeniable.

"Did they make him laser it off?" Trey had no tattoo now.

Lazlo laughed. "The Elders had their sweet revenge because the tattoo completely disappeared after a few shifts."

"So Trey was a typical young man. I don't have a problem with that. I'm sure you were a complete bore in comparison."

"But you don't seem to understand the expectation that everyone had for him to succeed his father as Alpha Leader. Trey's grandfather was the one who united the decimated European packs and brought us here. Only a few know the truth about Trey."

A uncomfortable inkling told CJ she wasn't going to like what Lazlo revealed. She didn't want to hear it. Betraying Trey wasn't part of her plan.

Lazlo leaned closer to her and spoke quietly. "He's weak. Weaker than me. Weaker than all the other males. Weaker than you, I suspect. Few of the pack could have gotten through my defenses the way you did the other night. Your strength is amazing."

He was too close. CJ shut the photo album and shoved it at Lazlo. Then she got out of her chair and made a move toward the door.

She didn't get far.

Lazlo's chest slammed against her back as his long arm reached out and took her waist in his iron grip. His smell oozed over her senses. "Why are you helping him? You want answers about your father? I can give them to you. Trey is just a weak and jealous man. He's using you."

She moved a leg behind, trying to use Lazlo's own weight to flip him off. Before she could strike, he released her and shoved. The strength of his push knocked her to the couch.

He leapt from the floor to land on top of her. His bent knees on either side of her hips. Before she could lift her arms he had them pinned at her sides. "He hates me, CJ. The breeding plan is just an excuse for him to attack me, because I know how weak he is. His mother was a weak female who should never have been allowed to breed with the Alpha."

"Lazlo, I'm warning you. Get the hell off of me."

"I just want you to listen to the truth. Though Trey had turned his back on me when I told him as a young man that I was competing in the next Alpha Succession, I held him close in my heart. My friendship for him did not die. I knew he would never succeed, so to save him embarrassment, I made sure I fought him in the first round of the Succession Challenges."

"So you fixed it."

"You stupid woman. Can't you see what I did? Because he lost to me, none of the other werewolves realized how truly weak he was. And how does he repay me? By turning my brother against me. By undermining my command with his position as CEO of Guardian."

"Trey owes you nothing."

"He owes me everything." He let her arms go and moved off the couch. He grabbed her shoulders and pulled her into his arms once again, his face mere inches from her.

She could smell the sexual arousal on him. Never mind his erection pressing hard against her thigh. "You are a strong female and though Doc Vogel hasn't discovered your true genetic structure yet, I believe you are werewolf enough."

Enough. Hell, she hoped he didn't want her as part of his breeding plan.

"With my genes and your incredible strength our child could very well be a full werewolf." He reached a hand into her braid and pulled the plait free. He brought it over her shoulder and brushed it against his face.

His breath invaded her space. Hot and too strong. Overpowering like his scent. Not like Trey's. The wolf was stronger in Lazlo. A feral fragrance, wild and unpredictable.

Couldn't he sense her repulsion?

"You are so beautiful and strong. I can feel your power. Why do you still cling to this loyalty to Trey? Did he not reject you the other night?"

She wedged her arm between his lips and her neck. "This isn't about Trey. This is about you and me, and I want you to let go—"

The edges of the room blurred. Lazlo's dark eyes glared at her. Was it anger? Fighting to hold off the vision, she desperately sought the smell of his emotion.

She couldn't. She saw his head turning. His lips moved, but she couldn't hear a sound.

When the haze cleared from her sight, CJ no longer saw Lazlo. She cringed at the sight before her. The white wolf lay unmoving on the ground before her. She itched to move. To flee. Her body wouldn't respond. A great wind gusted and knocked against her. A presence came. No fragrance or sound carried on the wind to ease her fear.

Her heart jumped as a great dark wolf emerged from the haze. Each strike of the wolf's paw upon the ground sent her body trembling.

The gold eyes of the wolf locked on her. She wanted to move, but she couldn't.

The wolf wasn't stopping. It lunged and she saw its hairy chest lurch into the air in front of her. She opened her mouth to scream, but no voice for her terror sounded. Its face came straight for hers. She braced for the impact. Felt nothing...

...nothing except the warm envelope of darkness carrying her away.

Chapter Ten

"Get the fuck away from me, you...you..." CJ's right fist cracked against the hard bone under his eye. The bone held under her assault.

Trey didn't flinch from her punches as she came back to consciousness fighting against her confinement. *That's my girl.*

He wanted to shift, but first she had to calm down. He couldn't release her. She might run, expose their cover. He knew what he looked like.

And she might think he was Lazlo.

She had been passed out in Lazlo's arms when he crashed through the cabin's door, so she had no memory of him taking her from Lazlo. He marveled he hadn't injured her when he sprang on the Alpha.

He could smell the fear from her. Her fighting instincts wouldn't let her stop long enough to see he meant her no harm.

It was so hard to hold her down and not cut her. Even as he tried to curve his claws away from her tender shoulders, they scraped the floorboard next to her head, filling the room with their evil sound. The hands of his Beast form were made for killing, not for gentle touches.

She stopped. He sensed an eerie limpness under his claws. He stared at her, penetrating the dark shadows of the unlit room with his heightened sight. Her eyes were closed, but her chest fell and rose with quiet breaths. *Faking defeat.* Smart fighter, not just a strong one.

Oh, his clever CJ. Of course, if he had wanted to truly kill her nothing would've stopped him, but he might have paused for a moment. A moment she could have used for a surprise attack.

She left no doubt in his mind. If the others caught them, at least the two of them would do some damage before they were killed. Trey guessed it would be a dozen against two. Lazlo wouldn't take any chances in this hunt.

Lazlo. His body stiffened with rage at the thought of him. It had taken every ounce of control not to kill Lazlo back at the compound, but he had fought through the blood lust and gotten CJ out of there before the guard werewolves came to their Alpha's aid.

What would Lazlo have done to her if he hadn't gotten back to the compound in time? Killed her out of fear? Raped her out of spite? Had power truly corrupted his old friend so much?

This was his fault. His own need for power had brought CJ to Seattle, and now she could die for it. He wanted to cry, but the Beast had no tears.

He lifted his hands from her shoulders and wrapped his gruesome limbs around her, her body so fragile. Too human.

She was completely human now, yet her fragrance affected him. Just as sweet and warm as the night they had shifted together. Heaven. Though every second was precious, he drew in her scent like oxygen, implanting it even stronger in his brain for when this gift would be taken from him.

But he'd lose much more if he kept waiting for the inevitable. He let her go and retreated slowly from crouching over her. He stood close to nine feet in this form. He ducked clumsily, his large thigh and calf muscles bunched and quivering with suppressed power. His rapid run across the city from the compound to downtown had shown him the awesome strength he had with CJ's powers. The Beast was itching to run again.

CJ scrambled to her feet, and stood frozen as she stared at his monstrous werewolf form. Her fear hit him hard as he caught it the air between them. Confusion marked her face as she inspected her surroundings. She gazed around the room, taking in the bed and spare furniture.

Trey willed her to look at him. He wanted her to see the truth. Their kind had been ashamed of the Beast for so long and yet tonight it had saved her from Lazlo. Once her attention was on him, he revealed his true identity.

"Trey?" Her words reached him as he made his body shift, felt the fire, the pain and then the completion.

"I should have never left you alone." Trey moved to her in his human form, naked and slick with sweat. He enfolded her in his arms. "Part of me wanted to believe there was still a sliver of honor in Lazlo. I'll never put you in danger again."

"It isn't your fault. I would have found my father sooner or later and when I did, I would have found Lazlo." She laid her head on his shoulder. He felt the breath move out of her, as she settled deeper in his embrace. "I'm just so glad you got me out of there. But how did you know?"

"Sebastian called me and told me Vogel had been sent to take you to Lazlo. When he said Vogel carried his bag, I was afraid of what Lazlo had planned, but even I didn't expect him to..." He ran a hand down her hair. "I shouldn't have left you."

CJ tipped her head, frowning as she probed his face with her questioning eyes. "How did you get past his guards?"

Now was not the time to tell her about the amulet. "I'll explain more later." He bundled her into his arms and carried her over to his bed. He had never seen her so pale. Like a porcelain doll. He wanted to strip those clothes off her because, to his now sensitive nose, they reeked of Lazlo. But that would have to wait. He wasn't done with the Beast yet. "I have to create a false trail so the others will follow those. I'm hoping this place carries so much of my smell and is so obvious they won't even bother with it."

"Don't leave me. Something's wrong with me. He did something to me," she said, her voice shaky.

"I know. You'll be safe here. It's a secret room next to my office. I was in here the other night when you broke in. No one else knows about this room. But I want you to take this." He removed the gold amulet from around his neck. Along with the amulet, he pressed a small piece of paper into her shaking hand. "Don't ask me what it is now, but if I don't return in two hours, put this amulet around your neck. Say this spell in a circle of these candles." He pulled out the basket from beneath his bed. "And then get the hell out of town as fast as you can. Change your name. Take your mother and hide."

"Wait—"

He bent down and kissed her pale lips. They were warm and full. His chest ached at having to leave her, but there were still a few more tricks up his sleeve. Lazlo wouldn't find them easy prey. "There's twenty grand in the bedside table."

He went to the secret door, resolve settling in his chest. CJ would have to wait. He prayed he could control this new supernatural strength well enough to do all he had to in the next two hours.

He crawled outside through the bathroom window, reaching back to close it as tightly as possible. The sun had been setting when he made his run across the city bringing CJ to safety. Dodging human sight. The darkness was falling fast. The shadows would help. He heard the distant cry of a wolf. Then an answering howl from farther to the east.

They had started the hunt.

He leapt from the fifteen-story ledge, shifting form seamlessly as he fell. His Beast hit the ground on all fours, stood and ran off down the alley.

৪০৪০০৪

CJ lay in the dark listening to the noise of the urban night. The car horns blared less frequently, so it was probably nearing midnight. Surely two hours had passed since Trey left her here. She couldn't be sure. There was no clock in the room and her watch was back at his cabin.

Trey's small bed creaked as she moved from her side to her back. She moved to caress the strange piece of jewelry hanging from a leather cord around her neck. She didn't want to risk losing it. She figured wearing it on her body was as safe as anywhere else she could stash it.

He had called it an amulet. In the dark she couldn't see clearly so she let her touch explore it, the middle stone smooth and cool under her fingers. The flat red stone lay surrounded by the strange carved runes, the tiny ridges revealing nothing of their meaning.

She found it hard to imagine why Trey thought it was so important.

The spell she had folded and stuffed into her pocket. She was afraid to even read the thing after experiencing the power of the shifting spell the other night.

He should have told her more. Maybe then she wouldn't hesitate to do as he ordered. The time drew close. She had to think of her mother. She should do as Trey asked, say the spell and hitch a ride out of Seattle.

Her mother's cruise reached port in Miami in a few days. She could make it there and then they could start over somewhere else. They were smart women. She'd make sure the werewolves couldn't find them.

So this was it. She had to leave. No closer to unraveling the mystery of her visions than when she had arrived. Trey claimed he had caused them, but did that mean they were over?

The sound of movement on the other side of the room stopped her thoughts. *Trey or Lazlo?*

Steadying herself with her arm, she attempted to sit as the room spun. Once the spinning eased, she stood and readied herself for an attack. If it was Lazlo, she wouldn't go without a fight. She sniffed the air and tried to smell the intruder's identity.

Panic took hold. Nothing. As if no one was there.

She pushed down panic. This was all wrong. Pulling her shirt to her nose, searching out the threads of scent she knew so well, she found nothing. Not even traces of Lazlo.

All she could smell was the barest odor of laundry detergent.

She swayed under the realization of why she felt so weak. Her power. Gone.

A breeze blew cool air on her face and Trey's voice pierced her stupor. "I told you to leave if I didn't come back in two hours."

He sealed the door and activated a switch she hadn't seen. The small eight-by-eight room became illuminated by a few recessed lights.

"What did he do to me? I can't smell anything. I mean I can smell some, but you don't understand, before I could smell everything." Tears streaked down her face. How could she make him realize what this meant to her life?

He reached her just before her knees buckled beneath her. He took her against his chest and let her forehead rest against it as she fought with her fears. "I understand. I do. Don't worry. You'll be able to smell again. I promise. That's what the amulet is for," he said quietly.

She clutched at the strange stone around her neck. "This? My powers are in here?"

Trey brought her back to the bed and sat on the edge with her. He ran his thumb over her cheeks, wiping her tears away gently. Once she got herself under control, she noticed he was dressed, but in clothes resembling rags.

He unbuttoned the filthy shirt he wore and tossed it to the floor. "Your powers aren't in the amulet. They're inside me." He touched his chest.

"You took my powers?"

"I had to. I couldn't get you away from Lazlo, away from the compound and danger without them."

"Stop." CJ swallowed the ache in her throat. "Tell me what happened back there. I had a vision while Lazlo grabbed me and the next thing I remember is some great hairy monster on top of me," she said. "Which thankfully turned out to be you and not him."

Trey took her hands in his. His warmth did little to settle her nerves. "There is a problem I haven't told you about. Something about me."

183

CJ just watched as he traced his fingers in a circle on her hand. He breathed slowly and clenched his jaw.

His voice was soft when he spoke. "The problem in our pack, the strange weaknesses which appeared about ten years ago as our younger werewolves reached puberty—"

"Like Mario's?"

"Yes, like Mario's. There was actually an earlier case no one noticed."

Lazlo's words came back to her. *"Weaker than all the other males. Because he lost to me, none of the other werewolves realized how truly weak he was."*

Trey swallowed. "When I was about six or seven, I realized I was different from other werewolves. I and a couple of the other kids, including Lazlo, were on a hike with Doc Vogel. One of our first days of school. He had taken us to a remote corner of the compound and began showing us berries safe to eat, if we should ever be separated from our pack while on a hunt. The day is as clear to me as yesterday," he said, running a hand through his hair.

CJ could read the pain in his eyes.

He continued, "Doc held up two red berries exactly alike. Then he sniffed it and told us the sweet-smelling one was poison and the stinky one was safe. I watched the other kids nod their heads in understanding. I had no idea what he was talking about. I knew what my nose was for, but everything *smelled* the same to me, because the truth was I couldn't smell anything."

"You can't smell. Anything?" She thought about her current condition. Living life as a werewolf who couldn't smell would have been impossible. "Why?"

Trey shrugged. "I don't know. It's the way I was born."

She parted her lips to speak but he shushed her with his finger.

He took his finger away. "There's more. I'm strong, but no stronger than any normal man my size. The only way I've hidden my secret was by becoming the martial arts expert in the pack."

Lazlo knew. He knew Trey didn't have incredible strength, but the Alpha blamed it on Trey's mother. "I think Lazlo knows about you." She hated having to tell Trey his secret was out.

"You're right." He rubbed his chin, looking lost in thought. "Lazlo found out when we fought in the Succession Challenge, but he doesn't know how weak I really am. I think my mom guessed about my lack of scent detection, but she'd never betray me. She's been convinced by Lazlo and his supporters it was her fault."

CJ found it incredible Trey had been able to hide his deficiencies all his life. "How did you get away with learning marital arts? Didn't the others find it odd?"

Trey sucked in his upper lip and gave an odd grin. "Remember Chuck Norris and Bruce Lee? I simply made them an obsession. Even at twelve, when I really discovered how extensive my problem was, I knew the danger of being weak. My father was the Alpha, my grandfather the hero who united the packs. I couldn't disappoint them. Everyone just thought I was an eccentric kid with a fascination for ninjas."

CJ pulled Trey closer and squeezed his arm. And she had accused him of not understanding what it meant to be different. No wonder he had taken Mario under his wing. He knew exactly what Mario was going through.

"You needed my strength." She lifted the amulet and studied the ancient marks on the stone she could now see in the lit room. "You used this magic stone to take my powers so you could be stronger than Lazlo."

"Yes, CJ, I did it tonight right before I rescued you. When Sebastian told me Lazlo had come for you, I snapped. My only thought became your safety. Smelling, having your strength," he whispered, "believe me, it all came second to you."

"But why *my* powers? Why take mine when werewolves surrounded you?" It didn't seem fair.

"I can't answer your question. All I know is that I've been trying to summon the power of smell and strength for the last six months since I first found the amulet." He blew out a deep breath, guilt in his voice. "Six months of trying and tonight I succeeded."

She stilled her hand on his arm. A cold fear took hold. Six months. Six horrible months. Her hallucinations. This is what he meant about causing her visions.

He has been trying to steal her powers all this time.

She moved to her feet. *Trey* was the entire reason her life was fucked up.

His eyes pleaded with her to understand. "I didn't know for sure until tonight. Don't hate me, please don't hate me. I didn't realize what I was doing to you. Didn't have any idea that, to have my rightful powers, I had to take them from you."

She turned from him. In the damn tiny room, she couldn't get far enough away. All along her visions weren't about her. He caused them. She could have stayed in Minneapolis.

"I think I can give them back. Using the spell I wrote on the paper." He got off the bed and pulled the basket of candles out from under it. "All you have to do is wear the amulet, sit in a circle of these candles, and repeat the spell."

She watched in amazement as he carefully arranged the candles on the wood floor. Was he serious? "After six months of trying to take them, you're going to give them back? But then you can't challenge Lazlo to be Alpha."

He didn't look at her when he replied. "I know. I've changed my mind. I can't take this from you. I've seen how you work. What you do is important. You need these powers. I'll find another way to stop Lazlo's breeding plan."

CJ wanted to see his face. Read his eyes. "Don't you want to be Alpha? Isn't that why you're doing all this?"

Trey rose and moved close to her. He took her face in his hand and held her gaze with his. "You think I simply want power? No, I must stop this breeding plan. I need to make Lazlo and the others see that whatever science they think can explain us, it isn't the answer. It is magic. We need to understand our magic, learn to wield it. Using it is the only way my people will survive."

"Then we have to go back and show them this." She lifted the amulet, letting the light glance off the etched runes. "What good is it hiding here? Let's go back and face them. Together."

Trey ran a finger along her jaw, his lips tight and unsmiling. "No, we can't return yet. I attacked the Alpha outside of a proper Challenge. Lazlo will easily convince the Council I should be condemned to death. We need to escape the city. Hide. Figure out a way to come back and prove I'm right."

Trey pulled her over to the candles. Their flames heated the small space and she could feel their intensity as she sat down in the circle. He moved a few inches away from the circle and lowered himself to the floor facing her.

CJ smelled the flickering candles. She noticed a faint odor of wax, but only barely. As if she was drugged, her world blurry without the scent threads so essential in her daily functioning.

187

"First, we need to make you whole again. I think you should be able to call the powers to you since you carried them for so long. Remember in our shift how we were together and you were strong enough to prevent me from stopping the shift? The powers obey you, too."

She reached into her back pocket and pulled out the sheet of folded paper. Carefully she uncreased it and held it open. The print blurred as her hand shook, from fatigue, from fear. Trey reached over the candles to hold it still.

CJ regained control and she nodded for him to release the paper. She saw the strange words and began to chant. "*Comus mir sawl. Comus mir lupus*—wait, what if I take your other powers, the hearing, the night vision, the ability to shift?"

"You'll have to stop the chant. I don't know if I'll be much help once the spell gets in full swing. If you went into that trance and had hallucinations while I was taking your power, I assume I'll do the same."

"How will I know? Will I feel each power coming into me?"

"Yes, I noticed each by itself. The olfactory sense entered first, then the strength. If you feel anything else, stop chanting and take off the amulet."

"You're willing to risk me having the power?" She folded her fingers over the amulet.

Trey shot her a tiny smile. "I trust you. Okay, let's try this again."

CJ focused on the paper and read the words carefully. Her voice softly uttered the verse, apprehension in every pause. "*Comus mir sawl. Comus mir lupus potére. Comus mir sawl. Comus mir lupus potére. Comus mir sawl.*"

The stone grew hot against her chest. She kept her eyes glued to the paper, the words coming automatically. She couldn't bear to see Trey helpless.

The flames seemed to grow several feet high and the heat intensified unbearably. Sweat poured down her face and dropped onto the sheet of paper. A strong, sweet aroma reached into her brain and grabbed her like a vise.

The candles. She could smell them.

Next Trey's hot, musky scent crept over her. She smiled in spite of the heat. His scent warmed her more than the candles ever could. Her breath steady and calm, she felt more in control with her nose back to its normal state.

It seemed like several minutes passed as she continued to chant. *"Comus mir sawl."* Slowly a pulse moved up her legs, as if a signal traveled to the rest of her body. *"Comus mir lupus potére."* It reached her brain. She fought down the urge to spring to her feet and break free of the stifling heat.

Was this what Trey meant? She needed to stop. She didn't want to take anymore from Trey. Her voice grew silent.

She looked over and saw Trey. His eyes closed as if in sleep.

She knew better. Were his visions as terrifying as hers had been?

The power still seemed to be growing within her—she felt it. The arrival of the wolf.

No!

The amulet. She ripped the cord from her neck and flung the amulet away. It skidded across the floor and landed against the wall.

The candles went out.

Trey opened his eyes. He tried to stand and CJ watched as his legs faltered.

She leapt to her feet and caught him before he collapsed forward into the candles. His weight nothing in her arms. "Are you okay? Did I stop soon enough?"

"Yes." He took a breath, exhaled slowly and stood back on his own two feet. He held his arm out in front of him and it shifted flawlessly into a black wolf's paw. Then he shifted his paw quickly into a monstrous hand with thick flesh, heavy hair and curved claws. The Beast. Trey curled his hand into a fist, the claws deadly sharp.

Trey's face showed obvious relief. She watched his arm and once again saw a man's hand. "We did it. We're back to normal." She pressed herself into his arms.

Trey pulled her as tight as he could, lifting her off the floor, and then tumbled back with her on the bed.

His touch wiped away the last hours, filling her with joy.

His smell, not so much. "You smell awful, like urine and oh, nasty stuff."

He got to his feet and peeled the pants from his body. "Is that the thanks for saving our butts? That putrid smell happens to be the best way to cover my own scent. Remember, you are the best tracker I've seen. The other werewolves are good, but they can be fooled."

"Did you steal those from some homeless guy and backtrack here?"

"In a way. I traded. Actually I took a suitcase of clothes I had stashed at a rented storage unit and gave my clothes away all over the city. Then I gave one guy another full suitcase, my credit cards, a plane ticket to Phoenix and enough cash to make sure he got on the plane. Tonight the other clothes are creating enough confusion out there that the pack is going to get frustrated."

"Wait, won't they come here first?"

"Why would I come to my second home? Without this room, I'd be a sitting duck," he said, calmly. "No one else knows about this room."

"But how long can we stay here?"

"If they follow procedure, they'll pull back in a few hours and do a more structured search of all the airports, trains stations and car rental places. Protocol should lead Lazlo to the bum I put on a plane for Phoenix. Hopefully, since the guy's had a glimpse of what's coming after him, he'll keep them busy while we sneak out of the city."

"What did you do to the poor guy?"

"A little...this isn't just a furry mask. Don't worry after a few weeks, he'll think it was just a bad batch of Wild Turkey."

"So we can just sit tight until morning."

Trey walked over to the far wall and pressed a small button she hadn't noticed before. The wall slid into a pocket and revealed a small but complete bathroom with a toilet, sink and shower.

"You thought of everything in this room."

"Well, looking at you on that small bed, not everything. I never thought the day I actually had to use this as a hideout, I'd be sharing it with someone like you." He stepped into the shower. "I was always prepared for my secrets being discovered."

The water ran for several minutes while CJ sat on the bed and absorbed the events of the last few hours.

She'd found out who her father was, discovered being the product of a human and a werewolf was or wasn't such a big deal depending on who you talked to, discovered Lazlo was a very dangerous man and, surprisingly, she now understood that both he and Trey seemed to have one objective—to save the werewolves.

And of course, she'd discovered Trey had been the source of her visions. He didn't want her powers anymore. No more life-disrupting hallucinations.

She was free. She had accomplished what she came here for.

Except there was one other thing that became crystal clear to her as she sat surrounded in that circle of magic a few minutes ago. When she was desperately trying to stop the spell before she harmed Trey, an unexpected realization dawned.

She was falling in love with a werewolf.

Chapter Eleven

CJ punched the balled up sheet for the hundredth time and tried to settle her nerves enough to sleep. Trey had taken the floor and the one pillow, while she got the bed and the blanket.

They had discussed plans for their escape when Trey came out of the shower. It hadn't taken long. Bouncing ideas off one another, they had devised a plan to leave the city tomorrow.

Trey knew the hunting technique of the werewolves and CJ knew what made a person hard to track. They made a good team.

The small room was soundproof, but Trey assured her the howls of the pack would still be echoing across the city. They probably wouldn't relent till they reached the outer suburbs sometime during the night or earlier morning hours of Monday. Hopefully one of the werewolves would have caught the decoy's smell at the airport. Once they tracked his credit card, which he was confident they would do, they would see he'd purchased a ticket to Phoenix.

Trey predicted Lazlo would send only their best available trackers, two werewolves CJ hadn't met, on to Phoenix. The rest of the pack would go back to regular business, since the Elders were meeting at the compound on Tuesday morning, less than forty-eight hours away.

By the time of the Elders Council, he and CJ planned to be long gone from the city. They'd hop the most crowded commuter train out to one of the suburbs at five o'clock tomorrow afternoon—rush hour. From there they'd buy a common sedan and head straight to Minneapolis.

The pack only knew her as CJ Duncan. She was positive she hadn't mentioned her full name of Clair Jane, so it would take them a bit longer to track her to Minneapolis. Her home city remained a secret, a small advantage. But sooner or later Lazlo would discover her full name. With that info, finding her would be simple. She would only have a few days to uproot her entire life and begin again.

She lay watching shapeless shadows on the ceiling, wondering what her mother would say when she realized CJ had put their lives in jeopardy.

Some daughter she was.

Even if Trey had caused her visions, she had set out to find her father. And everything she had been trying to save—her ability to do her job, her ability to help the lost—was over. At least until Lazlo grew tired of the chase.

The sound of Trey moving made her lean over the edge of the bed and watch his slumbering form. His bare chest rose and fell in a steady rhythm. She marveled how quickly he had fallen asleep on the hard wooden floor. He had warned her he might sleep until midday tomorrow, because being in Beast form exhausted a werewolf. He had spent a few hours zipping around the city using her incredible powers. He had explained how powerful she was in comparison to the others, but it was hard to understand because she hadn't really seen any of the others' Beasts to compare it to.

He had some theory about the power being so much stronger because she didn't waste any of her magic shifting.

Whatever. He had come back. His presence a comfort she never before thought she needed.

She didn't want to face running from Lazlo for the rest of her life on her own.

"CJ? Are you awake?" Trey's voice came through the darkness.

She started. "You know I'm awake. Did you sleep at all?"

"Will you be mad at me if I say yes? I was exhausted, but apparently not as spent as I thought." CJ heard him walk over to the dimmer switch on the wall. He turned the dial till a warm yellow glow pushed back the darkness.

In the soft light, his relaxed naked state took her breath away. She had never seen a man so unconscious of his body. Most men with Trey's build looked at themselves more than anyone else did.

Not Trey.

His face was bleak, his gold eyes dark as he sat on the floor next to the bed. He leaned his back against the wall, brought his knees to his chest and wrapped his arms around them.

"I really fucked this up." He spoke the words softly and rested his chin on the knee of his folded leg.

CJ reached out from the bed and laid a hand on his arm. "You? I was thinking the very same about me." She flexed her fingers around the solid flesh, extracting as much comfort from his nearness as she attempted to give.

"Well, then we're a perfect pair." He peered over his knees, "Yeah, I know exactly where you fucked up."

She lifted herself to her elbow and rested her head in her hand. "Oh? And when was that?"

He captured her hand and gently stroked her wrist in a soft sweeping motion. "When you decided I was such a hottie you had to track me down to find Mario."

She laughed at his bravado. "Hate to burst your bubble, but that wasn't exactly my thought process." She saw a smile sneak across his lips.

He peeked at her out of the corner of his eyes. "Admit it. I turned you on."

He looked amazing, sitting there next to her. Naked. Human. He smelled like sin and she wanted to jump in. Exactly how she had felt every time she lifted his handkerchief to her nose as she tracked him.

She tried to pull her hand back so she could sit. Trey held on tight.

"Okay, I thought you had a *hottie* scent. Happy now?"

"I'll take it." He lifted a finger to his lips and gently kissed it.

A warm blush heated her face. His warm lips made her think of other intimate kisses they had shared. Yet, he had made no attempt to share the bed when he emerged from the shower. He seemed to have no idea what his nude body did to her imagination.

The fact she still wore her T-shirt and panties while Trey curled up naked on the floor, only reminded her how the werewolves differed from other men. In her experience men got naked for one reason only. Sex.

Part of her saw him as the most perfect human on earth. Yet she wondered where was the Beast? Where was the wolf? They were both part of this man. He wasn't just a man to be used and passed on like her lovers before.

If she could even call him her lover after their odd night before.

CJ grabbed the wadded sheet from under her head as she sat up. She got out of bed, shook the sheet out flat and threw it over Trey's naked body. "I've got clothes on. You need this." She sat in front of him, her ankles crossed and knees bent. She, too, wrapped her arms around her knees.

"Thanks, but I'm not cold. Is that the only reason you covered me?"

CJ wanted to think there was an invitation in his voice, but after his rejection the other night, she just wasn't ready to take the chance. More likely he covered his shame with this careless flirting.

He hid his feelings well, but his quiet voice told her more troubled him tonight. "You didn't fuck up, Trey. You were doing what you thought best. You wanted to stop Lazlo."

He let the sheet slip and grabbed both of her hands. They sat silently. Facing each other, their knees bent, nothing touching but their hands. CJ couldn't meet his eyes, but instead stared at his thumbs caressing the sensitive skin of her wrists. She heard him take a deep breath.

"He'll destroy the pack. My pack. He's going to match everyone off in these superior breeding pairs. The weaker werewolves will resent the others, the stronger werewolves will become little more than breeding stock. It will destroy us as much as losing our werewolf abilities in the first place." He gripped her hands tight as his emotions ran hot. "Why can't he understand?"

CJ didn't want to defend Lazlo, but he hadn't witnessed the power of magic like she and Trey had. Maybe Lazlo would change his ways if they showed him. "He's on a power trip. But he believes the only way to save the pack is with proven

197

scientific ways. He doesn't believe in magic. As leader, he feels he must take action. He doesn't know magic is part of the equation at all." She almost didn't realize what she had said until it was out. Would Lazlo listen to their explanation, would he let them explain how magic had made Trey strong?

"I know what you're thinking and the answer is no." He pulled her arms closer and she tipped forward in between his legs. "You're not going back with me to prove that magic exists. I've got twenty grand in cash in this room. Plenty to get us out of town and to safety. I won't put you at risk again."

"I've been thinking about Mario." Leaving her little brother in the care of the pack ran against her every instinct. "Can't we get a message to him? Have him rendezvous with us outside the city?"

Trey brushed her hair from her face. "Lazlo doesn't want to kill Mario, but he's clueless to Mario's pain. Your father will be back for the Council. There's a chance he'll convince Lazlo to let Mario return to school."

"Just a chance?"

"Your father isn't a high-ranking werewolf. He's never rocked the boat before." He shrugged knowing that wasn't the answer she wanted to hear.

CJ rested her forehead against his dimpled chin. "I want to take Mario with us."

"CJ, Lazlo might very well want us dead. We're not going to put Mario's life at risk, too." He held her closer, brushing her hair with his cheek.

She let him comfort her. He was right. She wouldn't risk her brother's life. She just wished they would've had more time together. Forcing the sadness away, CJ immersed herself in the present. In Trey's body holding her tight.

His arms seemed so right around her. His chest warm and beating with a life force so strong it intoxicated her senses. "How many hours before we leave?" He had pulled her to him. Did he want her or was it the shift affecting him? Did she care?

He reached up to a small bedside table and pulled down his watch. "We've got fourteen hours."

In fourteen hours, Lazlo and the other could be breathing down their necks. If these were her last hours before she had to run, she would make them worth it. "I have a question for you. I know you thought ahead and have twenty grand stashed away." CJ's voice grew soft, she wasn't sure he wanted what she did. "But you don't happen to have a condom or two socked away in here?" She waited for his reaction.

A strange look came over his face. She went still, wondering if once again she had overstepped and misread his signals.

He reached back to the same bedside table as before and opened its one drawer. He grabbed something, then brought his hand over for her to see its contents.

Three day-glow orange condoms packaged to look like lollipops.

"The third floor is a gay rights office. They were giving these away in the lobby during AIDS awareness week last month. I didn't realize I had them in my hand until I got in here." He threw them on the bed above them. "Who knew?"

He pulled the rest of the sheet off and threw it over CJ's head. "Hey..."

Trey's warm laughter filled the room as she snatched the sheet off her head. CJ's heart tensed at the sound. She inhaled his powerful musk with each breath, letting his scent and sound pierce her tough girl defenses. She sat back and watched his muscles move as he bent over and grabbed the edge of the bed's mattress.

The dents on the side of his ass mesmerized her as he moved. So hard, so different than a woman's curves. Trey was all sharp angles and solid flesh. Tough and real. Strong enough to take her on. Maybe not in the supernatural sense, but in every way that mattered.

The thud of the mattress hitting the floor made her jump. She raised a questioning eyebrow at her smiling lover.

He ceremonially snapped the sheet in the air and let it drift over the small bed. "Shorter distance to fall when things get wild." With a sweep of his hands he smoothed the dark navy sheet over the mattress. He sank down on the edge and gave her a cocky grin. "Get naked and come here."

CJ's panties dampened at his firm tone. She did as he commanded, throwing her clothes to the side. This wasn't a striptease. This wasn't some enticement to send Trey over the edge. She was too eager for seduction. And way too wet.

She put a hand on his shoulder and joined him. A rare self-consciousness overcame her as his gaze roamed her body. He moved to lie on his side and propped his head on his hand. She twisted toward him, but he threw a leg over hers and held her still. The corner of his mouth curled in a mischievous smile.

"Not so fast, CJ. Let me enjoy you. I want you to be still." He eased his leg down a bit, but didn't remove it entirely. "Do you have any idea how beautiful you are?" He laid a hand on her stomach and rubbed her skin in gentle circles.

Old feelings of insecurity crept into her mind, "You don't have to say those words to me. You don't need to seduce me. I want you, Trey." Games weren't her style. "Just don't play with me and leave me hanging." Did he understand what he did to her last night?

He stopped his gentle touch and took her chin in his grip, making her look at him. "I didn't mean to hurt you. My desires carried me too far. I didn't stop and think about the shift making you so horny. I didn't want you to regret it in the morning."

She narrowed her eyes. She couldn't believe that had been his reason for rejecting her last night. "I wouldn't have regretted it. Please, I've been with men who finish in five minutes and expect me to rave about it. Those I've regretted. Is that the only reason you stopped?"

"I'm the one guilty of risking your life. I got you involved with all this." He pushed his hand down to her chest and laid it over her beating heart. "I am sorry about using you to distract Lazlo. I never meant for you to get hurt."

She traced along his jaw. He was a good man. A good werewolf. She had always been confident she could defend those she loved. Trey had spent his entire life too weak to defend his loved ones. He used his mind to win.

She didn't want the past to interfere with the now. "Forget it happened, okay? Lazlo didn't inflict any permanent damage. With you helping me get out of here, I won't get hurt. You're smarter than the others. Now, why don't you shut up and kiss me." She put her hand on his nape to pull his lips down to hers, but he stopped her.

A dark look in his eyes, he gently pulled away. "In bed that night it hit me for the first time. It wasn't by chance you followed my scent to find Mario. I was thinking about our shift together and how our powers were the perfect complements. I realized you had all the powers I needed. The powers I had been calling to me with my amulet."

"Why didn't you tell me?"

"Because if I was the one who had messed up your life and brought you to Seattle, then I was doubly screwing you over. Using you to stop Lazlo and taking your powers." Trey stopped

201

and lowered his eyes for a moment. "And truthfully, the thought crossed my mind maybe you knew more about your powers than you were letting on. You did break into my office. It occurred to me you might try and take my remaining powers."

CJ let Trey's confession sink in. Trey hadn't trusted her. But, what had she done to prove her loyalty? Broken into his office. Hadn't she been willing to bargain with Lazlo, until Lazlo pulled his *mate with me* stunt? "What about now? Do you trust me now?"

Trey's voice was calm and steady. "I don't have any more secrets, CJ. My heart told me you weren't here to steal my powers. But being so close to finally being the werewolf I felt destined to be, I just had to be sure. After I saw the way you went to Mario. The way it tore you apart seeing him injured. I realized you weren't deceiving me."

CJ wished darkness still enveloped the room. Trey's guilt so evident on his face, made her regret the anger she had felt. Anger that had almost led her to work with Lazlo. "Trey, don't beat yourself up. We both had our moments of distrust. It was pretty damn easy for me to figure out you were keeping secrets from me. I was pretty pissed at you by the time Lazlo called for me."

"Pissed enough to join with Lazlo?" Trey asked, his tone indecipherable.

"Not really, I had seen how he treated Mario. But, I was tempted." She leaned on her elbows as he rolled onto his back and stared at the ceiling. "I don't like secrets, Trey. I'm not going to change the way I am. No more, okay?"

Trey moved an arm behind her and hauled her on top of him. "It's a deal. I deserved your mistrust. You're a smart woman. I should have known I couldn't fool you."

CJ went down to kiss his beautiful lips, warm and waiting for her when she stopped a mere fraction of an inch away from contact, his breath calling her closer. "You're not afraid I might have some hocus pocus sex spell to steal your powers?"

He shifted beneath her and his erection rubbed hard against her slim stomach. Unconsciously she rocked her hips against him. Trey stilled her movement with his hand. "CJ, right now I don't care what you do to me. You could leave me a whimpering mutt. It would probably be worth it."

She ran a finger across his rough jaw. "Remember, you don't have anywhere to run. You're going to finish what you've started." She clamped her hand around his wrist. "Or else."

In answer to her threat, he tossed her onto her back and covered her body with his. His mouth claimed hers in a swift, hard kiss. His tongue urged her to open to him. One hand held her shoulder as his lips coaxed dangerous impulses to the surface. Her mouth flushed, he moved lower down her neck.

She arched at the sensation of his rough, hard kisses. He nuzzled her collarbone, caressing her skin with the edge of his teeth. Not gentle, but exquisite all the same.

Her nipples ached to be touched. As if reading her mind, he squeezed her breast in his palm. He drew his hand to the tip of her nipple and followed with his mouth.

He lapped at her nipple, sucking and kissing until her crotch swelled with anticipation. She squeezed tight wanting him now, but wanting everything else, too.

She clutched his hand and moved it between her legs.

He pulled it to her breast. Resting his chin on her breastbone, he measured her with his golden eyes. Magical eyes. "Always in such a hurry. We're not rushing this." He lifted his chin and laid a trail of kisses on her chest.

She curled her own lip under and bit it gently with her teeth. His slow seduction would kill her.

Trey's soft, wavy hair brushed against her as he nuzzled her chest and belly. She plunged her hands into his hair and broke out in goose bumps at the aroma she shook loose with her sweeping fingers. She brought her palms to her nose and breathed his scent deep.

Heat shot to her clit, already the promise of her climax building inside her. She instinctively rubbed her legs together. Trey's arm went down and held them flat. She could easily throw off his arm with a jolt of her hips.

She didn't.

She wanted him to take control. She just wasn't very good at obeying.

He moved his hand lower and placed a finger between her wet lips. "Hmm, this is tempting." He eased slowly upward until her clitoris was under his wet finger. He circled the sensitive nub as she clamped down the urge to flip him on his back and mount him.

He was definitely hard enough.

But that would have to wait.

The length of his erection brushed the skin of her thigh. The velvet head was slick with his evident desire. Curled around her, he slowly nibbled at her breast as his finger stirred desire deep within.

He slowed his teasing touch on her clitoris, drawing a moan of frustration from her lips. He bit her nipple.

CJ flicked his ear. "That hurt."

He brushed a cheek against her chest and smiled with a cocked eyebrow. "I know. Just reminding you I'm taking charge tonight."

She couldn't resist a challenge. "I thought this might be a give and take sort of thing."

"Let me think." He licked his finger and moved it back down between her legs. He pushed it into her.

CJ clamped down on the penetration.

He pulled his finger out. Plunged again. He hooked it and held it inside her. "I thought about it. I'm doing the giving tonight."

Before any retort left her mouth, a new, intense heat began building in her womb. He moved his finger. Stroked her hidden web of sensitive tissues. Inside her. Deep inside her.

She closed her eyes and pushed her head back into the mattress. The tension spread into her legs, up her spine. Filled her in a way she had never experienced. He kissed her stretched stomach, his lips hard. His mouth sucked her skin more than caressed it. Lower and lower he went.

Yes. Oh, sweet heavens...get there already. CJ clenched the sheets in her hand. She wanted so badly to just grab his head and show him exactly where she needed to be sucked. Explored. Time had slowed to a crawl with his steady strokes inside her and his wet lips without.

His mouth touched her clit. His finger went faster. He rolled her small pearl with his tongue. Faster with the finger, harder with his tongue. She lost reality as he worked her body into a frenzy.

Her fist pounded the bed. He worked her harder.

The orgasm engulfed her body and mind. Wave after wave kept coming. Her muscles constricted around Trey's finger and her heels hit his back in reflex. The colors behind her eyes blinded her until the final waves of pleasure eased.

She winced as he slowly pulled his fingers from inside her body. She lay there, catching her breath, slowing her beating heart.

Satisfaction filled every fiber of her body. "Thank you." She meant it, she really did, but she wanted more. "Now what do you plan to give me?"

Trey crawled up her body until his hands braced his weight on either side of her shoulders. He leaned down and kissed her nose. "Oh, so *now* you're okay with me giving and you taking."

CJ reached to the side, feeling the floor where she thought Trey had thrown the condoms.

He saw what she was doing and produced one between his fingers. "Looking for this?"

She gave him her most charming smile.

Trey leaned back on his heels and she sucked in her breath at the sight of his erection. Perfectly proportioned to the rest of him. Perfectly huge and full, with a wide shiny head slick with his excitement.

She was glad the condom he sheathed on himself wasn't day-glow orange like the wrapper. The dark purple of Trey's cock was too perfect to hide. He gripped the base when he was done and leaned back over her.

He pushed between her legs and with one hand lifted her buttocks off the mattress. He cupped her cheek and kneaded it with his hand. This time he was the one to bite his lip and moan. "You wanna know a secret?"

She nodded.

"I love your ass. It's perfect." He slapped her butt cheek for emphasis. "I'll have to show you how much some time."

CJ spread her legs wider as he cocked his penis down to her waiting opening. She arched her back and rose higher. He brushed her lips with his penis wetting it with her natural cream.

He pushed higher and tapped against her still swollen clit. Once again her womb warmed with anticipation. She wanted him closer. "Inside," she whispered. She grabbed his fist and placed the tip of his penis at her entrance. "Now."

With a low growl, he slid deep. He sat back up and placed his hands on her knees. Slowly he pulled out, only to slide back in as she wrapped around him.

They watched their joining in the silence of the soft, warm light. The playfulness disappeared, replaced by stronger emotions. Powerful primal passion. Slow and steady they rocked together. CJ felt the loss each time he withdrew and the satisfaction when he filled her again.

She opened her arms and reached for Trey. He released her knees and leaned down over her, again placing a hand on either side of her shoulders. His strokes grew faster.

She could smell his excitement in his sweat. He neared his climax. She let the salt and heat of his body enter her mind. Like glowing threads she reached for them and pulled herself along on his journey.

His pelvis tilted higher and he ground against her clitoris with every plunge into her. Spirals of pleasure coiled faster than she could control. She tightened around his cock, her body's sex aromas mixing with his.

He bent closer and lowered his mouth next to her ear. "You're mine, CJ. I'll never let you go."

Her heart ached as their climax spilled over them. His words echoed in her head. *You're mine.*

Trey ground his throbbing cock into her until he spent everything he had to give. With a groan, he withdrew and collapsed next to her on the mattress.

He pulled her head onto his arm and kissed her hair, before she heard the soft sounds of his sleeping breath. CJ snuggled closer to the man who had unexpectedly found a way into her heart.

With his thick, sex-soaked scent wrapped around her, she closed her eyes. *You're mine, too.*

୫୬୧୪ଓ

Trey watched his laptop screen with amazement. Lazlo lurked in Trey's outer office, downloading the firm's database of customers from Trey's desk computer. The hidden security camera gave a clear shot of the files Lazlo accessed. He had already downloaded Trey's address book and personal documents.

He didn't know Lazlo had the password to retrieve those files. Not that Trey had left any incriminating information on Guardian's network. The sight unsettled him. Lazlo had always given Trey the impression any dealings with the moneymaking arm of the pack was beneath him.

Trey had floated the idea of using some of his contacts from his days as an operative in the firm for their escape. Knowing Lazlo scoured Guardian's database made him scrap the idea.

He wondered if CJ had any idea how difficult their life might be on the run.

Life was different when someone hunted you.

CJ's warm breath tickled his neck. She moved in closer to look at the screen over his shoulder. She gasped when she saw Lazlo at Trey's desk, surveying the room.

The soundproof room protected them but Trey still spoke quietly. "Relax. If I can't hear him out there, he can't hear us."

"What about the security camera?"

"He knows there's a camera feeding to the master security room in the lobby. No one is aware I tapped into the closed circuit system so I could monitor the building from in here." He closed the laptop and unplugged it from the cable. He pushed it across the floor and against the wall.

He remained naked, while CJ had wrapped herself in the thin sheet. Her blonde hair was pushed behind her ears and the look in her eyes revealed her uneasiness.

The Alpha's presence bothered Trey, too, but he doubted for the same reason. He hadn't thought Lazlo would be out spearheading the hunt. Many of the Elders would be arriving today, including Trey's father and Rupert. Trey had expected Lazlo to be busy at the compound putting his spin on their escape.

Trey planted his feet and ran through their options. CJ wasn't going to like his decision. They'd have to delay their run from the city.

"Don't you think we should keep an eye on him? What if he finds the peephole like I did?"

"I covered the peephole. I really didn't need it." He inclined his head to the laptop. "Not with the security camera. Plus, because of your clever nose"—he touched the tip with his finger—"I discovered my little hidden room had a leak. I caulked it shut when I came to get the amulet."

He watched as she rolled her neck to stretch. She hated being cooped up. An idiot could figure it out. She had paced the length of the room while he prepared their late breakfast of spam, bread and peanut butter.

"Lie down." Trey pulled the sheet from her body and threw it onto the floor. Her pale skin glowed against the dark navy sheet.

CJ's eyes went wide. "He's right outside. We can't have sex."

"Unfortunately I agree. I seem to make you scream with pleasure, if I recall correctly. Don't want to test the sound barrier of these walls." They had gone through all three condoms during the night.

She tweaked his nipple.

"Ouch." He rubbed his chest that was glowing pink from her less than gentle pinch. Vixen. "I wanted to give you a back rub. Help you relax, cause I've got some bad news. We have to wait longer to make our run."

CJ groaned. "How much longer? I'm going insane in here."

"Tomorrow morning. I want to make sure Lazlo is at the compound and occupied. There's a reason he's Alpha. If anyone could catch our scent, it would be him. The Elders usually convene around ten o'clock. We won't have the cover of rush hour, but most of the experienced werewolves will be attending to the Elders."

"That's twenty hours away. What if they track down Roz and my mother before then? I have to at least warn them."

"Your mom's still on her cruise, right?"

"Okay, she's safe until she docks."

"Roz is only your roommate. The werewolves will watch her for a while, but they won't reveal themselves to her. We only kill humans in self-defense. It's the first thing we're taught. To kill a human is to risk the safety of the entire pack. She'll be safe."

"Don't I count as a human?"

"Sorry, honey. You broke Lazlo's nose. You're dangerous. As for me, well, I'm not setting a good example for the others. Disobedience like this won't be tolerated."

CJ lay with her stomach on part of the sheet, part of it still covered her cute ass. That would not do.

Trey moved the sheet down with the tips of his fingers, caressing her skin. The smoothness of her body fascinated him. Mating with a female werewolf left little time for such observations.

They seemed to like rough-and-tumble sex on the whole. CJ's humanness was showing. All it took was a gentle touch, a slow kiss and she melted underneath him.

Once he had her bare from her neck to her toes, he began stroking her with his fingertips. Watching her butt wiggle as ran his hands over it, made him regret promising only a back rub.

"You like this, don't you?"

"What woman wouldn't? It almost makes me forget Lazlo could come storming in here at any moment."

"He won't. We'd hear him as he opened the door and I'm naked. I can shift in the blink of an eye."

"Could you take my power that fast?"

"I won't do that. That power is yours. I'd expect you couldn't resist getting a jab or two in, even if he came raging in here as the Beast."

"Such confidence in me."

"I'm used to working as a team. The pack can do anything when we work together. Don't you have anyone you work with?"

CJ brought her arms up and crossed them under her chin. "Before I discovered I could use my nose to track down missing persons, I paid the bills working as a bounty hunter."

"You know, after feeling your left hook, I can believe you were a darn good one."

She chuckled. "Yeah, well they paired me with an old, experienced guy. He got pissed being assigned to work with a twenty-year-old girl. He got real pissy when I started finding the bail jumpers before he got his sorry ass out of the car. The whole episode kind of soured me on working with a partner. No one would ever be able to keep up with me."

He kneaded her muscles and thought about their life on the run.

What would it be like for them? She was much stronger. He would hold her back. He hadn't thought about the possibility before. Once they were out of Seattle, she'd probably do better without him. If Lazlo took the lead in the hunt, Trey could actually endanger her more than if she traveled alone.

He couldn't keep up with her. The truth turned his blood cold.

"Trey, is everything okay?" CJ tilted her chin toward him.

His fingers had ceased their deep caress. He pressed harder with his strokes. "How did you decide to become a missing person investigator?"

"There was a little girl. I volunteered at the family shelter where my mom and I would go when things got tough during those early years. We never forgot the despair of walking into our apartment building and seeing all our things thrown in the hall and the locks changed."

"I can't imagine how that felt. I always had somewhere I could go. A pack member who would help."

"Well, mom was a foster kid and we only had each other. It took her awhile, but she finally got through paralegal school and found a good job. She was with me when we went to volunteer. The shelter was crawling with police."

"Does your mom know about your abilities?"

"She knows I can smell, but she never wanted to talk about it. Not till that morning. When we found out a little five-year-old girl had disappeared from the shelter's playground, my mother took me aside and told me what I had to do."

"Did the police let you help?"

"Are you kidding? I couldn't get anywhere near the playground to catch her scent."

"Did you find her?" Trey's stomach sank at what CJ must have felt. A little girl's life in danger and being unable to stop it.

"We went to talk to her family and her mother was holding the little girl's teddy bear. I could tell from ten feet it carried her scent. My mother made up some story about a reclusive psychic she knew and they gave us the teddy bear."

"Like my handkerchief."

"Exactly. No one had seen a car when the girl disappeared, so the kidnapper had to have been on foot, at least for a few blocks. I pinpointed her scent across the alley from the shelter, but lost it in a parking garage."

"He had put her in a car. He cut off the trail." Trey had done the same thing with Mario at the club. But he had known a werewolf followed his trail.

"Almost. Following her scent I also caught the thread of her kidnapper. It was vile. I wouldn't have believed evil had its own smell, but that day I tracked it. The creep left the driver's side window open. I followed his scent for several miles."

"How did you follow it in a car?" Amazement in his question.

"My mom drove and I stuck my head out the window like a dog. It looked crazy, but I was so scared the wind would increase and I would lose the scent. We didn't have far to go. He had gone to a wooded ravine behind the freeway. I knew what he was doing to the girl. I wouldn't let my mom go with me. I thought I'd have to kill him and I didn't want her to see me do it."

"She let you go alone?" Trey stopped rubbing CJ's back and sat back on his legs, listening to her story.

"You know, I often go over that moment. My mother must have known what I intended to do. She didn't stop me. She just ran up the road to a gas station to call the cops."

"Do you think she understood you were part werewolf? Did she know the truth about Rupert?"

CJ pulled the sheet around her. "I think she did. I think she realized I could actually use what my father had given me for good. But she wouldn't talk about it." A lopsided grin played across her face. "Of course, if she had told me my dad was a werewolf, I would have asked her what drug she was on."

He thought about what she said. There was still a mystery he hadn't solved about CJ's werewolf powers. She hadn't just inherited Rupert's werewolf powers along with his DNA, somehow she had gotten Trey's powers instead.

Those were questions they couldn't answer on their own. Maybe someday, after they talked to her mom, after they had somehow made their peace with Lazlo...

CJ's voice was quiet. "I went down into the ravine tasting the man's blood with my nose. I had every intention of killing him."

Trey stayed silent. He would have been tempted to kill the man if it had been him, except it would have endangered the pack.

"He was raping her and had his hands gripped on her throat. I ripped him off the girl, put one hand on his jaw and one on his shoulder. One motion and I would've torn his head clear off. I *wanted* to do it. I could feel the strength to do it boiling through me. But her face stopped me. Her little eyes red with tears. I couldn't traumatize her more. I simply threw him against a tree. Broke his legs, I didn't want him to run, but my first priority was to get the girl back to her mom."

"She was okay?"

"Yeah, the city found low-rent housing for her family and my mother made sure the little girl got the counseling she needed. In their last Christmas card they wrote she was working on a nursing degree."

"What happened to the guy?"

"They let him out after ten years, stupid jerks, and he tried to do it again. Luckily a garbage crew saw him take this girl, they chased him up a fire escape and he tripped. Took a ten-story head dive."

"Justice." Trey pulled on the sheet and moved CJ into his arms.

"For one case. But there are others out there. Other monsters preying on the scared and weak."

"You're my one woman wonder."

"I just try and do what I can. I can't imagine doing anything else."

He kissed the gentle curve of her neck. The soft skin beneath his lips a contrast with the strength of the woman herself. She didn't think about survival or her place in the pecking order. She just used her very special powers to help people.

Damn Lazlo and his stupid pride. Damn his own pride. They had put her between them in their power struggle. The Elders might decide they had to keep her on the compound.

One girl had died because he'd kept CJ from doing what she needed to do. Other kids needed her, needed her to slay their very human monsters.

215

He couldn't let his pack stop her.

He'd go back and face Lazlo now. Even if they killed him, he had to make Lazlo promise to let CJ go home.

Chapter Twelve

The thick wad of cash weighed heavy in CJ's right hand. In her left, she held the note Trey had left for her on top of the money.

He had gone back to the compound.

His instructions were direct and simple. She was to take the money and go back to Minneapolis. He'd destroy her cell phone in his toilet tank and see if Lazlo would negotiate with him to let her go unharmed.

She knew exactly what Lazlo would want from Trey in exchange: his life.

She couldn't believe he had done this. They could've made it out together. They would have been strong enough to outwit the others. Or go back together and use the amulet in front of everyone.

Now he faced death at Lazlo's hands. Alone.

She had never felt so powerless.

Trey had thought of everything before he snuck out while she slept. The laptop propped open, the feed of his outer office, the lobby and the parking garage running at real time.

And the amulet.

The source of her visions, the one thing that could prove to the Elders and Lazlo magic was real. Prove Trey could save the pack.

CJ eyed the ancient piece of stone with its strange markings. Trey had left it beside the money.

For her safety he said in his note. He told her to take it far away and destroy it so nobody could take her powers again.

He was right on one level. Destroying the amulet was the sensible thing to do. If saving her own skin was her priority.

She understood Trey's thinking. Protect herself, Roz and her mom. Stay off the werewolf radar and maybe, just maybe, Lazlo wouldn't come gunning for her. Without Trey, she wasn't such a threat.

Without Trey to support Mario, Lazlo would find a way to keep their brother on a short leash. He'd probably threaten to kill CJ if Mario came searching for her. She carried no doubt of Lazlo's ruthlessness.

It all played out in her mind as she sat nestled in the sheet on the floor, Trey's scent still mingling with hers in the thin fibers of the cotton. She held it close, not wanting to let him go. Knowing his scent would fade, taken over by time and change. One day the only thing she'd have were her memories.

No. She wouldn't let them have him.

Fuck these werewolves and their damn laws. Their damn Council of Elders. They weren't her masters.

Trey was not her master.

She followed her own code. She was strong and she fought the monsters, human or werewolf. She didn't let the monsters win.

She grabbed her clothes she had thrown in a pile and dressed. The feed from the security camera ran as she plaited her hair into one long braid down her back. She kept an eye on the screen, watching for any of the few werewolves she might recognize. The people checking with the security guard were strangers to her.

Trey's office was empty. Trey had told the firm's human receptionist to take a few days off once Lazlo had ordered him to stay with CJ on the compound. Thankfully the woman was still gone.

Now CJ just had to figure the best way to leave without alerting anyone to her presence.

Exiting through the bathroom window was an option, but there wasn't a feed of the alley on the monitor. Plus, the other occupants of the building might get alarmed watching a woman scale down fifteen stories without a rope.

Trey had said the Elders met around ten. She noted the time on the security feed. It was already eight-forty. *Shit.* Only a little over an hour to get there and stop them from sentencing Trey to death.

She crouched down and observed the guard on duty at his desk. He ignored people leaving the building, so chances were she could exit easily enough. As long as he wasn't a werewolf, she could sprint past if he had been alerted to watch for her.

Once on the street, though, she'd need a car, preferably fast.

She spotted a Mustang as she scanned the parking garage feed. That would do. She had once learned how to hot-wire a car. She hoped it worked.

CJ grabbed Trey's laptop bag and stuffed the cash in a pocket. The amulet would fit, but she had a feeling she might need it. She slipped the leather cord around her neck and hid it beneath her blue blouse.

Next she bent to put the laptop in its case. If nothing else, she and Trey could pawn it once the cash ran out. She checked the screen one more time, as she put a hand on the cords to unhook the feed.

A woman had approached the security desk while CJ was looking away. She only noticed her now because the woman argued with the uniformed man, her hand movements sharp. Her fist hit the desk several times. She wore a chiffon scarf tied around her head. The old-fashioned garment hid her face from the camera, so CJ couldn't make out her face.

The strange woman raised her hand, opened it and blew some sort of dust on the security guard. If CJ hadn't been watching so closely, she would have missed it. A second later the woman stared directly into the security camera.

CJ blinked in disbelief.

Roz.

Her roommate proceeded to walk toward the elevators without being stopped. CJ felt helpless fifteen stories above the action, waiting for him to pop up and run after her friend. Instead, the man simply sneezed a few times, then went back to reading the paper splayed on his desk. He didn't even glance over his shoulder when the elevator door opened.

Damn, if she hadn't seen it she wouldn't have believed it. Roz had some explaining to do.

After disconnecting the laptop from the cable, she shut it and shoved it into its bag. She went to the secret door and activated the latch. With a quiet whisper, the door opened and she stepped into the dark closet. Trey had told her the latch was hidden on the closet rod. In the dark it took a moment, but she found a small bump at one end. She pressed it. The door to Trey's secret room slid shut.

She opened the closet door and walked out into Trey's office. Lazlo's unmistakable scent sent a shiver down her spine. She searched for Trey's and found it under the foul smelling rags he had arrived in Sunday night. She circled his office looking for any trail. He had left via the bathroom.

The door handle to Trey's office moved. A sandalwood and peach aroma filled her head. She jerked the door open and yanked Roz into the room. "Are you crazy? What are you doing here?"

Roz pulled the chiffon scarf off her head and red ringlets tumbled loose. "I came to save your in-over-your-head ass, that's what I'm doing here."

CJ's eyes brimmed with moisture. She knew Roz might worry after the last message, but she never expected her to hop on a plane and come to Seattle. Roz hated flying.

Roz wrapped an arm around her taller friend and wiped away CJ's tears with the scarf. "CJ Duncan crying? Don't worry. We're going to get out of whatever mess you've made and save this guy you've fallen in love with."

"How do you know I'm in love with Trey?"

Roz lifted an eyebrow and took in the rest of the plush office. "Well, I didn't know it was this Trey Nolan fellow. I got mixed signals on him from the cards." She paused a moment. "But I did a reading on you yesterday morning and it was as clear as day. You had fallen in love with *someone* and both of you were in trouble. Deadly trouble, according to the cards."

"And you believed them enough to get on a plane?"

Her roommate shrugged. "Well, with your tarot reading and phone message, coupled with the fact I've left like ten voice mails on your cell with no reply. You've never left me hanging so long." Roz stepped out of CJ's arms, a frown on her face.

"What?" CJ asked.

"Um, I just told you I flew halfway across the country because of a *tarot* card reading and you're not jumping me about it?"

CJ grabbed her friend's hands. How could she apologize for never taking magic seriously before? She couldn't. She could only make Roz understand she believed now. "Okay, remember what you said about big, bad, and scary—"

Roz held up two fingers in the form of the cross. "And evil. I saw it clear as day."

CJ pushed Roz's fingers down. "Well, they're not all evil."

"Who's not all evil?"

"Trey and his pack. My dad is a werewolf and so is my half-brother." CJ waited for what she just said to sink in. Would Roz think she had lost it?

Roz slammed her hand into her head. "Werewolves, of course. How could I be so stupid? You can smell as well as any animal, you're incredibly strong. Man, I can't believe they really exist."

"I sound crazy, but trust me. They're as real as you and me."

"CJ, you're the sanest person I know." Roz eyed her quizzically. "Though you've got to tell me who needs rescuing. If Trey is a werewolf, why does he need us? Is there something else evil out there?"

CJ looked at the watch on Roz's small wrist. Minutes away from nine. Time was wasting and she didn't have a real plan, though she had thought of someone who might be able to help her. She grabbed the laptop bag with the money and motioned Roz to follow her. "I'll explain on the way. I hope the guard won't remember you when we try to leave."

"Don't worry. The forget-me-dust I blew in his face made him forget I ever approached the desk."

They stepped into the elevator and CJ hit the lobby button. So Roz's card readings were true and she had something called "forget-me-dust". She turned to her friend, unwrapping the flowing scarf from around her head. "Roz, what's with the scarf? Is that like a witch's uniform or something?"

Roz rolled her eyes. "No, the only thing they had gassed and ready to rent was a convertible. I found this in the glove compartment. And since I don't know any other witches, I have no idea if there's a uniform." The elevator slowly made its way down. "I hope it's not black. I hate black."

"So you're a real witch? And you didn't know I was a werewolf?"

Roz pursed her bow-shaped lips and shrugged. "A witch? I don't know. All I can tell you is I've been practicing some spells, good luck charms, stuff like that for the last year or so. Nine times out of ten they've worked. I believe in magic, but I had no idea anything like a werewolf actually existed."

"How come I didn't know you were doing this?" CJ leaned against the elevator wall.

Roz twirled the end of her scarf in her hand. "You're my best friend and my psychic readings drive you crazy. I was afraid if I told you about these other things you might leave."

CJ smiled. "Well, I guess if you can stand living with a werewolf mutt like me, I'll let the witch thing pass."

Roz stuck her tongue out.

The elevator door opened and they stepped into the lobby. CJ scanned the area for werewolves, but smelled only humans. "Well, witch or not, I'm glad you're here. I just hope I don't get you killed."

"The convertible's parked across the street." Roz led CJ right past the guard. He didn't look up from his paper.

Once they were out the door, CJ checked the street. She didn't see or smell anything close to a werewolf.

"What are we going to do, just bust into their den and get Trey? What about your brother and your dad?" Roz asked as the dodged across the street.

"Well, it's not a den. They live in a compound. Several acres outside the city. My brother and dad aren't in danger. It's Trey. Lazlo might kill him and no, hopefully we won't have to break in."

They reached the car and Roz threw her the keys. As soon as they were buckled in, CJ handed the laptop case to Roz. "Look for an address book on Trey's computer. See if there is a cell phone number for someone called Doc Vogel. He's the only one who can help us now."

ଧଉଶ୦ଓ

A sticky ooze covered the concrete floor of Trey's solitary prison. He scooted away from the center drain that bubbled with the runoff from an early morning rain. Barely enough light came from the small window in the door to find a piece of dry wood to sit on.

The remnant of the bench Mario had destroyed in his beastly rage.

The guards, two younger werewolves not involved with any of the Elders, were so surprised when he strode up to the compound gate early this morning, they had simply let him enter and called in his arrival to Lazlo.

Within two minutes six werewolves in Beast form tackled him. He didn't resist. He had no desire to arouse their anger more. They quickly shackled and dragged him into this dismal cell. Lazlo was obviously taking no chances. No one had any idea the power he attacked Lazlo with was gone. Trey chose not to enlighten them. It kept the focus on him. So far Lazlo hadn't asked about CJ's whereabouts.

Trey heard the slurp of the damp ground as someone approached the concrete outbuilding.

"Trey? Here's some water." Mario passed a Ziploc bag full of water through the narrow slot. "I've got some energy bars if you're hungry." He held them through the slot, too.

Trey slowly rose to his feet and grabbed the bars. "I'll save them for later." He'd stash them in a corner for the next unlucky prisoner. "The water's just what I need." He reached over and poured the bag down his throat.

The morning sun shone bright everywhere except Trey's prison. The early morning clouds had passed and Mario had pulled on a cap, hiding his eyes from view. Mario kicked absentmindedly at the steel door as Trey finished the water. "Why'd you come back? A couple of the guys said they'd have to sentence you to death for what you did. They're wrong, right?" He stopped kicking the door and lifted his head to look Trey straight in the eye. "You've got some plan to stop Lazlo."

"I'll do what I need to do." He only hoped his life would be enough to satisfy Lazlo. "This is between your brother and me, Mario. Don't forget that. Don't attack Lazlo if they sentence me to death. It won't do any good."

Mario snorted.

"I mean it." Trey raised his voice, trying to compel the teen to listen.

"Hardly my decision, is it?" Mario kicked the door with force.

"I was just—"

"Trey, drop it. Okay, there's something else I want to say. I want you to know..." Mario brushed his hand across his cheek, the sunlight catching wet tears. "I wanted to thank you. For what you did."

His powerlessness had never seemed the curse it did now, watching his young friend choke back tears. He only had words to comfort Mario. "Hey, it goes both ways, kid. I've needed you to keep me going these last few years. Sometimes I think you and I were the only ones who realized what a monster Lazlo had become."

Mario took off his cap and ran a hand through his tousled hair. Trey marveled at how the seventeen-year-old seemed to have grown up overnight. His eyes held more pain than many werewolves who had lived a lifetime. "Actually, I wanted to thank you for saving CJ. Sebastian told me Lazlo tried to rape her." The undertone in Mario's voice rumbled dangerously.

Trey reached two fingers through the bars and touched Mario's knuckles. He couldn't let Mario lose control now. There was something he needed to tell him, before they took him to the Council. "Hang in there. I know it will be tough for you to be around him, but for CJ's sake don't provoke your brother."

"I know she's only my half-sister, but she was like you. And me. Different. Do you think I'll see her again?"

Trey leaned against the door, resting his head against the bars. He didn't have those answers for Mario. He prayed she stayed away from his pack forever. He didn't want her hurt.

But still, he couldn't leave Mario without hope. Once Trey was gone, CJ would be the only one who could help Mario control his Beast.

She believed in the magic.

Trey shook his head trying to force out the self-pity. He wasn't dead yet and he had some important knowledge to pass on. "Mario. Right now Lazlo is angry. I've threatened his standing and CJ is a werewolf he can't control. She's defied him twice. But listen carefully." He prayed what he said was true. "Since her very existence could cast doubt on the logic behind the breeding plan, I don't think he'll pursue her if she doesn't interfere with us."

Mario shoved the cap back on his head and stared at Trey. "You're telling me if I want CJ to live, I can't go near her?"

"At least not for awhile. When you're older. When you're stronger. Once you can get out from under his thumb. I think she'll help you to finally learn to control your Beast."

"I'll never be able to get away from my brother. Even if I ran, I can't use the power of the werewolf to escape his trackers."

Trey took a deep breath. What he was about to tell Mario could endanger the kid, but if he died today, he couldn't let what he had learned about the power of magic die with him.

He brought his face close to the bars and whispered. "Kid, I'm going to tell you a secret. It's hard to believe. But if you are careful, you might find a way to master your Beast. Learn the wolf shift."

"Doc Vogel's tried everything. I don't have the right shifting genes. He discovered it in my blood," said Mario, his voice quiet with shame.

Trey held the bars in his iron grip. "Doc Vogel, Lazlo, all the others, they're looking in the wrong place, Mario. The secret to our powers doesn't lie in our genes. We're magical beings. We have some sort of magical soul, an aura or something. I don't know exactly. CJ and I discovered it together."

227

Mario's eyebrow shot up. "What in the hell are you talking about?"

"You heard how I stopped Lazlo from raping CJ? And I'm sure you heard how I blew by all the other werewolves. Hell, I leapt over the compound wall like it was a bump in the road. You *know* I'm not that strong. How do you think I did it?"

"Cause you love CJ. I figured it was like when I get mad at Lazlo and no one can control me."

Cause you love CJ. The kid made it sound so obvious.

Trey's chest contracted as the truth of what Mario said filled his soul. Magic powers, werewolf blood. These aspects drew him, but it was CJ's spirit. Her absolute drive to do everything she could to battle the monsters. That was the woman he had fallen in love with.

No wonder Lazlo wanted her. He had to have everything meant to be Trey's. The knot around his heart cinched tighter as he thought of the Alpha trying to make CJ his own. He could never let Lazlo control CJ.

Trey caught Mario's gaze and held it. "It was more than my love." He didn't want to reveal CJ's strengths could be taken from her, but he could tell Mario about the chant and the amulet. "I found an ancient amulet and a spell book from a Spanish witch. I used them to increase my strength and save CJ. I used magic."

Mario raised his hands in the air. "Well, if you can do magic, use it now. Get out of here. Escape."

"No, Mario. I can't run from Lazlo. I don't want CJ to give up her way of life because of me." He thought about her moving from city to city. Never being in one place long enough to put down roots, build up her agency again. He felt the certainty of his decision in his bones. "This is the only answer. But you have to promise me something."

Mario took a deep breath and shoved his hands back in his pockets. "Just tell me. I'll do anything for you."

"During the Council while everyone is focused on me, go to my cabin. You'll find a small, red leather book written in several languages. I keep it next to a copy of *Poor Richard's Almanac* in my bedroom. Take it. Study it over the next few years. Find the magic that will give you the control and power you need."

"But where do I start?"

"Learn as I did. Study the magic books and shops. Believe me, you'll begin to see the real magic among all the cheap tricks. I think the magic inside of us lets us see the truth. You can do this, Mario."

"I don't want to do it alone."

"I'm sorry, Mario. There is no other way. Only when you're old enough to get away from Lazlo. Go to CJ. She'll help you." He could hear branches snapping in the forest beyond the dormitory. They were coming to take him in front of the Council. "Promise me."

Mario heard the others, too. He stepped away from the concrete building. "I promise." His face contorted with grief, he ran into the woods.

Trey couldn't see, but he heard his young friend's heavy footsteps mixed with stifled crying. He listened for the movements that would tell him if a guard went after Mario, but the steps of the six men continued toward his prison. They knew better than to risk angering Mario.

Sebastian stepped to the door. "It's time to go, Trey." He slipped the key into the door and swung it open. Bruno stepped forward to shackle Trey in heavy iron chains. Sebastian barred Bruno with his arm. "I told you, he won't need those. Lazlo did not say he had to be bound."

"But if he escapes," Bruno protested.

229

"He won't." His eyes met Trey's. "I'll take the consequences if he does."

Trey nodded. Sebastian understood Trey wasn't leaving the Council alive. "Thank you. I'll appreciate not being shackled like a dog during my trial."

Sebastian grabbed a bundle from one of the rear werewolves. "Here is at least a clean pair of pants, so you can get out of those rags."

"You risk Lazlo's anger for a dying man's dignity. Thank you." Trey had not expected anyone to show him kindness during his last hours. He should not underestimate the nobility of his kind.

Sebastian did not reply, he simply nodded and led the small group toward the Council Hall.

ഇയ

CJ's nose curled at the clinical smell of alcohol surrounding Doc Vogel's large cabin. She found it hard to believe the old werewolf could stand living next to such a strong odor, but perhaps he had grown used to it.

She and Roz carefully followed Vogel through the maze of steel tables and medical equipment crowding his small laboratory. She noticed several large computers and various test tubes filled with strange liquids. She sniffed trying to identify the contents, but the mix of alcohol and bleach interfered.

"Hurry, you two. I just hope the guards didn't alert Lazlo to my afternoon drive. He might wonder what I was up to, leaving the compound right now." He stopped in his tracks. "But, what am I saying. Lazlo would never think I aided the enemy." He gave a wide grin to both women and winked, before he moved toward the end of the room.

CJ inwardly smiled at his comment. That reason was exactly why she had contacted Vogel instead of Mario.

Roz had found Doc Vogel's cell number and the old werewolf had almost hung up when CJ pleaded with him to help them get in the compound.

Once she mentioned her plan to rescue Trey, he had stopped protesting and listened. It was such a simple plan. It would solve everything.

As she recapped the events of the last few days to Roz, she explained how feeling the power pass from Trey to her using the amulet had made her a believer in magic. It struck her then how simple it would be to give a demonstration to the Elders. She and Trey could exchange the powers in front of the werewolves. They would see Trey was right and Lazlo wrong.

She figured their magic would be a big enough discovery to the Elders, killing Trey for attacking Lazlo would fall by the wayside.

Doc Vogel had sputtered with delight when she told him of the amulet, the spell and how she and Trey shared powers. He hadn't questioned her at all, but rather quickly suggested he meet them a few miles outside the compound and he would smuggle them in.

Back in the car, as Roz searched for Vogel's number, CJ wondered why Trey hadn't thought of this plan himself, but her own words came back to a haunt her.

"The episode kind of soured me on working with a partner. I discovered no one would ever be able to keep up with me."

She hadn't been thinking of Trey, but he must have taken it to heart. He thought he would hold her back. Endanger her.

The words she didn't say would have changed his mind. Those words would have kept him next to her during the night. She hadn't told him she loved him.

Love.

Her heart hammered with the realization. Her passion for Trey was stronger than anything she had felt for a man. Her respect for his struggles. His inner strength.

He only made her stronger, but all her feelings were too late if Lazlo succeeded in sentencing Trey to death.

Vogel's sharp voice cut through CJ's thoughts. "Follow me through here."

Roz gave CJ a doubtful look. "It looks like a freezer door to me."

Doc Vogel twitched his bushy eyebrows with a smile at the two women. "Trey isn't the only werewolf with secrets. Come quickly, I think you'll be surprised at my cleverness."

He held open the door and pushed a button on the underside of the freezer ceiling. With a quiet creak, the back of the freezer slid open revealing dark steps leading down into a black cellar.

CJ smelled the air. Damp, but nothing vile oozed from the darkness. She went first.

"The light is at the bottom of the steps on the right." Doc Vogel swung the freezer door shut as Roz followed CJ down the steps.

CJ felt a switch with her fingers. The buzz of fluorescent lights echoed, before the blue glow illuminated the underground room for them.

She stopped in her tracks and Roz collided with her back.

It appeared to be some kind of basement or cellar, though much deeper than any she had seen. The ceiling had to be almost twenty feet high. Rough stones jutted from the wall, and the floor was a dull concrete.

"Keep going. You'll be safe here until the Council is under way. I'll have to go and take my place. You should follow me in about fifteen minutes."

Roz marched over to what appeared to be a wooden altar draped in velvet cloth. A large book lay open on a dais. Several candles dripping with wax surrounded it.

Roz's eyes widened in wonderment. "This spell book is ancient. How did you find it?"

Vogel joined her and touched it with reverence. "It is incredible, isn't it? I've spent my life studying it, but I can't take credit for finding it. My father collected occult artifacts. I suppose as a man of science, he found it to be a fascinating forbidden fruit."

Roz narrowed her eyes. "Do you believe in magic?"

Vogel took her hand in his. "My dear girls. I know you have seen fantastical things and it must appear to be some sort of strange paranormal power, but I am a scientist. I see all this, what you call magic, as simply undiscovered knowledge. But most of it is just make-believe."

Roz smiled. "Like mumbo jumbo or something."

"Exactly." He patted her on the arm and walked over to a table covered with vials.

CJ explored the room, which was larger than the laboratory upstairs. She guessed the length at around thirty feet long. She neared a small alcove at the end that held a large globe that appeared to be suspended in air by invisible strings. It rested above a golden bowl engraved with markings similar to the ones carved on Trey's amulet. She extended her hand to touch the large glowing ball.

"Don't," Vogel shouted from across the room.

CJ stepped back. "What is it?"

Vogel moved quickly to her side and grabbed her by the arms, moving her away from the globe, his grasp surprisingly tight. "It's a Victorian hexing orb, very rare and expensive. Supposedly a soul could be stolen and stored inside it."

"Victorian? It looks much older." She didn't want to say why.

"Well, the occult fascinated the Victorians. They often created objects to look older. I have many of their reproductions in my collection." He gestured to a table of ornate goblets and plates.

CJ couldn't take her eyes off the globe. Its energy reminded her of the luminescent scent threads she tracked. "But what makes it glow? And float?"

Vogel sighed in exasperation. "Simple chemistry. It's a gas lamp really and it isn't floating. There is a stand behind it."

"Oh." It didn't seem like any lamp she had seen.

Vogel put both arms around her and guided her back to where Roz stood, a deep scowl on her face, surveying a collection of wooden stocks and iron maidens.

The gruesome objects gave CJ the willies and she wondered why anyone would collect things that inflicted pain.

Vogel noticed Roz's interest. "Try them." He swung open a heavy-looking bar and pointed to the two wrist holes. "You might think the wrists became sore, but you'll find the angle of the stocks put terrible pressure on the victim's back and hamstrings. There are reports of people dislocating their shoulders when their legs finally gave out. Really, try it. I have a few minutes before I head out."

With a sigh, Roz leaned forward to humor the old werewolf and put her arms in the stock. He snapped the heavy wooden bar down and latched it on the other side. "Now just wait a few minutes and you'll see what I'm talking about."

CJ shook her head at his request. She supposed since magic was against the werewolf law or whatever, they were the first visitors to his macabre cellar. She needed to remind him of their real purpose. "Doc, don't you think we should talk about the plan. Do you have any ideas about how I can get past the guards?"

Vogel patted Roz's head and turned back to CJ. "Yes. Well, Sebastian will be at the door. He's next in line to join the Elders, so he acts as sentry. He has no love for Lazlo. He will help us. If you show no weapons and I tell him you are coming... Wait, you're wearing the amulet, aren't you?"

CJ touched the amulet she had hidden in her bra. "Yes, why?"

He held out his open hand. "You must give it to me. When you enter the hall, I'm sure Lazlo will attempt to make you leave, perhaps call the other guards to detain you. You may not be able to get the amulet to Trey. Unless you think you can perform the spell while defending yourself?"

CJ shook her head.

Vogel rubbed a hand over his gray mustache. "I'll throw the amulet to Trey so he can perform your spell. I can't see any other way you'll pull this off, without Lazlo interfering."

A momentary flash of doubt halted her hand from pulling the leather cord from around her neck. She felt the stone's smooth, cool surface in her hand and remembered Trey's warnings. This amulet could take her powers.

Whoever had it could take her powers...

"Lazlo won't let you enter unchallenged. He won't give me a passing notice." His voice was soft and reassuring.

Vogel was right.

She didn't know the layout of the hall and where Trey would be. Nor did she believe Lazlo would let her enter unchallenged. She had no choice but to trust Vogel.

CJ reached into her shirt and clutched the amulet. She pulled it over her head and held it out. Vogel grabbed it and examined it under the blue light. "I'm counting on you, Doc."

"Don't worry, I know exactly what I have to do." He put the amulet into a pocket of his suit coat and pivoted quickly on the concrete floor. "There is one more thing we must do for luck, my girls." He went over to a small cabinet.

She watched as he opened it and chose a bottle of wine from the several he had stacked inside the cabinet. Next, he moved over to a wooden table holding various small bottles, plates and cups. She couldn't see what he did, but when he turned around he held three cups in his hands, each filled with the rich-smelling wine.

"Don't know if Trey told you, but my birth pack was Ukrainian. Had a bad time of it after the War, but I've never forgotten my roots. You must allow me to bless our mission with a toast. To Trey's freedom and the hope he and Lazlo can come to some sort of peace. For all our sakes."

He gave CJ her glass, then remembered Roz in the stocks. "Oh, I'm sorry, dear." He sat the remaining two glasses down and went to open the heavy bar. "Damn it, I accidentally set the lock and I don't have a key to this stock. I'll have to get my wire cutters and snip it."

"Lovely." Roz cocked her head at CJ, her expression sour. "CJ can bust me out. If the Elders meet at ten you need to get over there."

Vogel checked his watch, "Yes, you're quite right, dear. But first, I insist. Our toast." He turned back to face CJ. "Indulge an old man?"

He gripped a glass and held it high.

She didn't like seeing Roz imprisoned. Accidentally or otherwise. "I'll get Roz out fir—"

"Oh, just do the toast, CJ. I hate wine anyway." Roz rolled her eyes.

CJ relented and lifted her glass.

Doc Vogel cleared his throat. "To our success." He clinked his glass with CJ's and emptied it.

CJ downed hers in one swig. The wine struck her as awfully bold flavored. She coughed a little as it went down, but Vogel seemed pleased she had honored his old traditions, if the smile on his face was any indication.

She moved to break the latch holding the stock over Roz's wrists, but a sharp stab in her belly sent her lurching for the floor instead.

Pain seared under her ribs and she felt as if her stomach constricted into her chest. She opened her mouth to vomit, but she only tasted the sour essence of the wine.

"CJ!" Roz's shout echoed off the brick walls of the cellar.

She jerked her gaze upward to see her friend's terrified face. With effort she moved her head and saw Vogel sprint up the stairs two at a time. He grinned as he dangled the amulet in the air for her to see. "I need to thank you for giving me Trey's amulet. I believe it is much stronger than the one I've been using all these years." He opened the cellar door. "Sorry the silver is so painful. I'm afraid there isn't any other type of poison that will kill a werewolf, so you understand, I had no choice."

Margo Lukas

With a final wave, he slipped through the door. The door slammed shut.

Chapter Thirteen

The pain subsided, but only because everything below her neck went numb. Drawing on every ounce of strength, CJ tried to push up on her knees and crawl to Roz. Slowly her arm edged out on the hard floor. The remainder of her body didn't obey.

As if the poison paralyzed her. *Silver* poison. How kind of the fates to make silver lethal to her when she wasn't a full werewolf. Strength and smell did little good now. Curses, why couldn't she shift?

CJ curled her fingers on the smooth surface and willed her body to inch forward. The pain became a pounding in her ears. The throb of the poison slowed her heart. Anger at her stupidity drove her on.

Vogel. Somehow he had weakened the pack. What did he have to gain by destroying the werewolves?

Shit, it hurt to think.

Roz yelled down to her from the stocks. "Don't move. Don't exert yourself. You'll just make the poison move quicker through your system. I'm going to try something. It's an old spell I found on a New England witchcraft site."

CJ lay on the floor, barely able to hear Roz's words. She couldn't twist her head to see anything other than Roz's sequined red flip-flops. Her eyelids grew heavy, but she kept them trained on her friend.

She couldn't pass out. Not yet. If she died down here, she wanted to know Roz made it out safely. She stretched her eyes open, fighting off the blackness.

The crash of shattering glass jarred her from approaching unconsciousness. CJ could hear the wind rushing through the room as if someone had opened a window.

The cellar didn't have a window. As the thought crossed her mind, her body was hit by the gust. It pushed her several feet, flipping her onto her back. The hard slam barely registered on her numb body.

CJ gazed helplessly at the hanging fixtures sweeping light across the room. From her new position, she was able to turn her head slightly and see Roz locked in the stocks. The wind, silent in the rest of the lab, had formed a vortex around her roommate. Roz's red curls whipped around her face hiding it from CJ's sight.

A piercing scream tore from Roz's throat, shrill enough to reach CJ's drugged mind. Helpless on the floor, CJ watched as a ball of blue flames engulfed Roz's arms and the stock.

Roz tumbled to her knees on the floor, blackened stumps all that hung from her trembling shoulders.

CJ couldn't pull her gaze from the horrifying sight. Roz raised her head and shouted strange words. The tunnel of wind swept back through the room carrying the acid aroma of burnt flesh across CJ's face.

She closed her eyes and wished for the blackness of death to take away the horrid smell of her friend's misery.

Roz's words grew louder and again CJ felt the fury of wind pelt her body, but this time a different smell came to her.

Sandalwood and peaches.

Soft hands brushed her face. CJ opened her eyes to see Roz kneeling next to her. Roz made a muscle with her one perfect, pink arm. "I can't believe it worked. Except for my missing sleeve, I can't tell it even happened."

CJ took a breath. "Can you get us out of here? We've got to tell"—she gasped for another breath—"tell Mario about Vogel. Get Trey."

Roz scrambled to her feet, grabbed a wooden stool from against the wall and tore up the stairs with surprising speed. She hit the door several times. In anger, she tossed the stool aside. "It's no use, I can't budge it and I don't know any spells that might open it."

"That fire trick?" CJ yelled weakly.

"No, I can't do my whole body. Only a few parts at a time." Roz sped down the steps. "Wait, I've got my cell phone in my pocket." She reached in and pulled out the silver flip phone. "Three bars of reception. Give me Mario's number."

Oh, shit. She didn't know it. Would he have the phone on him? She wanted to close her eyes so bad. She had never felt so tired in her life.

She could feel Roz squeezing her arms.

"CJ, don't you give up on me now. Think. There has to be someone we can call."

"I don't know."

"Okay, I'm calling 911, damn the werewolves."

The girl. Kaitlyn. She'd have Mario's number. "Call...Kait...lyn Roberts, Four...Five One Maynard Avenue...she'll...have number." She gasped for air. The world smelled like peaches, but it was fading.

As she lay paralyzed on the floor, the beep of Roz's phone penetrated a part of her brain holding on to consciousness. Three beeps. A long pause. Then a lot more beeps. Did Roz get through?

A cold nothingness overran Roz's peaches. The smell of death?

ஐ௫௦௪

Resigned to his fate, Trey kneeled before Lazlo on the cold tile of the Council Hall. Determination to save CJ kept Trey focused. They had secured him to a ring in the floor by a heavy chain attached to a leather collar around his neck. His wrists bound tightly behind him, he held his head steady and stared straight ahead.

Lazlo circled him, regal in his black Armani suit and perfectly polished wing tips. "Where is she?"

"Does it matter? You have me." In a few minutes, Lazlo would allow the Elders to enter and begin the trial. Trey would only go peacefully to his death, if he could convince Lazlo not to go after CJ.

"I command you to tell me where she is. I'm still your Alpha Leader."

Trey's gut roiled at Lazlo's arrogance. "You could be the fucking king of the world and I wouldn't tell you where she is."

Lazlo's fist caught him on the side of his head. He reeled, but the chain painfully jerked his neck before he went over.

"You think I won't find her? Did you think I would quit just because you surrendered?" Lazlo's shouted words echoed off the hall's glistening marble walls.

Trey spoke more quietly, trying to get his old friend to see reason. "Why, Lazlo? Why must you have CJ? I only wanted to use her to make the Elders question the science behind your precious plan. She has no interest in usurping your power, as I did. If you leave her be, I won't tell the Elders why I attacked you."

Lazlo stopped pacing. "Your reasons make no difference. The laws clearly state an Alpha Leader cannot be attacked in any form outside an approved Challenge. And I don't need to remind you it is illegal for the Beast to attack another werewolf unprovoked."

"Unprovoked? You don't think the Elders will be interested to hear you intended to rape CJ? Rape is against our laws, too." Trey thought of Rupert. Would he sit in this hall and let the man who almost raped his daughter escape punishment.

"It would not have been *rape*. You simply attacked too soon. I would have convinced her I was a better choice than you. She would have chosen me once she saw the truth of what you are." His voice dripped with venom.

"The truth of what *I am*? You are a depraved maniac. You treat my pack as nothing more than breeding animals. You think that emotions, that love aren't important to the survival of this pack."

Lazlo lifted his chin and yelled into his face. "You just revealed your true motivations. You said 'my pack'. The New World Pack is crumbling around us. Every new child with less and less power, and all you care about is being the Alpha. At least I have a plan to save us. All you offer is an example of disobedience. Dangerous emotional rampages."

Trey let his rage boil inside. Lazlo would never believe magic weakened the pack. In Lazlo's extreme insecurity, he perceived every action of Trey's to be about taking his power.

243

The pack. His family. They were beyond his help. Rescuing CJ had been the deciding moment. Maybe Mario would figure this magic thing out and convince the others. Whether Mario would be too late, Trey didn't know.

The pack wasn't his priority now.

He had to make Lazlo see the pointlessness of pursuing CJ. He couldn't fail at this, too.

He stared at the mosaic of tiles beneath him, his mind urgently searching for a plan. He needed to deflect Lazlo's interest away from CJ. Make her unimportant.

That was it. He spoke up clearly, "She has nothing to offer you. She can't even shift." He heard Lazlo's sharp intake of breath. CJ's inability to shift was a surprise to the Alpha.

Lazlo resumed pacing a circle around Trey. "What do you mean she can't shift? She has to have our power. I felt it. You were there when she broke my nose and Mario told me how she tracked you down. No, don't lie to me. She may be part human, but our genes our dominant. She can be of use to the pack."

"Really, or will she further undermine the pack's confidence in you? If you bring her back, she will accomplish what I intended to. She will make the others realize your grand breeding plan, a plan tearing apart lovers, is based on nothing more than your wishful thinking."

The Alpha stopped and shook a fist at the empty room. "When the first werewolves born from my plan mature. When they come into their power, you'll all see I was right."

"That's twelve or fifteen years away. In the meantime, others will defy you. How many werewolves will you have to kill? One, five, twenty? We are more than animals that you can breed to be strong. We're human, too. CJ will remind everyone of their humanity. The humanity you are taking away."

Lazlo crouched down to Trey's level and gripped the chain, jerking Trey's chin up. "Don't tell me about a werewolf's humanity. My father died because of our humanity. Our human side is frail and weak. Now, even in our other forms we are weakening. I will not stand by and see more of my kind suffer what my brother suffers."

"Your brother suffers because of you." Trey spat the accusation.

Lazlo snarled in Trey's face. The Beast flashing in his eyes. "My family has paid the price for our humanity. The werewolf will not evolve into a race ruled by our fragile humanity. That is why you must die and CJ must be brought back and her strength used for our purposes." Lazlo pushed him away and marched to the wide double doors, the only entrance to the hall. "Enough of your drivel. It is time for the Elders to decide your fate."

Lazlo threw the doors open and Sebastian moved aside to let the group of older, solemn men enter the hall.

Once the men had seated themselves, Sebastian closed the great doors. Trey caught his eye for a second before the sturdy werewolf took up his place outside the doors as sentry to the Council. The anger in his friend's eyes was not well hidden. At least CJ would not be without allies when Lazlo dragged her back to the compound.

He scanned the seated men for CJ and Mario's father. Rupert Le Croix chose not to be active in the pack's affairs. A capable operative when younger, he and Lazlo's mother had taken a semi-permanent post as the bodyguard of a British financier for Guardian.

The handsome man with gray-streaked hair worn long and loose sat in the back row. In the corner. If he had heard reports of CJ and her apparent relation to Mario, his face did not reveal it.

Trey could see his father, too. His bowed head was in the second row, fourth seat from the middle. He leaned forward, eyes cast down. No doubt to avoid not only his son's eyes, but the stares of his fellow werewolves. His reaction was no different than when Trey had lost in the Succession Challenges to Lazlo in this very hall.

Trey had always been a disappointment to his father, even after Trey made Guardian International more profitable than anyone could have imagined. If his father knew what he had discovered about their past, about their magical origins, would he be proud? Or would he still hold his physically weak son at arm's length?

Not that it mattered anymore.

Lazlo was making damn sure Trey wouldn't live to see tomorrow's sunrise.

Lazlo's voice carried through the hall. "I bring before the Elders Council, a traitor. A traitor not only against me, the Alpha Leader, but to the laws of our pack."

Every word he spoke was a slow burn to Trey's pride. The Alpha held him like a dog. Head jerked painfully upward by his hair so he could watch the reaction of the men who would condemn him. Three rows of ten men sat towering over him as he knelt in the semi-circular hall to be judged.

"The accused, Trey Nolan, in the form of his Beast, attacked my person, the reigning Alpha Leader, in my quarters this past Sunday. Furthermore, I was in my human form at the time of the attack. A clear violation of standing rules three *and* seven of the New World Pack constitution."

The murmuring of the Elders' whispers underscored Lazlo's triumph.

Once the chatter died, Lazlo resumed his arguments. "I was able to quickly shift to save my life from the extremely deep injuries I incurred during said attack, but I believe it was Trey's intention to kill me. If not for the quick arrival of several loyal werewolves, I fear we would have had a fight to the death right there."

The talk grew louder as the Elders exchanged their thoughts about what Lazlo had told them. Of course, they had heard about the incident, but hearing the definitive tale from the Alpha Leader meant the charges were real. They would have to sentence a fellow werewolf to death for such violations. It was their law.

The room grew quiet again. In all trials or disputes, the accused had a chance to either speak for himself, or appoint another to do so. They waited for Trey to speak.

Trey surveyed the men around the room. Would it matter what he said? He had clearly broken the laws of the pack. His father would not argue for his life. Trey could think of nothing to save his life, or protect CJ.

His gaze came to rest on Doc Vogel's face. Trey had called him a friend, but Vogel would never have condoned attacking the Alpha. The doctor's face changed for a second. He wiggled his eyebrows. Was it a message? Trey surged with last minute hope.

The old werewolf reclined in a front row seat, nearest the door. His hand covered his mouth as he looked down at Trey.

Vogel slipped his other hand into his jacket and pulled a fist-sized object from a pocket. The other Elders' eyes still focused on Trey. The doctor wanted him to see what he was doing.

Vogel brought out his hand. A leather cord hung down from his closed fist.

The amulet. CJ was here.

Vogel smiled at Trey then slipped the amulet back into his pocket. Why would CJ give Vogel the amulet? It was too dangerous to let someone else have it.

Lazlo stepped in front of Trey. "Is there no defense for this werewolf—"

The sound of something, or someone, hitting the outside of the door silenced Lazlo's closing speech.

While the commotion distracted everyone, Trey pulled at his chain. It dug into his flesh, but he could not pull it from the hook embedded in the floor. Damn his weakness.

Lazlo made it first to the door and flung it open, as if he had no fear of what might lie on the other side. He moved quickly to the side and the men in the hall gasped as Sebastian and Mario tumbled into the hall. The force of the fall sent the two sliding across the tiled floor.

Mario rolled to his feet and ran to Trey's side. Trey could see the panic in Mario's eyes. The teen fought with his Beast to keep it from emerging.

Once on his feet, Sebastian made no move to go after him and all others, including Lazlo, seemed to be frozen with amazement that another werewolf would dare enter the hall.

Mario grabbed Trey's chain in both of his hands. "CJ's in trouble. He's poisoned her with silver." He pulled on the chain, his young arms quivering with exertion. The heavy links tore free of the hook before the others could react.

Trey sprang to his feet, instinctively pushing Mario behind him to protect him from the others. "Where is she? Who's poisoned her?" Had Lazlo found CJ and tried to kill her while the Elders gathered here? Trey's veins pulsed as he stamped down his own Beast.

Lazlo stood facing them, a living wall between them and the door, fury engraved on his thin face. "I won't let you leave this hall alive." A few Elders jumped out of their seats and came to aid their Alpha, flanking Lazlo on each side.

"It was Vogel. All along it's been Vogel." Mario shouted the words, loud enough for Lazlo to hear. Loud enough to echo through the hall.

Vogel. All along? Trey couldn't process what Mario was saying.

But he was certain of one thing. He had to get that amulet.

Silver. Poison. Most werewolves could shift and expel it before it did them any harm. CJ couldn't.

And somehow Vogel knew CJ's weakness.

Trey had to get to her soon and give her his shifting powers. He had no alternative. He had to save her.

He glared past Lazlo, toward the empty seat of Doc Vogel. Frantic with worry, he steeled himself to fight. "Lazlo, get out of my way. I haven't betrayed our pack. It's Vogel. We have to go after him."

Mario pushed around Trey and found his father, standing alone in the Elder's gallery. "Your daughter, Father, *your* daughter is dying, poisoned by silver and unable to heal because she can't shift. Do something. Trey is the only one who can help her."

One of the Elders grabbed Mario by the neck and pushed him to the ground, grabbing the boy's arms and twisting them behind his back.

Before Mario wrenched his arms free, Rupert leapt across the room and knocked the other Elder away. He turned his back to Mario and faced the Alpha. His voice was raw with anger. "I have never interfered in your life, Lazlo. Even when I had to leave because of the cruel way you treated my son, I respected your position, but no more."

He took a long step forward and grabbed the Alpha by his silken lapels. No one made a move to stop him. "Rumor has it you tried to rape my daughter and I will not stand by and let her die because of your personal vendetta against Trey." Rupert directed his wrath to the shocked Elders who stood frozen next to their Alpha. "We are still the Elders and our vote can override the wishes of the Alpha. Before we condemn Trey and my son for their actions, do we not owe it to our kind to pursue the truth?"

Mario placed a hand on Rupert's shoulder "We don't have time for their support, Father. We have to go now."

Sebastian went behind Lazlo and opened the great doors. He ignored Lazlo's command to close it. "Go now. You have more allies than you realize."

Trey didn't wait for Lazlo to react.

Trey shot for the door unhindered, Mario at his heel. CJ his only concern now, he shifted to wolf as he leapt through the door. His paws skidded across the inlaid tiles of the outer hall as he hit the floor. His canine eyes checked to see if Lazlo followed, but instead his father's face looked out between the crack of the doors.

His father nodded and swung the massive doors shut. A formidable barrier to those who would destroy his son.

Sebastian's words echoed in Trey's mind.

You have more allies than you realize.

Chapter Fourteen

Vogel's cabin wasn't far from the Council Hall, but thorns and shrubs overgrew the path. The brambles didn't bother Trey in his wolf form. He flew through them, not waiting for Mario.

He heard Vogel before he saw him. The bastard had not shifted out of human form, at least not yet.

Trey didn't let up. Vogel fumbled with the amulet as he ran through the overgrowth, trying to put it on and run at the same time. The doctor realized if he shifted he couldn't hold the amulet in his paw. It would fall to the ground.

Trey growled as Vogel's foot caught on a branch and he stumbled inches in front of his cabin. A few more feet and Vogel would be his.

Vogel ran through the cabin door. Trey launched into the air and locked his jaw around his prey's ankle. Glass scattered as the doctor brought down a table of vials when he fell beneath Trey's wolf.

Trey let go of Vogel's ankle, snapping his jaw and trying to catch the amulet in his teeth, but Vogel thrust his arm beneath Trey's broad wolf chest. Using his superhuman strength, he launched Trey across the room.

Broken shards of glass tore at Trey's flesh when he landed, his thick wolf coat unable to protect him. His claws slipped on a steel table. He let himself fall to the floor where he steadied his legs underneath him. Trey searched the room with his wolf's razor-sharp vision.

He couldn't see Vogel anywhere. He took a step away from the smashed table with his paw, skirting the shards of broken glass, when a strange haze began filling the room. Trey focused on the far end of the room where he had last seen Vogel, but the details quickly disappeared in the thick gray fog.

The fog cleared slightly. A white wolf lay prone on the ground before him. He attempted to get closer, but he couldn't move.

A hallucination. Like CJ's. Only he knew the wolf was CJ.

The wolf whimpered in pain. He could hear it clearly. She needed him.

She had to be calling his powers to her. Somehow she had found a way to call his powers without the amulet. But Trey didn't feel any lessening of his own powers, as he had when she had taken them after her rescue. His present wolf form resisted the spell. A physical tension pulled on his body. The power did not want to leave him easily.

He remembered how she had talked about visualizing herself walking from the wolf to get out of the vision. Could he visualize himself shifting to a man, so he could send his shifting powers to her?

A strange silver liquid mixed with bright shiny blood gushed from a wound in the white wolf's stomach. The poison. Time was running out.

ะเ๊ะ

CJ heard a voice, but she couldn't understand it. From brow to limb her body burned with unnatural fever, leaving her grasping for consciousness. She took a deep breath and gagged on the heavy smell of burning oil candles, their odor repulsively horrid, like singed flesh.

Her chest contracted from the smell and a slick liquid spilled from her mouth. Blood? It didn't taste like it. She lifted her hand to wipe herself clean. Where was she? Had someone attacked her?

Slowly the heat subsided and she sensed the hard, cold floor beneath her. Feeling the darkness of sleep receding, she lifted one eyelid slightly.

A bright blue light flashed in her tender eyes. She squinted against the painful glow and slowly forced them open.

"CJ, hold on. You're changing. You're almost there."

Roz's soft words. CJ recognized her voice. *What does she mean I'm changing?*

Before she could think of an answer, her stomach convulsed violently. As if it sucked back into her spine. The slick liquid poured from her mouth. She fought to breath. She placed all four limbs on the floor, heaving.

It ended. She took a deep breath, rose up and opened her eyes.

She stood in a circle of candles. Horridly huge candles, stinking like burning meat. A gentle touch around her ankle made her swivel her body and look down.

Roz knelt inside the circle of candles with her. She held the huge book from Vogel's altar and something else. Some sort of necklace with a stone. CJ gazed at the stone. So like Trey's amulet, only smaller and without the rune marks.

She moved her gaze to Roz's face. Her friend's eyes brimmed with questions and CJ could smell her fear among the stink of the candles.

CJ remembered the slimy liquid. Silver.

She had been poisoned. Vogel had laced her wine with silver and left her to die. Only one thing could have saved her...

The shift.

CJ lifted her hand and saw a great white-clawed hand, coarse hair traveled up her arm and across her torso. She had shifted into her Beast form. A glitter on the floor caught her eye. Poison. Splattered across the floor where she had expelled it during the shift.

The sound of a slamming door tore her attention away from her changed body. She cocked her massive head to see who entered the lab.

Doc Vogel stood at the top of the stairs, frozen in disbelief. "It can't be. I have the amulet." He touched the jeweled stone around his neck. Anger contorted his face. "No matter. I can still defeat you."

He shed his clothes and said something very similar to the chant Trey had taught her. Soon he yelled like a madman as he jumped the final few steps to the floor.

CJ felt the beginnings of something powerful in the air. An electric current about to let loose, like a storm coming across the prairie. Her instincts told her to cover Roz. She lowered her great body and cradled her friend beneath her. As Roz tucked her head under CJ's chest a yellow burst filled the room. The candles of the circle danced in response. Anxiously CJ scanned the room trying to figure out what Vogel had done.

Light flared from the glowing orb hanging next to the altar, a halo of yellow and gold colors. It grew outward several feet, then retracted into the globe. Shocked horror took hold of her as the golden glow of the orb arched across the room *into* Vogel.

The old werewolf shifted into his Beast form, but his body grew much higher than she remembered Trey's Beast. Yellow shone from his eyes and great fangs protruded from his jaw, grotesque canines that resembled tusks more than teeth.

The light from the orb transformed Vogel into some kind of über Beast. She gazed at her clawed hand, repulsed, yet hoping she had enough strength to stop him before he grew any stronger. They needed to break the arc of power coming from the orb.

Small hands grabbed at her arm, turning her attention from Vogel.

Roz pushed CJ off and stood. "It's the orb. You take Vogel. I've got an idea to stop the flow of power." She sprinted away from CJ and ran to the alcove. She took the smaller amulet she held and wrapped its chain around her fist.

CJ watched in horror as Roz thrust her hand into the orb. With a loud crackle, the golden arc of light wavered crazily then folded back into the orb.

Every piece of furniture in the room shook as Vogel's howl of anger reverberated over the stone and concrete. In the next instant, he launched off his massive legs toward Roz.

With an ability CJ didn't recognize, she vaulted into the air, colliding with the giant Beast, and sent them both crashing to the floor.

ಬಿಞಧಿಐ

Mario had tracked Vogel's scent to a hidden door behind a fake freezer. Trey could not believe the sight that met his eyes as they pried open the door to Vogel's secret cellar.

Two Beasts, one horrifically huge and one white, grappled among the strewn tables in a strange occult laboratory.

CJ. She lived. Awe filled him as the strangely beautiful, pale Beast sank her deadly teeth into the dark fur of the other monster's shoulder.

His relief at finding her alive evaporated as Vogel slashed his great claws into her side, sending blood streaking down her white fur.

She wasn't strong enough. They had to help her. "Shift, Mario. She can't fight him alone."

The younger man's face tensed as he searched for the power within. Tears of frustration streamed down his face.

Trey gripped the boy's shoulders. "Don't worry. We'll find a way."

A female scream echoed through the room as the fight shattered a rack of glass vials against a wall.

Mario pointed to the back of the room. "Look. I think that's Roz. The one who called me about CJ."

A tiny, red-haired woman stood next to a large glowing orb, but he couldn't see what she did.

Vogel's Beast made a lunge for the woman. CJ caught his leg and yanked him back into battle. She held Vogel, but her bloodied body told Trey she was losing ground.

Trey shouted above the din of the fighting. "Vogel is trying to get to Roz. We need to get to her first. She might know how to stop him."

They raced to the bottom of the stairs, the two Beasts oblivious to the running men. Between the smashed tables Trey and Mario dodged the monsters.

Trey reached her first and stopped short at what he saw. Roz's arms were plunged into the side of the glowing orb, surrounded in an aura of yellow light. The small woman, shaking with exertion, eyed the men with hope. "Please tell me you're Trey and Mario."

Trey put his arms under hers and let her collapse against him as her arms wavered in the globe. He didn't understand what was happening. "We've got to do something. CJ can't hold off Vogel much longer. Why is he after you?"

Roz shouted above the sound of the growling. "I think this orb is a storage container for magical power. We saw Vogel use your amulet to draw the power into him as he shifted into that freaking monster."

Mario caught Roz as she teetered forward, her legs finally giving out. He glared over her head at Trey. "*Our* powers. He took our powers and put them in here, didn't he?" His face flushed with fury.

Trey saw Mario's eyes lengthen, an ominous sign that Mario's own Beast yearned to burst forth.

A cry of pain pierced his eardrums before he could answer Mario. He jerked his head around and watched in horror as Vogel clamped his jaw on CJ's neck.

Roz shook with the orb's power, Trey and Mario her only support. "I've got Vogel's amulet. I used it to bring your shifting power into CJ. I thought the amulet could absorb the power of the orb, but there's too much. I don't think the amulet will hold much more. I need to send the magic somewhere or I'm afraid it will feed into Vogel again. He'll get stronger."

Helplessness overtook Trey as he glared at the orb. Shit, why didn't he know more about magic? His spell books said nothing of orbs and power. He was a fucking werewolf. A magical creature. Why didn't he know what to do?

The answer hit him as the Beasts howled in anger. Vogel was a werewolf, too.

"Use me." He removed his arms from Roz's waist, letting Mario hold her and stepped up to the orb. "If the power can go into Vogel, it can go into me. I'm a werewolf. I'm magic."

He went to grab Roz's arm back from the orb, but Mario stopped him. Trey felt the scratch of Mario's claws in the boy's touch. "No, Trey. What if it doesn't work? CJ needs you here."

Trey could barely understand him as Mario's mouth elongated into its monstrous canine form.

Roz screamed when Mario's Beast claw reached in to take the amulet from her hand. She dropped it into his hand, then stepped back against Trey. He gripped her tight, protecting her. Could Mario control his Beast?

Mario drew his lips back in a snarl as the yellow light of the globe grew brighter.

The orb exploded.

The force blew Trey across the room. The cold stone cellar walls bit into his spine with brutal force. Roz crumpled to the floor next to him. Her eyes opened wide with fear. Eerie silence filled the cavernous room.

Roz clutched at his arm, trying to squeeze her body between him and the wall. "What the fuck is that?"

He turned his attention to where she pointed. What he saw made even his werewolf blood run cold with fear. *Mario?*

Standing over a shattered orb loomed a monster only vaguely resembling Mario's Beast. Familiar canine teeth hung exposed in a snarl. The large eyes, the hanging arms and spread claws were the werewolf at its most gruesome. But, beyond that, Mario had become something else entirely.

His ears lay flat against his head, flesh instead of fur.

His chest and stomach rippled with the chiseled muscles of a man.

Instead of the animalistic legs of the Beast, he had the massive, sculpted legs of a man that ended in sharp, gleaming black hooves.

And, clearly hanging behind him, whipping around in agitation was a long, razor-tipped tail.

It, Mario, this new creature, whatever it was, stood still. Watching. Its glare moved between Trey and Roz huddled against the wall and the two creatures locked in combat.

Vogel and CJ continued to grapple. Had they sensed the presence of this new threat? He let Roz wiggle further behind him as he waited for Mario to make his move.

He prayed Mario still lived in that creature.

Hot air rushed across his face. Roz dug her nails into his arms as she held on to him. He jerked his gaze toward the hovering creature. "How can a werewolf have wings? What the hell did Vogel have in that lamp?"

Above them, flapping shiny black wings to stay aloft, Mario stretched his arms wide. His face was a mask of fury.

Roz's voice came quiet, but clear. "I think Vogel collected power from someone besides the werewolves." She edged out from his protective cover. "He looks like a demon. Do you think Mario remembers who he is?"

Almost exactly at the sound of his name, the creature lifted its snout and a piercing howl rang out.

Trey winced as the sound bounced off the hard cellar walls. "Hold on, because I think we're going to find out."

Mario arched his wings back and tore down to where Vogel had succeeded in pinning CJ to the ground. Mario's claws clamped down on Vogel's head. The old Beast instinctively let go of CJ to pry Mario's hands from his head.

Trey wanted to run to her. Wanted to pull her out of the fight now that Mario joined in, but one thing stopped him.

This was her fight too.

Vogel had hurt CJ as much as the werewolves he had stolen from. At least, she didn't fight alone.

Now she had Mario.

And Roz. And him.

Trey scanned the lab seeking a weapon he could use to kill Vogel. Either CJ and Mario had to behead the giant Beast, or Trey and Roz had to use magic to kill him. The splatter of blood and silver glinted in the light.

Silver. Its deadly effect on werewolves, that had to be magic.

Trey just had to figure out how to get the silver poison into Vogel without harming CJ or Mario. "Roz, when you searched for the amulet did you find any knives?"

She scrambled across the back of the room toward the altar. He followed, staying out of range of the fighting monsters. She flung open an altar drawer filled with deadly blades.

Roz snatched up the largest and handed it to Trey. "But it's not silver. I don't know what good it will do."

He grabbed her hand and pulled her down to the floor. He pointed to the ugly pool of silver liquid surrounded by a thin layer of blood. "Stay here out of the way. I'm going to go in there and dip this blade in the silver. Hopefully I'll see a chance to get close to Vogel."

"Will one knife be enough to kill him? Where is your target?"

"The one place that can prevent him from shifting to survive."

Vogel fled up the stairs, obviously feeling the strain of fighting two other monsters. Trey had to avoid getting caught beneath them.

Trey saw Mario lift into the air with one of Vogel's arms in his jaw, leaving a few feet of clearance for Trey to sneak under them and get to the silver.

He scrambled around the broken heaps of furniture and dove for the puddle. He stopped short of touching it and flung out the blade to coat it in the thick liquid silver. Satisfied the poison covered its surface, he pulled it out. As the shiny liquid ran down the blade, he flinched when the liquid hit his hand, but the pain never came.

He had been wrong before. He wasn't a magical creature anymore. CJ had all the werewolf powers. *He was human now.* Silver couldn't hurt him.

Trey jumped to his feet and swiveled away from Mario's whipping tail. Mario still had his jaws clamped on Vogel's arm while CJ attempted to pull Vogel's claw away from Mario's wings. Mario's size almost matched Vogel's, but the doctor must have pulled more power from the orb than the kid. CJ and Mario's battered bodies proved it. Vogel was wearing them down.

He had to act fast. Watching for Mario's tail, he jumped between CJ and Mario onto Vogel's legs. Busy with the other two, Vogel couldn't claw Trey off.

The knife clamped between his teeth, Trey clutched a thatch of Vogel's foul hair and pulled himself astride the Beast's chest. Vogel brought his head forward to bite him, but CJ reached across to wrap her claws around Vogel's gruesome snout. The slash of her razor-sharp nails spattered blood across Trey's face.

With a great sweep of his wings, Mario lifted off the ground and held Vogel's other arm far away from Trey's tender flesh.

Trey reached for the knife and raised it high above his head to use all of his human strength to plunge it between Vogel's eyes.

Fear flashed across the Beast's face. Vogel bucked his body. Trey went sprawling over the monster's head. The stone steps slammed into Trey's side. The knife whizzed into the air.

Trey watched helplessly as the knife spun in the air, unable to reach it.

CJ let go of Vogel's face and shot her hand out. Her long claws snagged the knife before it fell to the floor, its handle now dripping silver liquid. She closed her hand around it and Trey saw the withering of her flesh as it made contact with the poison.

She didn't drop it. Not his CJ.

With all her supernatural strength she drove the blade between Vogel's eyes, burying it to the hilt inside the werewolf's skull. As the silver oozed into his demented brain, Vogel's flesh and bones melted into a blackened mass.

Vogel cried out, his howl weak and screeching. One hand shifted to that of his human self. Vogel lifted it, as if trying to pull the knife from his skull, but the silver struck too fast. The hand fell back to his side. The rest of his body contorted in the gruesome form of his dying Beast.

Sensing the life ebbing from his opponent, Mario released the dead man. He flew to the cellar's ceiling and hung there in mid-air, a look of confusion on the distorted werewolf face. He howled again and beat a fist against his own raw chest. Vogel had wounded him. His body was covered with lacerations.

Trey feared some cuts could be deep. If Mario was unable to shift, he might die.

A few steps below Trey, CJ staggered to her feet with Vogel's dead Beast in her arms, her body as bloody as Mario's. Bunching her damaged muscles she summoned the strength to heave the silver-soaked carcass to the floor of the cellar. The force of her effort sent her stumbling after.

Trey's heart stopped beating as she fell backward off the steps. He lunged for her, grasping only air. Her pale blue eyes held his golden ones for a second.

"Shift, CJ. Shift," he yelled, praying she could hear him.

Her Beast twisted and buckled in mid-air. Hope swelled in his chest as her body compacted in size, her bloodied fur replaced by a silky, snow white pelt. Wounds healed as if Vogel had never touched her.

By the time her paws hit the floor, she completed the shift to the white wolf. Her nimble animal form landed easily before she darted to where he lay helpless on the stairs

She moved her snout under his arm and helped him sit up. He buried his face in her fur-covered neck. Her life force beat against his cheek. Feeling her alive, next to him, his own injuries seemed inconsequential.

Though he could no longer shift to heal, the fight had not mortally wounded him. A cold knot of dread formed in Trey's stomach as Mario hovered in the air, blood pooling beneath him on the cellar floor. His wings were intact, but Vogel had shredded one his shoulders and slashed Mario's thigh deep enough to expose bone.

Would he be able to shift into a wolf form to heal. Or would the powers of this strange winged creature save him?

Trey stretched out his hand. "Mario," he spoke quietly, trying not to spook the creature. "Remember who you are. You're a werewolf. Our friend. You're hurt. You need to shift to the wolf inside you. It will make the pain go away."

CJ howled to her brother, filling the underground lab with her calm and comforting call. Her plea for Mario to join her in the shift.

The creature howled in anguish.

Still clinging to the wall, Roz scurried over to the bottom of the steps, her eyes locked on Mario. "What's the matter?" Roz had grabbed Vogel's book of spells and crammed it under her arm. "Can't he understand us?"

"I think he understands. He must be having trouble shifting. He couldn't do it on his own before." Trey watched CJ go down to her friend and bury her nose in Roz's free hand.

CJ whined and rubbed against her friend. Roz gently stroked the wolf, as she smiled at Trey. The wolf form was much less scary than CJ's Beast.

"How much have you figured out about the orb? Is there a chance Mario didn't absorb the power to shift?" Trey asked the woman who seemed to know quite a bit about magic, considering she had used Vogel's amulet and spell book to help CJ.

She sat the book down on a step and opened it. "I don't know. This is the spell that was bookmarked. I recognized some of the French and Spanish words, so I took a chance and tried it on CJ, but it's just a spell for summoning powers." She flipped through the pages. "I'd have to study it. Try and finds some notes Vogel made—"

CJ let out a warning growl. She ran past Roz and Trey, stopping at the top of the stairs.

A moment later, Trey heard the men picking their way through the mess of the lab upstairs.

Lazlo strode through the cellar door. The winged creature with a werewolf torso and the feet of a demon stopped him in his tracks. "What the hell is that?"

Trey scowled at the Alpha. "Shut up, Lazlo. You better leave. It's Mario."

"Mario." Lazlo shouted the name.

Mario let out a growl and dove for his brother. Lazlo leapt out of the way, but Mario simply kept flying. The wall between the cellar and Vogel's upstairs lab collapsed under his assault.

CJ, Trey and Roz jumped clear of the tumbling wall and landed hard on the floor. Once he made sure Roz was unhurt, Trey saw Mario in the sky above a large hole in the cabin's ceiling. Lazlo threw off the stones that had tumbled around him.

Mario wasn't watching his brother. He peered upward. To the sky.

Trey noticed the wounds on Mario's body were gone. He had healed without shifting. Relief poured through Trey. Mario was finally strong enough to survive.

On his own, if he had to.

Lazlo stood free of the rubble. "Mario. Don't do it. You need us. You belong here."

Trey recognized Lazlo's misjudgment. So did Mario.

With a burst of speed faster than any werewolf, Mario shot above the trees and into the afternoon sky. The birds scattered, their cries filling the forest.

Mario claimed his freedom. He had wings. No werewolf would ever be able to stop him now. Not even Lazlo.

Unable to follow, all they could do was stand and watch until he faded into a speck in the distance.

Then he was gone.

ೋೋೊೋ

CJ could hear Roz and Trey laughing downstairs in the kitchen. She tried to make out their conversation. She found with this new, improved hearing it was harder to block out the background noises in human form.

She smoothed out the Soul Asylum T-shirt she had put on after her shower this morning and pulled on her jeans from a pile on the floor. She dug in her bags and found her brush to wrestle the tangles in her hair.

Ignoring Lazlo's protests, Trey had led her and Roz back to his cabin yesterday after Mario flew off. She had been exhausted after the fight and wasn't sure she could have taken the Alpha.

CJ found her Nikes and shoved them on. With practiced efficiency, she twisted her hair back into a loose knot, stuck in a clip and headed down the loft's stairs.

The smell of Trey's burnt bacon wafted from the kitchen and stirred her stomach. Last night Trey had shown her how to catch a rabbit while in her wolf form, but she had refused to try. Once she shifted back to human, she had informed him raw meat didn't cut it.

Another scent swept past her. She smiled.

Coffee.

She entered the small kitchen to find Trey tearing into a plate of bacon and eggs, while Roz sipped a brimming mug of black coffee. Amaretto flavored by the smell.

Trey pushed back and stood, holding his plate in his hand, and offered CJ his chair. She waved him back down. "You finish, just give me some coffee for now." Roz pointed to the counter where a brand new high-end coffee maker sat. CJ poured herself a nice full cup. "Where'd this come from?"

Roz smiled behind her mug. "When I sent Sebastian out for antiseptic and bandages, I asked him to bring some instant coffee for me. This was here when I woke this morning."

Trey snorted.

CJ laughed. Little Roz always did have a way of making men bend to her will. After watching Roz in action down in Vogel's cellar, she wondered if there was a little magic in that as well.

She took a sip and inwardly smiled at the way Trey and Roz interacted. It thrilled her they had hit it off. Besides her mother and Mario, they were the two most important people in the world to her.

Roz finished her coffee and got up from the small table. "I'm glad you're awake. I found some interesting stuff skimming through Vogel's old spell book. I'm gonna get it."

Once Roz left, CJ grabbed a plate and stole some of Trey's bacon. "I slept like a rock. I thought being in the wolf form would make me all well and rested."

Trey took a gulp of orange juice. "Usually it does. But the Beast form takes more energy. Plus Vogel did some serious damage."

CJ reached into her shirt and pulled out the amulet. Trey had taken it off Vogel's dead body and insisted she wear it last night. "I'm better now. I think you should take this so you can summon your werewolf back. We have Roz here to help. We can do it in a minute." They had argued last night after she shifted back into human form.

CJ wanted him to take his powers back.

Trey wanted her to keep them, because he wanted her safe and felt the werewolf powers were the only way he could make sure of it.

He set down his fork. "I told you, I'm committed to learning to live as man. As the CEO of Guardian, I sit behind a desk, while you're out there everyday dealing with the bad guys. You're not going to be able to perform the spell when someone has a gun pointed in your face."

"This isn't finished." She downed another gulp of coffee.

Roz popped back into the room, the huge old book in her hands. She came over to the table. "Move your plates, I want to show you this."

CJ marveled that Roz could make sense of any of it. Most of the words appeared as gibberish to her.

Roz flipped to the page she had marked with a gum wrapper. "Let me have your amulet for a second." She took it out of CJ's hand and laid it on the open book.

Trey and CJ both stared in amazement. The runes on the amulet were identical to the illustrations framing a small spell in the center of the page.

"Yep, I thought those looked familiar last night." She switched back to a page Vogel had marked. "This page is the spell Vogel used to summon power from the werewolf fetuses." She tapped her finger on the bottom stanza. "Most of this verse is French, which I read fairly well, and it talks about storing the power of another."

Trey put a finger on the page. "This is the one you used to get my werewolf powers into CJ?"

Roz shook her head. "Not all of it. I left off the last stanza. I didn't want your powers jumping into Vogel's stupid orb. But, you guys, I knew you two were soul mates. I've read it in my cards. I just summoned the power using the first part of this spell and it automatically found its way to CJ."

CJ sat back in her chair in awe of her friend's knowledge. How different things might have been if she had believed Roz all along. "But why does the other spell match the runes on Trey's amulet?"

"The amulet you have isn't just a run-of-the-mill amulet. These runes specifically represent the flow of energy between the elements. Energy or power, I think to magic it's all the same." She pointed back to the spell. "I can make out French, but also some Latin. Specifically, this is a spell to make a woman have twins. It splits the magic power between two fetuses. My guess? Vogel tried this spell first, not really knowing what it said. And you two are the result."

Trey gazed in wonder at Roz. "How did you figure that out?"

Roz giggled. "Truthfully, it wasn't all my incredible deductive powers. I skimmed through this tome because I couldn't sleep last night." She wiggled her finger at Trey. "For some reason, I kept imagining a werewolf jumping through the door. But anyway, look here in the corner of this page." She reversed the book so Trey and CJ could see. "I found these notes all over the book. He dabbled with lots of spells, which is why I'm guessing Mario came out of that orb as more than just a werewolf."

CJ gasped sharply. She read the faint words written in pencil. "'May 7, 1973. Baby N. Failure.' Baby N...you think that is Baby Nolan. Vogel did this spell on Trey?"

"And look at the date. Your birthday is in December. Your mom was barely pregnant with you. Vogel must have cast the spell, thinking he could steal Baby N's powers for himself, but since you were the only other werewolf fetus and this is a twin spell, instead some of Trey's powers went into you because your dad was a werewolf."

A salty smell caught CJ's attention. Trey's eyes filled with tears. She sprang out of the chair and wrapped her arms around his shoulders.

He swabbed at his eyes with the hem of her shirt. "Sorry, didn't mean to ruin the moment. It's just that, I always thought…" His fist hit his chest. "Believed, that some great evil had stolen my powers to keep me from my destiny. My desire to defeat that evil, to take back my rightful powers drove me on. Kept me motivated when I wanted to give up and reveal my secret." His tears changed to a strange, sad laughter. "And to think it was just a mistake. The fucking mistake of a demented, power-crazy werewolf."

CJ hugged him closer. "But Trey. You did defeat the evil. Vogel was evil. He almost destroyed your pack. It just took the other part of the *mistake*, to do him in."

ഇൽൽ൪

Trey had just finished his second helping of blackened bacon when CJ heard the front door slam open. Trey's face tensed with unease.

He stood slowly and placed his empty plate in the sink. "Well, at least they gave us time to rest. I'll go first. CJ, you watch Roz's backside if Lazlo's decided to be a jerk."

CJ about suggested she go first, but the set of Trey's jaw told her this wasn't the time to remind him he was no longer an almost indestructible werewolf.

Roz had bandaged Trey's few scratches, but he refused to be taken to the hospital to be checked for any broken ribs. She had wrapped his ribs with the tape last night and loaded him with ibuprofen. Waiting for the healing would try his patience.

The air carried two distinct musky male fragrances. Neither Lazlo. She took that as a good sign.

One of the men smelled familiar.

His scent thread almost identical to Mario's.

Her father.

Trey went into the room and she heard his sigh of relief. Roz followed, then CJ came through the door. Rare butterflies danced in her stomach. Rupert Le Croix. She knew he was on the compound grounds, she just hadn't expected to meet him outside the Council.

He stood in front of the fireplace, his hands behind his back, staring at her. The reserved study didn't last long. He smiled. A real smile that spread all the way to his eyes.

CJ grinned back. Her dimples mirroring her father's. She went to him first, passing the other man who she recognized as Trey's father. Not knowing what else to do, she stuck out her hand.

He grabbed it and used it to pull her into his arms. "God, you look so much like Karen. I've never forgotten her. Never."

She stepped back a bit, overwhelmed with his aroma and his embrace, but he held her tight. "Um, I need some breathing room here, Rupert."

"Oh, of course." He let her go.

CJ moved to stand by Trey. Everyone just stood looking at each other. Roz finally rolled her eyes and took a seat on Trey's couch. The werewolves remained standing.

She checked out her old man from head to toe. Mario had his height, but any family resemblance ended there.

Rupert Le Croix reminded her more of an overgrown chocolate lab than a werewolf. His hair hung to his shoulders, long and wavy with streaks of gray. His eyes were deep brown, and his smile greeted her with warmth and sincerity. She could see why a lonely foster kid, like her mom, and a young widow, like Lazlo's mother, would gravitate to a man with Rupert's demeanor. He oozed kindness.

Trey gently placed his hand on CJ's elbow. "Let's sit down for a second. I think CJ has some questions for you, Rupert. I'm guessing you two have some questions for us as well."

The older werewolves exchanged a glance. Rupert pulled up a side chair, while CJ and Trey joined Roz on the couch.

Before Trey's father sat, he held out a hand to CJ. "I'm sorry we couldn't meet under different circumstances. I can tell my son is quite taken with you." He gave her a guarded smile and an appraising once-over. "I'm Avery Nolan."

She took his hand and nodded. Once he had sat down, she turned her attention back to her father. "Well, there is one thing I want to know from you." She took a deep breath, prepared to hear the worst. "Did you have any idea that my mom was pregnant with me?"

Rupert's face fell. "Oh, man, no way. I wouldn't have deserted her like that." He stole a glance at Avery. "I would have done anything to make sure she and the baby were safe. If I had known, I would have never let Trey's grandfather ship me off to Europe."

Avery spoke up. "You see, I found out how serious their relationship had become." His voice grew quieter. "I told my father, who then commanded Rupert to break it off. None of us realized that she was pregnant. If I hadn't gone to my father first, but instead confronted Rupert, he would have had more time with her and discovered the truth." He ran his hand through his hair.

"It's in the past, Avery. Don't blame yourself." Rupert's face grew grim. "I was ordered to end it. We met at a place we liked to go, a park near where she lived. I was a wreck when I told her we had to break it off. Her tears tore me to the core. I didn't notice the three hoodlums until they jumped us. They had guns."

Even now, thirty years later, CJ smelled Rupert's scent change. His adrenaline pumped, reliving the attack as he told her the story.

He continued, "I didn't kiss her good-bye. I just shoved her behind me and told her to run and not look back."

"Hate to break this to you. She looked back." CJ could just imagine what she had seen. No wonder her mom had run all the way to Minnesota.

Rupert ran a hand through his hair, looking older than his fifty-odd years. "I lost control. My Beast killed those men." His lashes lowered. "I endangered the pack, left Karen to raise our daughter alone with that nightmare hanging over her head."

Her father moved his gaze from the floor and peered into her eyes. "Can you forgive me for putting your mother through that hell? Do you even want me as part of your life?"

Trey put his arm around her. She took strength from his closeness. "Rupert, your mistakes were a long time ago. My mom may not be a werewolf, but she's the strongest person I know. She gave me a good life. I'm ready to give it a try." She directed her gaze to Trey's father. "Unless Lazlo and the Elders have a problem with it," she said, her voice thick with sarcasm.

Avery and Rupert exchanged a glance before Avery spoke. "Speaking for the Elders, we won't interfere with your relationship. We've actually decided to discuss all the policies on human and werewolf relations. As for Lazlo, he won't be a problem. He resigned as Alpha last night. He left early this morning. Said he won't be back until he finds Mario."

Trey tensed next to CJ. "It's pointless. Lazlo is the last person Mario will trust." His voice carried an angry tone.

Rupert interrupted him. "No, if there is going to be peace between those two, it's best to let them figure it out on their own. Lazlo has much to atone for and he knows it. He has to do this."

This time it was CJ who comforted Trey. She placed a hand on his thigh. "Okay, so Lazlo won't be a problem. What about Trey's trial? Because I'm telling you right now"—she looked between the two men—"we're not going down without a fight."

Avery raised a hand. "No, the Elders have no interest in punishing Trey. But we have met and talked about the implications of what happened to Mario and Vogel. The pack is uneasy. This *magic*. It's a phenomenon we don't understand. If we understood it once, the knowledge has been lost."

He took a deep breath and stared his son straight in the eye. "We'd like you to take Lazlo's position. Since both Roz and CJ seemed to have had some success using Vogel's spell book we'd like them to stay and help us. Trey, would you accept the position of Alpha?"

CJ's heart tightened in her chest. Alpha. It's what Trey had always wanted. It's what had kept him searching for answers all these years.

She held her breath as Trey met his father's questioning look. "Excuse us for a minute." He took her by the hand and led her to the door.

The cool spring air washed over her as they settled on the top step of his porch. She hugged her knees to her chest. The calm beauty of the pack's wooded compound contrasted with the turmoil inside of her.

"CJ, I have a question for you." He brushed a loose strand of hair from her face. "Do you want to stay here? In Seattle? With the pack?"

With the seemingly endless forest spread before her CJ wanted to believe she could be happy here. A part of a whole. Connected and safe. But her mother had raised her to be more. To stand on her own. To follow her own instincts, not the dictates of some lofty old men. "Part of me does, but my life is back home. With my mother. My friends, my work." She spoke quietly to Trey. "No, I can't live here."

Trey stared quietly into the woods, too. Her answer no surprise. CJ wasn't a follower. The structure of the pack would drive her crazy. "Think Roz might stay? A witch, some werewolves. Not a bad match," he asked, avoiding the obvious question.

CJ shrugged. "Can't see her going for all this obey the pack stuff. But she might surprise me and stay."

"I think my father and the other Elders are hoping she does. They're more shook by all this magic stuff than they're letting on. Roz's coolness under pressure impressed them." Her quick thinking in Vogel's lab had saved a lot of lives, including CJ's. He'd always be indebted to the little red-haired woman.

"A witch for a roommate. Damn, has my worldview changed in the last week." Her matter-of-fact tone revealed nothing.

"You're not the only one." He meant it. His own life, his dreams had been turned on their head. "Think about my pack. Besides having to relearn our magical lore, they're without a leader. Werewolves need a strong leader."

"What do you mean? They have you. Your father just told you." Her brow furrowed in confusion.

He took a deep breath. Stamped down his nerves. "He asked me, CJ. I haven't accepted the position yet."

Her eyes went wide. "But this is what you always wanted. I thought being Alpha was your destiny— Wait, it's because of the powers." She reached into her shirt and slipped off the amulet. "Here, take it. Take your powers. I don't want them. All I need to keep is the ability to smell, to track."

Trey covered her outstretched hand that held the necklace. He peered in her eyes, making sure she understood. "No, CJ. I'm not taking your strength. And I don't think it'd be such a bad idea if you kept the shifting, too. The creeps you deal with might warrant use of some Beast whoop ass."

Her silence said everything.

"I mean it. I want you safe." He pressed the amulet emphasizing his request.

"But what about being a full werewolf? Being Alpha?" Her face broke, blue eyes brimming with tears. "I don't want to make you choose me or the pack."

"You're not making me choose anything. As far as I'm concerned it's not a *choice*. The pack is safe. That's all I really wanted. I've opened their eyes. The truth is out. They're going to be okay." He brushed her tears away from her cheek. "I love you, CJ. Werewolf or man, it's you who makes me strong."

She smiled, though her lips quivered. "Heaven help me, I love you, too."

His heart leapt at her words. *Her love.*

CJ wiped more tears away with the back of her hand. "But you're a werewolf, Trey. Can we really make it? Together?"

Trey arched an eyebrow. "Technically, right now, you're the werewolf."

She reluctantly chuckled, her eyes brighter. "Got me there." She cupped Trey's face in her hand, somberness in her voice again. "Is this really what you want?"

Trey folded an arm around her shoulders and pulled her closer. He wanted to keep her in his embrace forever. His lips brushed against her hair. "You've got the super nose. You tell me what I want." His blood raced with wanting her, his jeans straining against his desire.

CJ responded by nuzzling his neck. "Trey, your dad, my dad. They're right inside." She whispered her meek protest.

Trey's hand moved from her shoulder to her hip. He squeezed her tighter. His woman felt so right next to him. "I'll tell them my decision and send Roz over to Vogel's lab with them. We can have the whole cabin to ourselves. Make our own naughty magic."

Epilogue

The cicadas filled the warm evening air with their song as CJ stood on the deck sipping the cool lemonade her mother had served with supper. Her mother had just bought the two-story A-frame cabin on the remote Minnesota lake.

Her mother said she planned to retire there someday. It's the story she told everyone, but CJ knew the truth.

Karen Duncan adored her new son-in-law and Trey had missed the freedom to run free in his wolf form since he moved to Minneapolis with CJ. Karen had sensed his restlessness.

Trey had protested when Karen had spent a good part of her retirement to buy a cabin. She just stared him down and told him no one told her what to do. Like a good son-in-law, Trey hadn't pushed the issue.

CJ wasn't worried. Their new investigative firm was doing well financially, so her mother wouldn't miss the money when she retired.

She fingered her half of the gold amulet and said a silent prayer for her younger brother as she gazed into the starry August night. No one had heard from him since he had flown off that afternoon over fifteen months ago. Lazlo had checked in with Sebastian, the new Alpha, a few times. The guilt-ridden Lazlo had found nothing but dead-ends, yet he vowed he wouldn't give up.

Lazlo and Trey had yet to talk. Ten years of distrust wouldn't be fixed overnight. For Mario's sake, she had offered Lazlo her contact lists in the missing person's community. The humbled former Alpha had accepted it gratefully.

To everyone's disappointment not one blip on Mario had come across the wire. But CJ wasn't the only one relieved that stories about a flying demon hadn't popped up either.

She hoped wherever her little brother was hiding, he'd come home to them soon. When he did, she prayed the other werewolves were ready to accept the man he had surely become.

The smell of vanilla drove away her sad thoughts. Trey hated the northland mosquitoes and practically bathed in the fragrant extract to keep them away. She didn't turn around as he slid the glass doors closed. "Got those dishes washed for Mom?"

"Dried and put away." He curled his arms around her. "I'm going for a run. Do you want to come with? I'll even let you be wolf first."

She twisted in his arms to face him. His handsome jaw was scratchy with his five o'clock shadow. Since giving up the office job at Guardian, he had let his hair grow longer and didn't shave quite so often.

CJ thought the look suited him just fine. *Dangerously* fine.

She put her hand on her growing belly and felt their child kick. "Well, Junior seems to think it might be fun, but I'm exhausted after the drive. I'll be waiting in bed when you get back."

Trey unbuttoned his shirt. "Well, I guess it will be a short run then." He slipped his shirt off and tossed it over the deck railing. His jeans followed shortly. The man insisted werewolves didn't wear underwear.

Her body warmed at the sight of her naked husband. It amazed her that at seven months pregnant, she could be stirred to such lust. She hoped it was a short run.

He slipped his half of the amulet over his head and gave it to her. She put it around her neck. Though they always wore the split amulet, it had become nothing more than a symbol of their union.

After a few months together, their powers had begun to pass between them with a mere thought.

Roz had initially split the amulet so both Trey and CJ could call the full powers of the werewolf as they needed. A risky undertaking, but both felt so strongly about the other having the power to shift and heal, Roz had finally suggested it.

CJ pulled Trey close in the wonderfully rich night air and ran her tongue up his rigid neck. The vanilla wasn't bad, but it was Trey's scent that made her wild with desire. "On second thought, I'll meet you in the shower."

He put his hand on her jaw and pulled her mouth to his. "Yet another reason I fell in love with you." He reached around and grabbed her ass. "And here's another."

"Get out of here before we embarrass my mom." She slapped his bare butt as he jumped off the deck. By the time she leaned over the edge, he was a black shadow disappearing into the trees.

CJ put her hands on her stomach and yelled to the darkness. "I love you, too."

She laughed as an answering howl echoed through the forest.

About the Author

Margo Lukas began her love affair with the romance novel as a young girl when she worked with her grandmother, the town librarian. Margo loved to escape into new worlds where a happy ending was guaranteed. Having a romance story published is a dream come true. To learn more about Margo Lukas, please visit www.MargoLukas.com or her blog at www.margolukas.wordpress.com. To contact Margo, send an email to her at MargoLukas@yahoo.com.

Seth Kolski, a werewolf, hides his heritage and passes for normal. Until he meets Jamie.

The Strength of the Pack
© 2007 Jorrie Spencer

Since his sister disappeared two years ago, Seth's solitude has intensified. Despite his deep need to be part of a pack, he sets himself apart, wary of humans who fear the wolf in him.

When Seth hooks up with his teenaged crush, loneliness and physical desire overcome his distrust. Jamie welcomes his attentions, albeit a little shyly, and Seth rationalizes they can have one night together before they part.

For Seth can never be part of a regular family. No normal woman is going to accept his freakish nature, nor his past violence. Especially a single mother determined to protect her family. However, Seth and Jamie's bond runs deeper than he knows. He cannot return to the shadows. Yet exposure may bring danger to them all.

Available now in ebook from Samhain Publishing.

"Would you like whiskey in your coffee?" he asked over the burble of the coffee machine.

"No, thanks."

He added a dollop to his mug, then stilled. She might not have recognized the tension in his body if she hadn't been watching closely.

"I had a crush on you, you know," he said abruptly.

Her cheeks warmed as she sat on a stool behind the counter, putting a barrier between them. She didn't want to get too emotional, something she was quite capable of, as Derek had pointed out oh so many times.

"I'm flattered." Her words made it past the tightness in her throat as she realized they were going to make love. She was unlikely to back out now.

He hitched a hip on the edge of the counter. "Now you are. You wouldn't have been flattered back then."

"I liked your company." She remembered the skinny, awkward teen. He'd followed her around when Tom was off playing with other friends who didn't want to hang with the unpopular Seth. Derek—they'd just started to date—had teased that she had an admirer and she'd laughed, not wanting Derek to know she enjoyed the attentions of a fifteen-year-old boy. Derek would have given Seth grief.

Other memories were sweeter. "You thought everything I said was wonderful. Pretty heady for an eighteen-year-old girl." With a college boyfriend who made sure she knew who the smart one in the couple was.

"I was obviously devoted." He crossed thick, muscular arms. Despite his leanness, this was a man with a good amount of upper body strength.

"I didn't quite figure that out."

He raised an eyebrow in doubt.

She shrugged. "I didn't think about it like that."

"You didn't think about me much," he corrected. "Understandable. I was young."

"You were Tom's friend and Tom's friends were first and foremost from another planet. Including the nice ones, like you."

"So, I was nice."

"Oh, yeah. Aren't you still?"

He blinked at the question. "I try my best."

"You were nicer by far than my then-boyfriend Derek. Even if I thought he was great at the time." She didn't hide her bitterness.

"I think it's better we don't discuss Derek." His voice was solemn. Part of her wanted to complain about her ex, but it would spoil the mood.

Instead she watched him pour coffee, hands now steady. She, too, felt more at ease. Casual sex scared her, but this no longer felt casual, or at least thoughtless. They didn't have much history, but they had something.

He picked up the two mugs and walked past her. "Come with me." His elbow pointed towards the doorway.

He exited the kitchen. His straight back and strong shoulders mesmerized her, bringing alive a desire that had long been buried deep. She entered a cozy den. A place for friends. Though the thrum of excitement beating through her veins contradicted that thought. Since she'd set eyes on Seth, her body had its own ideas.

He placed the mugs on the coffee table. As he settled into one corner of the couch and she in the other, she was tempted to scoot over and cuddle up to him. She liked his caresses, his firm arms around her. The space between them suddenly seemed daunting.

He held out his hand to her.

She opened her mouth but the word "I" stuck in her throat. Indecision grappled with desire, tangling her words.

"Whatever you want, Jamie." He dropped his arm, eyes pale and watchful. Attentive.

"I don't know what I want. How's that for sophisticated? Though presumably I knew when I accepted your invitation to drink coffee."

"You wanted coffee," he suggested, drinking his. She hadn't thought that eyes twinkled, but Seth's did.

"Truth is, I never drink coffee at night."

"You don't have to drink coffee for my sake." His rapt attention flattered her. It had been years since anyone focused on her like this.

"I know." She set down the mug and he reached over to snag her hand. "I just—"

"You don't have to talk, either." He closed the space between them.

Don't talk.

He pulled her next to him, smelling of musk and male and outside. His fingers ran across the back of her neck and she shivered. The other hand came under her chin and he turned her face towards him, brushing a thumb across her lips. The feather-light touches had her trembling and he'd hardly done a thing.

"I don't usually—"

"Shhh." He brought a thumb back to her lips.

He was right. He didn't want to know she'd left Derek two years ago and their sex life had stuttered to a halt before the split. He might want to know her belly was knotted with desire, but he was going to find out before long.

As his arms came around her, she forked a hand through his dark hair and remembered the buzz cut his father used to insist Seth wear. "You have gorgeous hair."

He stiffened slightly and she wouldn't have noticed if he hadn't just pulled her into his lap. Maybe he feared she saw him as some kind of trophy. He *was* handsome, as well as physically fit. But what drew her were his volatile eyes, his soft, persuasive voice, his frank interest.

"I wouldn't be here." She evaded his lips though she did want to kiss. But she couldn't make love without talking. It wasn't her way. "If I hadn't known you ten years ago."

His mouth explored her neck, giving her goose bumps.

"And you used to rescue frogs the other boys captured. Put them back into the pond where they belonged."

He drew back, his eyes crinkling with humor in a way she hadn't seen before. "My unpopular actions have had long-term benefits, I see."

"I couldn't have gone home with anyone else."

His hold on her tightened. "Be careful, Jamie, if you do go to bars on your own again. Don't go home with a stranger."

She had to laugh. "Are you trying to talk me out of this?"

His serious, somewhat guilty expression puzzled her. She reached up and touched his face, rough from shadow that had formed by the end of the day. "I want to be here, Seth."

"I sure don't want you to be anywhere else," he said roughly.

She grinned. "Maybe it is better if I don't talk."

"Let me think about how I can arrange that." His mouth skimmed hers and her lips parted, wanting more. Which, she suspected, was how he wanted her to feel.

He took her mouth with his.

9 781599 986340